JOHN DORY

Also by John Murray from Flambard

REIVER BLUES (1996)

JOHN DORY

John Murray

First published in England in 2001 by Flambard Press
Stable Cottage, East Fourstones, Hexham NE47 5DX

Typeset by Barbara Sumner
Cover design by Colin Brownson
Author photograph by Jonathan Becker
Printed in England by Cromwell Press, Trowbridge, Wiltshire

A CIP catalogue record for this book
is available from the British Library.

ISBN 1 873226 46 2

Flambard Press withes to thank Northern Arts
for its financial support.

To the memory of the poet and critic

WILLIAM SCAMMELL

and with love to Jan

And if any man think that he knoweth any thing,
he knoweth nothing yet as he ought to know.

St Paul

Author's Note

Anyone who knows the real Maryport and its aquarium will realise I have taken considerable liberties with the geographical layout of both. This is because *John Dory* is a work of fiction and all the characters are my own invention. Only the fish are real.

Last Things First

He was writhing and apparently clutching at his belly. That's literally impossible so what I mean is it must have been me sympathetically clutching at my belly as I watched him. As for his motion it was drunken and staggering, yet at the same time completely sober. It was also pure and it was also immaculate, and I defy anyone to deny me the use of those words.

He seemed to be moving up and down as he wrestled with his situation, and his face was the most poignant representation of pure pain. He must have been in agony. But that was what entranced me. The pain in his face was extreme and at the same time he bore it with what I can only describe as a humble, heartfelt endurance. He reminded me of a child, of a tiny, tiny child.

I was reminded of something else. When I went with my daughter Anne for her hospital ultra-sound, and I saw her tiny foetus that in a few months' time would be my grandchild Clare, I saw something of that same inexplicable radiance. Infinitely tiny yet infinitely huge. In infinite weakness you discerned the most enormous strength. The most accurate word has been done to death and perverted so many times, I hesitate to use it. But yes he was suffering with his meekness as well as with his agony.

I know what you're thinking and in one way you're right. It's a deliberate red herring. You need patience to understand, unfortunately, and if you're anything like me it's one thing you'll always be lacking. Patience perhaps explains the way in which he endured so tenderly his extraordinary condition. He rolled around the little rocks as he struggled for some sort of relief, some purging, some pitying release. None of which was permitted him all the time that I stood there.

He took it all like a man, like a real man. A really real man that is. A real man so movingly tiny he was a legendary giant. A real man so impossibly, mythologically gentle he was a genuine and unselfish hero.

He was pregnant, God bless him. He was carrying his child. I mean, his young.

> Roll, roll, roll it away
> Roll away your agony...
> *Hippocampus...*
> *Hippocampus fuscus...*

Penniless villagers go out to catch you, then dry you, to sell you as a seaside trinket.

They even catch you when you are carrying your young. They love your heartrending novelty, your two in oneness. The fish that's a horse, the horse that's a fish.

Your tiny woman left her seed inside of you.

And you, Hippocampus, are left to bear the precious load.

I saw you going through labour the day after I saw Wright. Which was when I realised I knew enough by now.

1

People are intrigued to learn that I sell as much of my regular stock to adults as to children. For example, it's almost exclusively the grown-ups who indulge themselves in my fifteen flavours of Authentic Italian Ice Cream which I get from a manufacturer down in Ashby-de-la-Zouch. To tell the truth, the sociological spread of sweet-eating is very baffling. As far as I know, I haven't a single adult friend who eats boiled sweets from a paper bag, yet it's only the grown-ups who purchase them from me. Obviously little kids can't afford quarters of Needler's Fruit Thins or Fox's Glacier Mints or Callard and Bowser Mint Toffees; they only have enough to buy the penny mixes or twenty-pence chocolate bars displayed on the counter. As for the gangs of teenagers, they always buy from the cheap jars right at the front, those nasty little sweets that are coated in coarse sugar and as rough and abrasive as scrubbing brushes. All blushes, moodiness and bad skin, these problematic youths will shuffle off with a quarter of cheap confectionery made in Wigan or Garstang or Bacup or other hard-as-nails towns. Five minutes of sucking away at that sort of rubbish and it feels as if you've been shaving the skin inside your mouth. Later these pimply kids will spit disbelieving into their hands, then gleefully confirm that, yes, in among the coloured spit there is blood from the razor edges of the Black Bullets or the Pear Drops or the Lemonade Rock or the Tobermory Tatties...

You only get what you pay for, my old mother would have informed them briskly. A Needler's sweet is *not* a child's sweet, she would have loftily maintained, nor is it within their limited

13

price range. She mentioned that heavenly pairing Callard and Bowser with the same tremulous reverence with which others mutter names like Harley-Davidson or Bang Olufsen or Huntley and Palmer's. If you had said to her with a mock-Shakespearean gravity: What's in a name? – she'd have said: Every bloody thing, George. Callard and Bowser are to quality confectionery what Wedgwood is to fine china and Mr Rolls and Mr Royce are to the most refined in automobiles.

You might think I'm exaggerating but today, inside my kiosk, I flicked through the telephone directory for Cumbria and North Lancs, and this is what I confirmed. There wasn't a single Bowser in the whole bloody book. There wasn't a single Callard either. Later this afternoon I walked into the town library, my regular haunt outside of the confined geometry of this kiosk, and sloped into the reference where they have all the phone directories for the whole of the country. I looked through a dozen directories, trawling patiently through Hunts, Cambs, W. Yorks, N. Yorks, Staffs, Fife, Orkney, Dyfed, Humbs, Lincs and more. I found people called Bumstead and Longbottom and a dentist called William Snowball and a plumber called Derek Duck. I found a Chinese carry-out in Newcastle-under-Lyme called Bum Suk, and another in Chorley called Wang Phuk, and another in Newton-le-Willows called Ding A. Ling. But neither a single Callard nor a solitary Bowser, and the more I thought about it the more it hit me that Bowser especially is an improbable bloody surname, isn't it?

Make of that what you will, I mused to myself in the library. Maybe their real names are Belcher and Furbelow, and they feel they have to call themselves something more wholesome and attractive, these bogus Caledonians.

My mother also sold every possible brand of fag from her dockland shop, which I adamantly refuse to do. She smoked sixty Capstan Plain a day until well into her eighties and her finger ends were as black as pitch rather than as pink as mellow old age. Every so often she would have a desultory go at those stained mitts of hers with pumice stone, but no one in this little backwater minded the state of her thin little fingers back in the Sixties and Seventies. It was a proof of her genuineness that she consumed all her own toxic wares and to excess. By rights she ought to have had lung cancer ten times over by the age of fifty but she died aged eighty-two of, as far as I can see, aggravated boredom. She made the mistake of retiring at eighty-one and moving into a pensioner's flat in sheltered accommodation down by the docks. It finished her off quicker than if she'd increased the Capstans to a thousand a week. One night in her sheltered flat she put the grill on to do herself a chop and then sat down and lit up her forty-eighth Capstan of the day and then walked off into the parlour and forgot all about the grill and the chop. You can imagine all the rest. Smoke alarms, evacuation (including of an old lad's bowels next door when he thought he was going to go up in smoke as well), marshalling a dozen single or widowed old folk in front of the harbour in the freezing cold at dead of night, eventual diagnosis in my geropyromaniacal mother of incipient Alzheimer symptoms, subsequent psychogeriatric assessment in the nearest mental hospital annexe, i.e. the one in the twin coastal town of Whitehaven.

I went to see her there in Hensingham Hospital, and found her the only one awake in among about twenty of the senile confused. They were all fast asleep, presumably sedated, and it was only six o'clock. Hiding each one in her fist, she was working her way through a packet of crumble cream biscuits concealed in the depths of her purple Woolworth's handbag. She believed she was in a hotel and that she was on holiday, and she asked me when my Dad was going to join us. My Dad had died in 1968, two decades earlier, and I pointed this out gently and with a smile. I smiled as if to say, we are all a little barmy, or we are all potentially a hell of a lot barmy, or let us say in certain instances some of us are so hopelessly unimaginative with our words and hopes and anticipations that we might benefit from a little tonic insanity, ma dear. She snorted and asked me what the bloody hell I was grinning at, like a smirk-

15

ing great chimpanzee. I wiped away my smile and told her by way of news that my daughter, her only granddaughter, Anne, had just had a little baby. I said that I spent a fair amount of time babysitting for her and Sol, as Clare was my first grandchild and I was very proud of the beautiful little girl. At long last, in late middle age, I knew what it was to dote and be unashamed. My mother took in my news stonily, and muttered: 'That still doesn't explain why you're always grinning like a monkey? Do you get paid to do it?'

My mother had fine, sensitive features and sometimes a welcoming and generous temperament. But she could also be as aggressive and acidulous as any hot-blooded Mediterranean.

I smiled at her again and said inaudibly, 'I have to smile sometimes to stop bursting into tears. Now that you appear to have lost a little of your reason, ma.' Then louder. 'No, as I say, I do a lot of looking after Anne's baby, Clare. Her hair is so blond and so fine it looks like gold to me.'

She looked at me suspiciously, then boasted with a certain maudlin plaintiveness. '*I* happen to have a baby as well you know! Didn't you know?'

'Oh,' I blinked, and a cold shiver ran right up my spine.

She gazed around the ward with narrowed eyes and fingered a crumble cream very tensely. 'But they won't let me have hold of my little girl as much as I want to.'

'Oh yes?' I said with a quivering mouth. I ought to have felt sad to hear this bizarre disclosure, but instead I felt oddly hysterical. 'So... so what's it called, your baby, ma?'

'Shirley MacLaine.'

I was momentarily speechless. Apart from anything else I was amazed that Mildred Singer had even heard of Shirley MacLaine, as all my mother's favourite films were made before 1940.

'Oh,' I sighed. 'Oh is it?'

'Yes it bloody is! Chimp!'

Terse by nature, she had never been as aggressive as this in real life, something must have happened to her brain chemistry

16

at the molecular level. I watched her return to her clandestine crumble cream feast. An old man stirred in his sleep, the packet shot back into her handbag, and she wiped away every crumb from her mouth with amazing alacrity.

While musing on what she said I suddenly remembered Nikita Khruschev visiting I believe it was Hollywood in the Cold War Sixties, on a diplomatic tour of the USA. From behind the set he had watched the beautiful young film star Shirley MacLaine doing some sort of burlesque dance scene for a forthcoming movie. Afterwards, most impressed, he had turned to his American host and said apropos their privileged rear view that on balance he preferred the sight of Shirley's handsome face to her handsome backside. Of course that kind of colourful anecdote will always linger in the mind, something to do with the random association of faces and backsides and totalitarianism, I suppose. But I still can't imagine why my mad mother should think the baby that was being denied her by the hotel staff here in Whitehaven Hospital was called Shirley MacLaine.

My unusual progenitrix Ma Singer ran her legendary hole-in-the-wall shop on Maryport docks from 1920 to 1987. She was born in 1906 and I was born, her only child, in 1936. She was so prosperous, thanks to the takings from her never closed shop, that by the time I was eleven she was able to send me to a fee-paying grammar school. Thus without giving it a second thought she changed me into something from which I can never, as it were, recoup my notional pristine working-class West Cumbrian identity. Nevertheless although Mawbray Grammar School near Silloth was a hellhole in most respects, it was also full of some very bright teachers who knew how to teach. Also they knew how to push – bugger me did they know how to push you and stretch you. They turned me into a brain-box, and as kiosk vendors go I am exceptionally academically overqualified. In a dull hour I might easily be reading a philos-ophy or science or history book which I always have concealed inside my outspread copy of the *West Cumberland Times and*

Star. The trick in life is not to frighten ordinary people, especially those on whom you are financially dependent, with extraordinary ostentation. No good vaunting a great fat tome on Leibniz or a volume of Needham's *History of Chinese Medicine* if it's going to stop an innocent customer coming and buying a Mars Bar or a Straciatella or Cappucino ice cream made in Ashby-de-la-Zouch, is it?

*

Imagine me as a quiet but ruminative fifty-six-year-old citizen of Maryport, which for almost two decades now has been trying to market itself as The Gem of the Solway. For over twenty years (I was a bookseller before I was a kiosk vendor) I have been a member of the local Chamber of Trade, which for a very long time has been taxing itself with the same overwhelming problem. Our town started on its exponential economic, sociological, ecosocial, socioanthropological decline about seventy years ago, once the countless number of tiny uneconomic West Cumbrian coal pits started to adjust themselves to the waning demand and to close down one by one. Lord Lonsdale's massive forests between here and Flimby used to be full of little pits in the old days. Seven decades on, the workings are still buried away in the remotest woodland depths. You clamber up the sides of great concrete air shafts full of water, then peer down into the abyss and shout to hear the macabre resonance of your inane and pitiful halloo. You drop the little pebble and wait a very long time for the sad and ghostly splash. Up in those woods there are remnants of primitive colliery drainage systems, water boxes just like enormous wooden tomato boxes, linked by metal pipes and trailing down from the dead pit to the living beck and then the vigorous Solway Firth. You realise that long ago people, men your age and half your age, once worked away inside a forest cut off from the prosaic outer world, just like in a fairy tale, just like in a bit of improbable folklore.

By the Twenties and Thirties this little town was one of the poorest in the country, the huge docks had all but silted up, there was nothing to celebrate apart from the coming of war and of work. It sounds a dubious paradox but once the war was out of the way we were back to square one. By the early Fifties when I was a teenager there was a little industrial estate and a few struggling factories making spectacle frames and electrical parts and wellies and biscuits and dog biscuits. By the time the second recession arrived in the mid-Seventies (the rest of the country's first recession that is) there was nothing else to do but declare ourselves a tourist draw, a heritage, a matchless Gem of the Solway...

*

I mentioned that the town library was my favourite haunt but that's not strictly accurate. I get almost as much pleasure from the wonderful new aquarium that sits about two minutes' walk away from here. When business is slack I leave my assistant Karen to man (I mean woman, I mean superintend) the stall, and I slope off either to lose myself amongst books and magazines, or to lose myself amongst the sharks. They let you pat the sharks in the aquarium, a fact I'd have found grotesque if you'd told me about it two years ago when the aquarium didn't exist. When I first went in I walked the sedulous schoolparty route from start to finish, looking at wrass and pipefish and bream and sea urchins and a sprawling colony of sleepy-looking starfish. The sharks are the *pièce de résistance* and therefore almost at the end of the sequence of displays, otherwise there would be extreme congestion at the start. They are in a vast open pool, with a little raised bridge spanning its radius. You can either stand on the bridge and gaze down at the sharks, or remain right next to them, if you choose, as I always do, to lean at the perimeter.

As well as several harmless species of shark, there are numerous rays and flatfish to be found inside the pool. On my first visit I watched in amazement as little tots, some as young as two years old, began boldly patting the miniature sharks. Others not much older were stroking the backs of the turbots and the larger flatfish. At fifty-six I was frightened of doing what these babes in arms could do without a flinch. After about twenty minutes of pathetic deliberation I gingerly reached my hand towards the smallest dogfish, which is a type of shark and is also known as 'rough hound'. With a single finger I touched its back expecting it to feel like slime or plastic or a cold bit of bacon or something equally as unpleasant. Instead it felt anything but repulsive. It felt *gentle*, which I suppose is the most important adjective in a difficult lexicon when it comes to describing the tactile sense and the piscine world. Five minutes later I was stroking the dogfish's entire back, and the dogfish, while neither admitting nor denying that it found my dog-patting behaviour agreeable or otherwise, certainly did not bite or snap at me.

As for the flatfish, the flapping great rays and the whopping great turbots, this is where I was set on my heels so to speak. The turbots are the most delicate looking of the flatfish, they have a cream and brown hue that spreads like winter light the vast arctic area of their huge but vulnerable backs. Their behaviour towards the human spectators is quite extraordinary. They flap along the bottom of the pool, but often when they see a friendly human hand approach they rise up to the surface and lift themselves up from the water. It's as if they are straining on tiptoe to take a naive note of what's going on in the bemusing world of dry land. Touchingly, the turbots, like the rays, have wide-spaced and very human looking eyes. Human I mean in the childlike anthropomorphic sense. They have eyes like a friendly cartoon fish character might have in a comic or a Disney animation.

On that first occasion in the aquarium, I was busy patting a rough hound when one of these cream and brown animals noisily lifted itself up from the water. Simultaneously it turned its rotating eyes directly towards my astonished face. It sounds like trite and inaccurate metaphor but it looked almost exactly like a lazy old cat that was jumping up for a kindly pat. If it had miaowed or even barked at that point I would not have been surprised.

I stared at it. The turbot rotated its eyes and stared back at me. It winked, I swear to God it winked at me. As if to say, go on, give me a pat, that's all I'm asking! Powerless to deny it such a simple request, I timidly stuck out my hand. The turbot obligingly raised itself higher and seemingly placed its back right under my hairy old palm for a tender stroke. I looked at its astonishingly childlike face and again it gazed dreamily, apparently affectionately back at me...

*

Then it smiled at me. Honest to God, the turbot smiled at me. It smiled just like an angel might have smiled...

*

What was that? Could you say that again, please??

At this point you might reasonably respond that you lost all enthusiasm for animal fairy tales once you abandoned the gullible innocence of early childhood. But hear me out and listen very carefully before you start to smirk. I am definitely not indulging in glib hyperbole when I swear that there was the most abundant and beautiful animal *tenderness* radiating drunkenly from that turbot's smile. To be as sincere and precise as I can, there was the vastest ever effusion of tenderness I have ever seen emanate from any living creature ever...

All of a sudden I felt very faint. Then I staggered back from the pool as if I'd been stung by an electric eel.

'I don't believe it,' I exclaimed, though I don't believe that anyone overheard me.

At this point let's just pause and pose the obvious questions. Let's marshall the proper forensic detail. Had I been drinking? Was I hallucinating? Was I without my prescription spectacles? Had I a long history of mental instability? Was it a whimsical trick of the light or a crassly poetic example of emotional projection?

No, emphatically, is the answer to all of those...

My stony late-middle-aged breast filled up with an access of trembling emotion. I was moved beyond words. It sounds very extravagant and arch to admit it, but I was moved beyond the confines of my being. Others more spiritually sensitive than someone like me might be lucky enough to see a radiant smile like that from a statue of the Virgin Mary, or from a depiction of the piety of some long-ago martyred saint. It seemed like pure sacrilege in comparison, but in my unique case I had seen my beatific smile from a humble fish...

I turned quivering to a ten-year-old boy wearing a blue woolly hat and thick spectacles, and said, 'Look at that fish. Look at it smiling.

The lad frowned and squinted uncritically at me and then resumed his back-patting of a ray.

'It's remarkable,' I said to him, as if to someone my own age. 'That turbot over there, it smiled at me like a... like a tiny little baby.'

'Ah,' said the lad thoughtfully to the thornback ray that he was stroking.

'I would swear to God it was smiling at me like an angel. No one ever told me that a fish... that an animal as primitive as a fish was able to do that .'

'I've never noticed,' replied the boy judiciously. 'But it's probably just a trick of the light.'

'It smiled,' I mumbled, feeling very dizzy, 'like one of those old pictures of a haloed saint. It feels ridiculous to say it, but it's the truth. It's something quite beyond words. I... '

Not long after, I staggered off to the aquarium coffee bar and found myself tingling as if in response to some major revelation. Attempting to steady myself with a double espresso, I felt tremendously uplifted as well as immoderately shocked. After a few minutes' sober reflection, there seemed to me to be two possible options with regard to this preposterous anthropomorphic encounter with a primitive animal species. The safest was to dismiss it from my mind and believe it had no more significance than those quaint melodramatic claims made by countless doting dog lovers. To the effect that: She's almost human my little poodle Mitzi, she always seems to know exactly what I'm thinking. The other was to keep an open mind and discreetly share my amazement with someone who wouldn't immediately laugh their head off. Pondering the latter, I looked around the aquarium café for the nearest intelligent and discerning adult. Eventually I spotted a sensitive-looking lady teacher who was wearing long jade ear rings and was in charge of a dozen squabbling infants. However she seemed extremely harassed by her anarchic little charges and I decided that discretion really was the better part of indiscretion. I remained glued to my table for about half an hour, then walked back to my kiosk and stayed silently preoccupied for the rest of the afternoon.

That night I told my daughter Anne about the beatific smile of the aquarium fish, and she laughed uproariously because of course she thought I was pulling her leg. With a wry expression, I showed her how completely serious I was. I was as baffled as the next, but I was definitely not making anything up. Anne is a very bright young psychologist of twenty-eight who has already published weighty books on child development and Melanie Klein. Nothing in the last analysis is capable of surprising her. She seemed at first anxious when I told her, but finally she just laughed. She suggested that I must have had that *rara avis* known as an interspecies paranormal encounter. She was teasing me, of course, and I felt moderately annoyed by her playful scepticism. Anne has the most reassuring and tolerant smile, and as a senior clinical psychologist she can disarm even the most suspicious of her clients and professional colleagues.

23

Yet impressive as hers was, it was definitely not in the same transcendent category as the one that I'd glimpsed in the harbour aquarium.

*

The next day I spent an hour in the biology section of the library and endeavoured to find out everything I could about the turbot. It sounds mad of course, but I was hoping to find something about its possibly unique psychology and idiosyncratic emotional life. After all, if dolphins can work with mentally handicapped and autistic children and demonstrate palpable altruism and kindness and massive intelligence, it didn't seem that outlandish to think that turbots might be notable for their radiant, almost human smiles. Eventually, after a frustrating search, I found an old tattered hardback on ethology, the science of animal behaviour. Encouragingly, there was a great deal in it about the behaviour of numerous species of fish. However it was all rather disappointing and inconsequential stuff, at least from the point of view of depth psychology and the turbot. A lot of it was about visual perception and how it related to the mating urge in the male fish, in this particular instance a male halibut. Wonderingly I perused these old line drawings illustrating experiments done with replica female halibuts made out of wood. Replica A looked exactly like the genuine female; correct shape, correct size, down to every last painted detail, but without a swollen belly full of unfertilised eggs. Replica B, though of similar dimensions, was just any old block of wood, a featureless sausage-shaped thing that bore no resemblance to any fish known to man. However the sausage in question had a vastly swollen wooden belly halfway down its length...

Place these two false females equidistant from the lusting male in your experimental pool, and imagine what you observe. Namely that old Romeo always bursts his bags and goes like a

24

madman for the pregnant wooden sausage, while supinely indifferent to that perfect imitation of a female halibut.

'There are several glosses you could put on that one,' I thought to myself sceptically. 'That the male fish has only one thing on the brain. That, if you're a halibut, you don't look at the mantelpiece when you are poking the fire. That maybe Jack the Lad, the male halibut, needs a little pair of glasses.'

The brand new 1991 *Encyclopaedia Britannica* with its Micropedia and Macropedia was a grave disappointment. It had nothing to say about turbots at all, and I rued the day the library had turfed out the 1946 set which I always found had five thousand words about everything under the sun, whether it be the botany of the chickpea or the sex life of the loris. In some desperation I turned to one of those Time-Life colour books about Mediterranean sea life, and eventually discovered a couple of sketchy paragraphs on the turbot.

The turbot, it explained, is found in the East Atlantic, West Baltic and Mediterranean waters, and is in the same family as the brill and the megrim. A left-facing flatfish, its body is almost diamond shaped and is studded with bony tubercles...

'Tubercles,' I whispered wonderingly, and I balanced the word on the end of my tongue. 'Copiously studded with bony tubercles.'

The turbot's colour varies from light to dark brown, and it is spotted with green or black. The blind side is white...

'I must have seen its blind side then,' I decided. 'I could swear the one that I saw was cream.'

To my disgust I discovered the most comprehensive information inside an old illustrated cookery book. It told you all the sordid details to give to your obliging fishmonger, and how to cook the rare delicacy, and something else I found remarkable if saddening after yesterday's experience in the aquarium. The French, all round sybarites and gormandisers that they are, have invented a special fish kettle called the *turbotière*. A *turbotière* is diamond shaped, of course, just like the fish itself. Also, the cookery book informed me, small turbot weighing around two pounds are known as 'chicken' turbot. These are best cooked simply in a *court bouillon*. The necessary ingredients are thyme, parsley, white wine, bayleaf, twelve peppercorns...

'Why that specific number?' I whispered to myself in a very ruffled state of mind. 'What sort of imbecile would count out precisely twelve peppercorns?'

I snapped the book shut and walked out of the library feeling depressed. That exotic Mediterranean fish yesterday afternoon had smiled at me with the effulgent – of course I blush to say the next word – *love*, of some small disguised angelic being made manifest in animal form. I stared at the library swing doors and then stopped at the bottom of the stairs. Hold your horses, Singer, I urged myself with some anxiety. Angelic beings and angels, what on earth can you possibly be babbling about? Believe you me, I don't for a minute swallow all that arcane stuff about metempsychosis or transmigration of souls, and I don't think you or me or even a butcher like Genghis Khan will ever come back in the form of an elephant or a dung beetle. And yet the sight of that gently smiling fish had at least convinced me that it possessed an enduring something. Let me be sceptical, judicious and self-protectively vague, and call it a metaphysical *core*... and a considerable metaphysical core at that.

The discovery seemed to me to be momentous. Though I wasn't as yet sure what the ultimate implications were...

2

From that day on I stopped eating fish in all its forms. For one who had whiled away half his Greek and Portuguese holidays in seafood tavernas and Algarve marisqueiras, this was a considerable about-turn. Not only were truta grelhada and barbouni a thing of the past, I would no longer eat tuna sandwiches or smoked mackerel baguettes from the local sandwich bar. I resisted every fish and chip shop in the town, one of which is of country-wide renown. When Anne one lunchtime offered me grey mullet that she'd purchased that day at Carlisle market, I apologised but said I would only eat the vegetables. My daughter was visibly irritated and dismayed as she and I have always shared a conspiratorial fondness for really challenging Continental cuisine.

Her reaction to my gastronomic disloyalty was reasonable enough. People's addiction to their bellies is a powerful thing. I have a friend, a computer fanatic called Thompson Williamson, a retired local government officer, who came back recently from a fortnight of touring the Republic of Ireland, a place he had never been before. Anticipating an interesting exchange of notes about the tea shops of Kilfenora, the bizarre lunar geology of the nearby Burren, the Irish-speaking fishermen of the Dingle Peninsula and so forth, I was treated exclusively to an account of the various restaurants he and his wife had visited when they toured Clare and Kerry and Sligo. Mouthwatering *ossobuco* in an Italian trattoria in Sligo (he had no memory whatever of what Sligo itself was like); a swanky fish restaurant in Galway where he had had sea bass with ginger for the very first time; a specialist vegetarian bistro in Tralee where he had tasted what were classed as gourmet pecan fricadellas at ten Irish punts a go, but turned out to be rather bilious little nut rissoles straight out of a Vegimix packet at £1.25 a ton.

As I said by way of justification to Anne, my first visit to the aquarium had had far reaching effects. Not only could I no longer eat fish, including such amorphous, absolutely unfish-like fish dishes as fish fingers or fishcakes or sardines on toast. My psychology as well as my belly had been affected by my experience in the aquarium. More important than simple dietary restraint, my inner life, and in particular the memories of things long forgotten and discarded, had begun to stir and rise up to the surface like some sort of glittering colloidal suspension. Alternatively you could say these disquieting memories were rising up to nibble at the surface, a bit like a shoal of nibbling minnows. There was nothing I could do about it but stop in my tracks and quietly gasp at some of these quivering chimeras within myself. These memories, long shelved, abandoned and forgotten, were of the same intensity as the radiant expression in that aquarium fish's eyes.

Among other considerations, I was obliged to recast my assessment of my mother Ma Singer. The predominantly iron, strong-willed matriarch, who kept the family going by her miraculous steely industry, would surface in these forgotten memories with a temperament quite the opposite. Despite myself, despite herself, I kept seeing her in certain confusingly gentle, even poetic, even spiritual lights. You have to remember that the last significant experience I had of her was when she had Alzheimer's and kept addressing me as 'chimp'. She was also punily secretive with regard to her crumble creams, her clandestine store of childish oral comfort. It is a commonplace to say that when people are on their last legs the repressed and often grotesquely distorted side of their personality finally emerges. Vicars blaspheme, saintly givers turn stingy and suspicious, lascivious roués suddenly become all prudish and pious. My mother was all sorts in her heyday, but the last thing she was was stingy. Mildred Singer had a finger in every pie in the town, she was an organiser, a committee woman, a finagler, an operator, but only, give her her due, for the common good. She wanted her town to prosper, to hold up its head and compete and trounce the places that smugly believed themselves better. She always insisted that Maryport could do anything better than Workington, even if it was a quarter of the size. She even said her home town was more go-ahead than Whitehaven, which apart from hosting the biggest hospital for miles around (including my mother's psychogeriatric annexe) always considers itself the most progressive, *au fait* and cosmopolitan of West Cumbrian townships.

Everything is relative and structural in this regard. Progressive Whitehaven, which got there first with the wine bars and the Middle East carry-outs and the Georgian renovations, puts its hand to its mouth and titters at its dingy competitor Workington, regardless of how much the latter has doggedly struggled to enhance itself in the last decade. Workington likewise titters at Maryport as a joke town because of its all too recent squalor and East European unemployment levels and a vast acreage of docks that not long ago was silted up to a deathly dereliction. Everyone laughs at someone else and to make matters worse the rest of the county laughs at the whole of the primitive west coast. And then most infuriatingly the rest of the *country* laughs at the whole of our bloody county. At bloody comical *Cumbria*, God's apparent gratuitous joke when he was resting between the creation of England and the creation of Scotland.

What, you say, *de haut en bas*? What price that rock-hard stuff, Kendal Mint Cake, as chewed by Edmund Hillary – the snow-white Cumbrian elixir that got him and Sherpa Tensing shinning up Mount Everest like greased lightning when all else failed? Or what price John Peel, Master Lakeland Huntsman, who inspired that sacred ditty that will still be sung and resung when the Beatles and the Schola Cantorum and Placido

Domingo have all vanished into a musty oblivion?

We in the backward provinces operate by our own laws. We deny Newtonian Physics and syllogistic logic, and instead we work on the principles of coagulation and agglutination. We pick up a bit of this and a bit of that and it sticks to us like glue. Also like the repetitive motion of the see-saw or the whip and top, we demonstrate a charming childlike predictability. Seventy years of recession produces a comprehensively ambient melancholy in a populace that doesn't even know it is sad. Even though things are improving a bit they are still standing still. The harbour developments have got in more tourists but not enough. There is insufficient spin-off, the town overall is not benefitting, just my ice cream kiosk and the marvellous aquarium are putting away the dividends in any significant quantity.

*

In the remote provinces, needless to add, people can get away with anything. Thus my own Maryport childhood, now that the aquarium experience has forced me to examine it, seems quite incredible in its wilder aspects. At times I seriously disbelieve the improbable fairytale absurdity of my earliest memories. For example, forty years on, I can barely credit that my best friend between the ages of five and twelve rejoiced in the name of Squinty Bar Radish...

Mentioning that little boy's ludicrous nickname, I recall that this was the point where things began to get really peculiar. Because it was immediately before I began to remember my mysterious bond with old Squinty Bar that I had my second encounter with that extraordinary harbinger, the fish. This time the experience was not even inside the aquarium but within the non-aqueous confines of my dockland kiosk. Simultaneously I was upset by a jolt of recollection so potent and so overwhelming I had no option but to desert the kiosk at once. That disturbing recollection was about a time in my childhood so very early that I hadn't even got to know the infant Squinty Bar. I was obliged to explain to my mystified assistant Karen that I had had a sudden stomach upset and was off home to rest for the afternoon. Instead of doing which I took myself off to the quietest backstreets in town and paced around them in distraction and embarrassment. After about half an hour of this repetitive wandering, I spotted a couple of acquaintances down below on the harbour front. I hesitated briefly, then headed back to my house by a circuitous route. Light-headed and feeling remarkably exhausted, I sat down in the parlour with some coffee and some tranquil piano music from my cassette player. It was a tape of Fauré, and something about its benignant melancholy and tender pastoral intensity seemed to subtly clarify the perplexing identity of the flickering ghosts I had glimpsed only half an hour ago

Let me explain. In the kiosk as well as ice cream and sweets I also sell a certain amount of rock-bottom stationery and assorted toys and knick-knacks. A few outsize pencils with *Maryport – Gem of the Solway* written on them, a few Pritt sticks and staplers and bags of rubber bands. I also sell a very few ornamental dollies, again with *A Present From Maryport* printed on their dresses. One of these dollies, which was manufactured in South Korea, happened to be a Barbie-type blonde of surpassing blandness, with a singularly vapid expression on her smirking mug. It must surely be the East taking revenge on the West, I often reflected, the Korean toy designers gleefully depicting the pampered Brits in their true depleted colours. However what caught my eye about this little sixty-pence gargoyle was not her face but her dress. She happened to be wearing a brightly coloured skirt which was decorated at the hem with some glinting crystalline material, as vivid and enchanting as the little coloured crystals one sees tumbling inside a child's kaleidoscope.

As I stood and stared in the glittering sunlight at the dolly's glinting hem, two things happened in quick succession. First of all there was a hallucinatory half-second when the image of the

31

levitating fish from the nearby aquarium flickered across my gaze and bestowed on me, as a personal and intimate gift, its mesmerising radiance. I saw the aquarium turbot raise itself and smile, and my heart started to thump at the delicate vividness of that beautiful, quite unworldly experience. I almost wanted to weep at the sight, and sheepishly decided that perhaps I was feeling the summer heat today. Instantaneously the piscine simulacrum – I use the fustian Latin just to distance myself from the raw force of the thing itself, from its uncanny, unnerving aura, you understand – seemed to evaporate and at once was replaced by a picture, a tableau, a memory. Gazing in a hypnotic rapture at the dolly's hem, I suddenly saw something that I hadn't seen or even thought about for over half a century. It was one of my greatest, most hidden treasures, one of my very finest hours, and it had all been buried away and forgotten like lumber in a loft or attic.

*

It was Christmas Eve, 1939, and our front parlour had been carefully arrayed with glinting holly, silver tinsel and an incalculable quantity of Christmas cards. I was three years old and I was all on my own in that beautiful room. It was early evening, perhaps six o'clock, and there was no sign at all of my mother in the house. She must have been out doing a duty visit to an exceptionally unbearable relative, one of those pitiful and insufferable rarities not invited to our house for Christmas Day. Because it was Christmas Eve, she had shut her kiosk at lunch time and wouldn't open it until the day after Boxing Day. My Dad was outside in the back garden chopping wood by the light of an outsize torch he'd purloined from the pit. The curtains hadn't been drawn because he was keeping an eye on me while he prepared his special stack of yuletide faggots. Inside the parlour, relishing my perfect solitude, I was standing by the firelight and examining the room and that breathtaking ornamentation. I was only a scrap of an infant and the state I was in was one of immobile rapture. It was all so terribly beautiful that I could hardly breathe. The gas light was off and my Dad had lit a few red candles and placed them up in dishes on the old mahogany sideboard. The room was hallowed by the dance of firelight and candle flame, and I, who was not accustomed to the flicker of candles, was staring at the heightened world of tiny festive ornament and sculpted shadows and waking euphoria...

The Christmas tree was both a sovereign deity and its exact opposite, a humble draught animal. As I stared at it, I was reminded of a kind and somnolent horse. It was about twice my height and was decked with very beautiful baubles. The baubles seemed to be vibrating and shimmering on the tree, though it was just the dance of the fire and the candle flicker that made the sly miracle of their turning. Those melting hues were so deep and so strong that they had ceased to be distinctive colours and had become the pure anonymous essence of light itself. The purple bauble became a vanishing colour of ecstasy that became the burning inside of my singing belly. The purple melted inside my guts and the colour of it was deep joy and my joy was in the purple. And that joy was deep inside me, and I was the dancing bauble too. That holy purple tenderness was dancing upon the tree and it seemed to breathe a word I knew. I believe, though I wouldn't swear to it, that it said l-o-v-e. By which I mean it spelt it, but it didn't say it.

Dimly I heard my Dad chopping the wood. It was a meek, self-effacing sound that did not intrude on my private ecstasies. I was breathless at the burning, glistening green of the viridian bauble as it turned on its axis of spilling tenderness. Inside my belly was such an immeasurable joy. The tiny scrap called George Alfred Singer was floating up towards a nameless heaven. My first sight of paradise was up there in those burning little baubles on the Christmas tree...

As for the dark crimson one that was leaking its l-o-v-e into this shadowy room, that colour was surely the same as my young mother. Mildred Singer always wore maroon and magenta when she was trying to express what was really inside herself. That steely abrasive woman who stood there smoking in all weathers, keeping the world on its toes with fags, sweets, candles and string and everything that mattered, was a rich baroque magenta woman. She had a fine crimson brooch she always wore at Christmas, and I treasured the sight of it, as if it belonged to me rather than her. It was my mother on her own, unaided, who had been supernaturally inspired to decorate this room and make it the extraordinary palace it was. She was as hard as rock, but in some magical, specially-aided fashion, she had created a temple that burned, danced and flickered with all this l-o-v-e...

Aglow with reverence, I turned my gaze up to the heights. Right at the top of the tree was the Christmas angel. She was looking down at me and smiling so infinitely tenderly. She beheld someone very small who was lost in the huge shadows. Of course I have seen hundreds of Christmas tree angels since, but she was the only one ever to give me a glimpse of the world we never see. She was the cheapest angel ornament in existence and she must have cost no more than threepence when Mildred bought her from Woolworth's in 1926. She was only a bit of printed cardboard, artlessly designed to resemble a demure pink-cheeked young woman from the Twenties. But her smile was perfectly pure, so very pure that when she smiled down at me I was brimful of deliquescent yearning. I looked at that kind and beautiful young woman's face and my heart rose up with a great heavy weight of longing. It lifted up like a fish and it glowed and smiled and exuded all the limitless power of its three-year-old intensity.

The tender leaking from my belly did not come from inside me, but from somewhere beyond me. The radiance of the baubles did not come from the the baubles, but from somewhere beyond them. The little cardboard angel's power and dominion over this room came not from her but from something perfect, loving and invisible. I stood there fainting at all the radiance in this room, and I felt myself swooning away with the endless joy of it. Nothing could be finer, more finished, more eternal than this cluttered and forgotten little Cumbrian parlour on Christmas Eve.

I was still in my rapture when my Dad came in from the yard. He picked me up and laughed and told me that fat old Father Christmas was coming down the chimney tonight. I groaned with a painful joy. My father was thin but Santa Claus was fat. I would have to go upstairs to bed where my pillowcase bolster was hung out for his gifts. My father gently carried me upstairs. I was fainting and happily dying in a languor of joy. I doubt that he, quiet, patient, temperate Joseph Singer noticed my condition. I doubt if anyone notices the signs of spiritual trans-fixedness in a tiny infant. But I think now that Clare my grandchild has just turned three I shall start looking for signs of her having glimpsed the world of angels.

*

I started from my trance as a middle-aged German approached and nervously asked me for a pistachio and cappucino ice. I served the puzzled tourist in a daze and then apologised to Karen that I had had a bilious attack and wouldn't be back this afternoon. Later, alone in the old house that had been my parents', I went into the parlour and reflected that it was here fifty-three years ago I had known that special Advent ecstasy. I felt sad, mournful, somehow bereaved, as I could not even faintly recreate the experience in the house where it first took place. For over half a century the memory of it had eluded me. It had been buried away like... like insignificant Christmas decorations shoved away in a loft or attic. I'd have given fifty fortunes, fifty lottery millions just to have held in my hand intact that little cardboard Woolworth's angel. Incredibly Mildred Singer had tossed that unique little thing on the fire on Christmas Eve of 1948, before purchasing an expensive and hideous plastic replacement from Workington.

So much for tender relics. So much for these innocent doll's house images of the holy and the infinite. You forget what they mean and you chuck them on the fire in a fit of carefree amnesia. Then you buy yourself a costly synthetic angel with a smile not beatific but rather more like a grinning bag of chips...

I felt greatly displaced by the sheer intensity of those memories of the Christmas parlour. I also felt puzzled and painedly melancholy as I couldn't really comprehend what their significance amounted to. The next day as I stood distractedly inside my kiosk, I kept vainly trying to reopen other hidden doors of significant memory. Back in the Fifties as a student at Durham University I had doggedly struggled my way through Proust's *Remembrance of Things Past*. Like everyone else I had felt that my own pitiful childhood souvenirs amounted to nothing in comparison. Even now I didn't seriously think either the turbot or my Woolworth's angel had much in common with the depths of that great artist's recollections. Marcel Proust happened to be a genius of illimitable proportions. Unfortunately I wasn't anything like a genius, at best I was only a dedicated amateur. So feeling very irritated and thwarted by my constricted imagination, I racked my brains impatiently for other magical advent calendar doors to early infancy, other special pathways to other special worlds.

*

I assume that after first seeing that radiant fish, I was unconsciously looking for the mysterious, ineffable faces of Advent angels. But instead, all I could focus on with any constancy at all was something quite the opposite. Or did this process perhaps involve a chagrined reassessment of what constitutes the genuinely angelic and what does not? At any rate, what came to me unheralded and repetitively in my ice cream kiosk was the same old image of the same extraordinary face. It was the puzzened, dubious, thoroughly unprepossessing countenance of a very unlikely apparition. That apparition happened to be called Squinty Bar Radish...

Squinty Bar's real name, which no one apart from his parents used, took some considerable effort of memory. It was Thomas Ernest Johnston. Yet even grown men and women would refer to him in the third person or address him jovially face to face as Radish or Squinty Bar or Squinty Bar Radish. He had been given this nickname when he was only three years old, by a boy called Bazzer Clough. In 1939 thirteen-year-old Clough had the deepest gruffest voice in the whole of Maryport. He called the little Johnston kid Squinty not because he had a squint but because he was precociously nosy and was always peering and grimacing at anyone who went by his Wood Street villa. Clough called him Radish because he noticed that the three-year-old had very waxy as well as protuberant ears. Clough's extravagant idea was that there was so much wax in those lugs that Johnston could easily have grown radishes in each of them. Finally, and this was the surreal touch of a frustrated poetic genius, Bazzer Clough called him Bar Radish to indicate that although radishes might easily have been grown in all that waxy muck, Squinty did not choose to plant any there, and thereby drew attention to an unconsolidated status. Hence he was 'bar' (without) any radishes, and his glaringly radishless status needed to be given a name...

For several years Squinty Bar and I were taught in Ellenbank Junior School by a certifiable lunatic called Miss Blood, or 'Bloody' as she was affectionately known. Miss Blood was in her late sixties, past retirement age, when she was hauled out of her Sea Brows cottage to contribute to the war effort by teaching children of junior years. She had been born to very elderly parents in the late summer of 1870, hence was three years younger than Arnold Bennett, or four years the junior of H.G.Wells. However she had none of Wells's or Bennett's ameliorative outlook or idealistic vision, but was a seasoned flagellomaniac. She identified with a much earlier literary generation, and displayed it in her zestful Dickensian bent. The original model for Dotheboys Hall is reckoned to be near Brough in Cumbria, which perhaps explains why Bloody modelled herself so closely on Mrs Wackford Squeers.

Every morning in her class we tackled a great many mental arithmetic questions which she had chalked up on the blackboard. Regularly there would be sixty additions, subtractions, divisions and multiplications arranged in four rows of fifteen sums. Once each row was completed the pupils had to take their exercise books up for marking at Bloody's desk. All correct answers were given a tick and a gruff approval, all errors were promptly punished on the spot. Your hand was seized and your wrist slapped hard three times per incorrect sum. Thus if like Squinty Bar Radish or obese Jennifer McCumiskey you had made seven errors out of fifteen, you would be slapped twenty-one times before returning to your desk. This would take old Bloody at least five minutes to administer, and she would be panting and sweating, not without a pious slavering relish, by the end of it. Radish was regularly slapped twenty-one, twenty-four, twenty-seven, all the way to the forty-five limit. Despite this pedagogic rigour the unteachable idiot could never master his three-times table. In fact all the weak mathematicians, despite Bloody's belabouring, stayed innumerate. If asked Miss Blood would probably have admitted she did not slap to improve their skill but because their woodenness made her infuriated.

Once Miss Blood was holding forth we were only allowed to speak if so requested and only if we had raised our hands first. The exception was a girl called Jinny Pettigrew who had wide staring eyes, a lugubrious smile and frequent epileptic fits. Jinny did not have to raise her hand before taking a fit, and as far as I recall was never slapped at all. If you tittered or whispered and were seen to do so, Bloody summoned you to the front and you were bent over for all to see. The boys were struck three times across the top of the thigh by her rough old palm while the girls had their skirts hauled up and were chastised across their knickers. Of course the boys, some not too far from masturbating puberty, frequently enjoyed the sight of the girls' abasement. Once I myself grew noisily hysterical at the sight of Jennifer McCumiskey's exposed underwear, principally because she had a large hole in her coarse navy-blue knickers. As soon as she had finished with blushing Jennifer, Bloody signalled for me with crooked finger and I too was bent over and clattered for laughing out loud in class.

It was during the previous war from 1914 to 1918 that my mother Mildred Singer had also known Bloody's hand across her backside. She believed it had satisfactorily toughened her hide against most small calamities, as well as making her fault-less at mental arithmetic. For her to run her all-hours kiosk single-handed on the docks from the age of fourteen, it was imperative of course that Mildred should be proficient at computation. Thanks to Bloody's slappings Mildred knew her twelve and twenty multiples better than anyone else in Maryport. She could convert £3/12/11 into pennies, halfpen-nies, farthings, nearest number of shillings, nearest number of florins and nearest number of half-crowns at the speed of a prodigy. Remarkably she could also manage this on her deathbed, and indeed the more florid she got with her Alzheimer's in 1988, the more she would conjure out-of-date calculations in pre-decimal coinage for pre-war sweets, fags and tins of snuff. Sixty Strand at 11d for twenty, change out of a ten bob note was 7/3d. Twenty Players Weights at 1/2d. Jujubes and jap nougat at twopence a quarter...

Miss Blood was mad not only in her discipline, but also in the stupefyingly senseless nature of much of her instruction. There was precious little point even in 1914 in forcing little Mildred Singer and her classmates to learn every last detail of apothecaries' weights and troy weight, in addition to the stan-dard avoirdupois system 'used for all general merchandise'. But Mildred Singer had had to parrot the whole lot, and in old age could still recite all the units verbatim and with pride, wholly indifferent to the fact she had never once in sixty years needed to use any of it in her kiosk. Nor for that matter had any

of her classmates, some of whom had also turned out successful Maryport shopkeepers. No doubt even Maryport boasted a
precision jeweller during the First World War, yet it's unlikely
its proprietor would have known, as my mother certainly did,
that one diamond carat was equal to four diamond grains...

Which was not to say, my old mother insisted sternly, the
same as four *troy* grains. A diamond grain, she simpered
approvingly, was the equivalent of only 3.2 troy grains.

'In troy weight,' Bloody growled at us on a warm June
morning in 1943, nearly thirty years after she had growled the
same thing at Mildred Singer, 'twenty-four grains make one
pennyweight. You already know that it takes twenty penny-
weights to make one ounce. Which means there are how many
troy grains in one troy ounce, George Singer?'

Just to confound her, I had been aping doziness and staring
out of the window at some sparrows having a dustbath. In fact
I was as sharp at mental arithmetic as my mother before me,
and Miss Blood devoted much of her energy to trying to catch
me out. She sensed a wilful rebelliousness in my effortless
memory for formulas and tables. There was something all too
sly and lazy about my ability to flick from daydream to
studiousness without apparent struggle.

'Please Miss, 480, Miss.'

My wooden double vocative irritated her all the more.

'Supposing, George Singer,' she said, lingering threateningly
by my desk, as prelude to a difficult question, 'supposing it was
jewellers' measurement instead?'

'Miss?' I bounced back defiantly.

She pouted her pendulous lips and struggled to think of an
absolutely impossible computation. 'Seeing you're always so
sure of yourself, so cocky, Singer, I want you to tell me how
many diamond carats there are in one troy ounce.'

The whole of Standard One whistled and for once Bloody
acknowledged the strength of the challenge she had thrown.
She did not rebuke them all for murmuring in class. It would
have taken a good half-hour to bend everyone over and clatter

the whole of the form's backsides in any case. Nonetheless she looked a little dismayed at having set me this outrageous calculation. Self-evidently she wasn't capable of answering it herself.

'Please Miss,' I began, 'if there are 4 jewellers' grains in every carat, then you might think the answer would be 480 grains divided by 4. Which is 120 diamond carats...'

'Mm,' she conceded doubtfully, glancing swiftly at her tattered arithmetic primer, 'you might think that if you were barking up the wrong avenue, Singer.'

'However Miss,' I continued, before stopping abruptly. I knew that she hated me using conjunctions like 'however', as they indicated an insufferable precocity in a seven-year-old, 'however Miss, 4 diamond grains equals only 3.2 troy grains. The answer must be 4 over 3.2 times 120. Which is 5 over 4 times 120, which is 150 is the correct answer, Miss.'

Bloody took an appalled glance at her 1893 pamphlet, *Imperial Weights and Measures Tables for Instruction in Elementary Schools at Home and Abroad*, and confirmed that I was right. Furious at not being able to confuse me with pointless conversions between obsolete mensuration systems, she turned on my best friend Squinty Bar Radish and decided that he would be the exemplary sacrifice. If she couldn't punish me for ignorance she could punish my pig ignorant friend instead.

'Thomas Johnston!'

Squinty Bar swallowed, knowing exactly what the precedent was here. Radish didn't even know his three-times table, much less what he regularly fondly misconstrued as 'carrots' and 'toy weight'.

'Johnston! What is a scruple?'

It was something that Bloody could have profited from. Squinty mused nonplussed at her meaningless sentence. 'Please Miss, what Miss?'

'Are you hard of hearing? Wash all that disgusting dirty wax from your ears and you might hear what's being said. I'm asking you what is a *scruple*?'

Squinty smiled in a debased and fawning manner, as he pretended the question was an amiable sort of riddle.

'I think it must be a vegetable.'

'A vegetable? Come out here, you little fool!'

Squinty Bar Radish trudged out with his wrist held out ready, as if for inoculation. Bloody picked up her ruler and rattled him twice as hard as expected. Radish winced but allowed no tears in his eyes. Bloody was busy caning me as well as her scapegoat, even he realised that, and adjusted his pain threshold accordingly.

'A scruple is a unit of apothecaries' weight! And what is an apothecary?'

A tense wondering silence filled the dingy, stuffy classroom. Squinty Bar squinted at her as if she had asked him the meaning of 'ontological phenomenology'.

'A type of wart?'

Subdued, fearful titters. Bloody glared at the rest of us and bared her pearly little teeth.

Crack! Crack crack crack!

'It's a chemist, you fool! A dispensing pharmacist in other words. A chemist needs to use very tiny measurements with his medicines and drugs, so as not to poison us. Hence the need for apothecary units, it's a matter of life and death. Very well, how many grains in a scruple?'

Squinty fingered the inside of his left nostril for good luck.

'A... a hundred, Miss.'

Crack! Crack, crack, crack!

'There are twenty grains in a scruple! I must have told you so at least twenty times. Three scruples make one what, Johnston?'

Silence again. Outside we could hear the cries of mourning seagulls circling over the docks. The thirty seven-year-olds opened their mouths and breathed through their noses at the nearest thing they had ever seen to Live Theatre. It was the Theatre of the Absurd and the Theatre of Cruelty before they ever existed.

'A potterkerry, Miss?'

Crack! Crack, crack, crack!

'A dram, boy. A *dram*. Tell me how many drams there are in an ounce!'

'Sixteen.'

'Gah!'

Crack!

'No there aren't, there are only eight! Let me give you something easier. I'm sure that even a clod like you will remember how many ounces there are in a pound?'

I saw Radish's wary eyes light up at the realisation that one unit at least had fixed itself in his brain. But it was a trick, a cunning trick she often used to catch us out, one only a fool like Radish could fall for. I was wriggling with suppressed excitement at my desk, bursting to shout out: No, Radish, no, it's not what you think, it really isn't the obvious answer.

'Miss, there are sixteen ounces in a pound.'

'Agh,' I sighed to my favourite pink india-rubber.

Crack! Crack! Crack, crack!

'Nitwit! Only you could make such an idiotic mistake. There might be sixteen avoirdupois ounces in an avoirdupois pound, but there are only ten apothecary's ounces in an apothecary's pound! Repeat what I've just said, dunderhead!'

'Yes. There are sixteen av... sixteen av...'

'Go on!'

Crack!

Radish blurted the rest out in one suicidal rush. He knew it was going to be nonsense but he had to say something or stay there all day. Rather than a hundred separate blows he might as well get all his hammerings in one fell swoop.

'Sixteen avoid-a-piss ounces in avoid-a-piss pound...'

'What!'

'And... and... only ten Bother Eric's ounces in Bother Eric's pound.'

The whole class erupted, including epileptic Jinny. Even I, Radish's best friend, could not contain my hilarity.

'Quiet!' screamed Bloody, snorting at the nostrils. Her face was part purple, part red, part blue. 'Or I'll tan the whole blasted lot of you, even if it takes all day.'

She turned on Squinty Bar and laid on a volley of feverish strokes in her fury. Crack! Crack crack crack crack crack crack crack crack crack crack crack! Yet he had intended no deliberate coarseness with his avoid-a-piss. It was simply how he always read that incredible foreign word on the back of his bright red exercise book.

'Avoirdupois,' she growled.

'Havwadooper!'

Crack!

'*Avoirdupois*!'

3

On the way home on that hot, intoxicating June afternoon, Bar Radish fulminated against mad old Bloody and her lack of justice.

'Shite to her scruples,' he muttered viciously. 'Arseholes to her pottybloodykerry.'

We stopped by the dockside and Squinty leant against a big metal capstan. He said that he would love to ambush her at dead of night, then upend her and bray her fat old arse with a joiner's T-square. He would love to kick her into the deepest stretch of harbour mud and watch her gasp and choke like a frog. I sighed and told him that my mother treasured the instruction she had had off Bloody and especially the canings. Radish grunted and said his own stupid mother was the same. Mrs Mina Johnston ran a guesthouse on Wood Street for a better class of travelling salesman and bachelor teacher. She worked day and night and was whiningly irritable as a result. Whatever Bar Radish said to her, whether it was a statement, a demand, or innocuous silence, always brought out a rebuke. He could do nothing right and she could do nothing but nag him. His Dad Joe was a collier, a strange man who cut his own jail-cropped hair in front of the mirror with his razor. He was a quiet, mysterious sort who never went near a pub and had a confusing way with his humour. Whenever I went round and said 'Is Thomas in?' he would always answer 'Yes' with a vacant look of inquiry. Minutes passed before I realised I had to ask a second question or I would be stood at the door all day. It amused him to take my question literally and leave me standing there until I learnt to phrase my requests more intelligently. Both he and Mrs Johnston insisted on rigid table manners from Squinty Bar Radish. If their only child wished for a sandwich or a piece of cake, he must put up his hand, like at school, and ask for it first, not just reach over and take it. Joe even barbered Squinty's hair with a razor so that the Johnston son also looked jailcropped and the wax in his lugholes was even more on display.

We stopped by the kiosk and I asked my mother for twopence worth of sherbet. I passed across my own money and she pushed it back mock-grudgingly. She was melting with sweat inside her little wooden hut and was making herself continuous cups of tea on a spirit stove. She seemed helplessly irritated by the sight of our freedom and even more so when I asked if I could eat my tea out in the back garden, it being such a roasting day. My Aunty Elsie always made my tea if my mother was working and I knew she would only say yes to a picnic if her big sister Mildred had approved it first.

'Very well,' she finally conceded, too weary to do battle on a day like this. 'But you have to carry it all out and clear it all away yourself. Don't have Elsie traipsing in and out like a pub skivvy.'

'And Radish,' I added audaciously. 'Can Squinty Bar Radish have his tea out in our garden as well?'

Radish looked as perplexed as she did. Back in 1943 provincial working-class children didn't have tea at each other's houses unless it was a birthday or a bereavement. But I felt a naive, rebellious wish to do something different. I wanted to have an impromptu picnic to celebrate the sunshine, and I had the even more expansive desire to enjoy it with a pal. I was expecting Mildred Singer to say no, but then I saw her eyeing all those weals on Squinty's wrist, all twenty-five, and deciding after all that perhaps that daft-looking boy might deserve a little spoiling.

'Very well. Provided his mother says yes. Make sure you ask her or I'll crown the pair of you.'

As if Squinty would have dared to dine out without seeking prior permission. The next stage we both acknowledged had a ten percent chance of success. I doubted whether Mina had picnicked even once in the garden of her own house in the thirty years she had lived there. Even in sweltering heat her guesthouse residents – whom she always referred to as 'boarders', and Radish was rattled across the ear if ever he called them 'lodgers' – were never allowed to dine outside. It was a bizarre foreign absurdity to picnic in your own grounds and to risk midge bites, bee stings and damp-induced rheumatism. A picnic was alternatively something you did on a church outing, and you had it in a field or a park where you weren't subject to the impudent scrutiny of your neighbours.

Radish almost chickened out but I pushed him through the door of his substantial villa, a three-storey townhouse that managed to host six guests and the Johnstons. I swore that if nervousness made him lose his voice I would intercede and explain my peculiar proposal to his mother. Mrs Johnston was there in the kitchen, hot-faced over a huge pan of tatie pot, a heavy and hearty Cumbrian confection of string beef and black pudding and carrots and potatoes. It is typical winter fare, of course, meant to toughen farmhands against frostbite and drenchings, and nobody but Mina Johnston would have served it on a broiling June evening. No doubt it was meant to punish her pampered residents who could gallivant around the shore or dally and stroll about the sea brows while she was forever tied to the house.

Radish hesitated. He raised his hand and coughed, as if we were still in Bloody's class.

'Miss. I mean Mam,' he whispered inaudibly. 'George Singer wants me to have a picnic in his garden.'

Mina had the hearing of a hunting dog, and she turned on him as if he'd said he was about to smoke opium in the Maryport Lifeboat Club.

'You *what*?' she said amazed.

I realised it was going to be impossible unless I spoke on his behalf with subtle eloquence. It was inexplicable, but Mina Johnston, who liked no one very much, seemed reluctantly fond of me, or at least to allow me some grudging admiration. She and my mother had been close schoolfriends and perhaps that had some bearing. I was very sharp at school and Bloody had a real job finding reasons to cane me, and this also impressed Mina, this extraordinary immunity. So I lied and glibly informed her that it was a special invitation from my mother, encouraged by my Aunty Elsie who had suggested the summer treat this morning. Elsie had insisted I ought to bring my best friend Thomas Johnston on the grounds that a treat enjoyed on your own wasn't really much of a treat.

Mina scrutinised me sceptically. Then she turned to Radish whose stuck-out ears and oddly shaved head seemed to be saying something piquant in their uncouthness. He was her flesh and blood after all, and she also noticed the weals on his wrists, and, though not critical of Bloody's unmistakable signature, thought perhaps a little pity was in order today. Some glimmer of good nature stirred in the abyss of her irritation.

'Go on then,' she said with a waning flicker of amity. 'It's a lot of clart and bother for Elsie, Mildred and me. But go on, you little buggers, just for once.'

Squinty Bar Radish was in a state of petrified shock. Permission! Permission! He had permission to do something out of the ordinary...

Just as quickly regretting her liberality, Mina barked: 'But you needn't think you're going to waste your tatie pot! I've sweated over it all afternoon, and I'm damn sure I'm not feeding it to the dog. Come here. I'll put your helping in a steak dish. You can take it across to George Singer's for your wassacommee. For your pic...nic.'

She spoke the word as if it was a debauched orgy or a drunken spree. Wide-eyed I watched as she doled out an obscene portion of gristly string beef, black pudding, taties, turnip and carrots into a chipped porcelain bowl. It looked, that malodorous stew, as if intended to loosen the bowels of the

48

entire Allied troops. It was Radish's idiosyncratic contribution to our picnic. A sizzling bowl of emetic winter tatie pot.

'Bloody hell,' I whispered to myself. 'Only Squinty Bar Radish could take black pudding on a picnic.'

Mrs Johnston commanded her gangling son to go upstairs and change out of his school clothes. I smiled, then told her I would go home right away and tell my Aunty Elsie we were ready for her treat. I shouted to salivating Radish to bring his dish of tatie pot direct to our back garden where the spread would be laid. Then I dashed off, wondering even at the age of seven how it was that so many adults had no conscience at all with regard to embarrassing their miserable offspring. Who had ever heard of supplying bubbling farty-smelling meat stew for a summer picnic? And his moody Dad, Joe Johnston, who gave him a haircut that would have been stylish only in the Maryport workhouse of a hundred years ago? By comparison Mildred and Edward Singer were the last word in liberal example. Once a month I went to a proper barber's and paid all of sixpence for my haircut. I sat in croaky old Jimmy Hounihan's chair, and the only indignity I suffered was the molten ash from his permanent Woodbine dropping onto my hair. When I combed my hair after leaving Hounihan's, as sure as shot a heap of fag ash would come tumbling out, like soot dropping out into a grate.

Luckily Elsie hadn't started tea, and I was able to bully her into giving us a feast of elaborate sandwiches and assorted fancy stuff in place of something hot. Ironically I called this sumptuous alternative a 'plain' tea, and I hovered over her, importunately supervising the overall plainness. Aunty Elsie was very plain herself, as well as vague and easy and often morose. Her young fiancé Harry had been killed by tank fire in Africa and she had been taken in by my mother as a kind of live-in housekeeper, as a spare mother for me, and as an occasional help in the kiosk. At thirty she was six years younger than my mother, who treated her with rough kindness and a terse authority. I knew that there was some blackmarket tinned fruit in the back larder (a straight swap with Billis the Senhouse

49

Street grocer, who took under the counter du Maurier from Mildred in lieu of the unsmokable Pasha Cigarettes) and I chivvied Elsie into giving us those pineapple chunks.

'Bloody pineapple,' she spat remorsefully, once she'd clumsily doled them out and I'd refused to give them back. 'Mildred'll kill me. These are meant for funerals and Christmas Day. Fancy anyone wasting blackmarket chunks on Squinty Bar Radish.'

I also stole some unprocurable Cadbury's chocolate biscuits once Elsie was back in the kitchen. I shouted through that I would carry it all out and her dozy trustfulness allowed me to augment the picnic with a few more illegal dainties. By the time I heard Radish fiddling with the latch on the garden gate, I had made us a picnic that would have done justice to the Royal Family, to Princess Elizabeth and little Princess Margaret if they'd been anywhere near Maryport in 1942.

'Hell's bollicks!' gasped Squinty Bar, as he sat down beside me on the little patch of lawn. With a hostile scowl he placed his still sizzling bowl of tatie pot at a good distance from the spread. He gaped bewitched at the tinned pineapple, the corned beef and fishpaste sandwiches, the melting chocolate digestives, and the two stone bottles of ginger beer.

'Where the shite did you get all this?' he asked suspiciously.

I smirked at my effortless larceny. 'I persuaded Elsie to give me some of it and I gaffed the rest.'

'You'll get bloody killt!'

'I don't care,' I said, shovelling in four chocolate digestives at once, and becoming instantly unintelligible. 'Shno thisrmintsme...'

'Eh?' Radish guffawed. He tipped up his dish with the chunks in them and slurped and gnashed at them like a rude cannibal. If his mother had seen him then, she would have chopped his head off without remorse. After five seconds I had masticated my four digestives, and explained: 'I said this reminds me of the book Bloody reads to us on Friday afternoons. *Great Expectations* by Charles Dickens. Do you

50

remember when Pip pinches all the ham and pies for Uncle Pumblechook's Christmas Dinner and when Mrs Joe wallops him with Tickler?'

'I think bloody Bloody wrote that bloody book. She's Mrs bloody Joe, the old cun–'

Three-quarters of the way through our gormandising, I suddenly thought of something. What, I interrogated Radish, was he going to do with his smelly bowl of tatie pot? It was sat there untouched, and Mina Johnston would surely be outraged to see it wasted.

Radish turned and studied the bowl and its excremental contents with loathing. He stood up and brushed off four troy ounces of fishpaste, corned beef and digestive crumbs. He stepped over and picked up the tatie pot and mournfully examined its still warm contents. Without a word he walked across to the compost heap that my father had laid in the corner nearest the house. I watched intently as he clambered on top of the heap. Still silent, he squatted down on his thin hunkers and dipped his dessert spoon into the porcelain bowl. Then he reached behind himself and noisily dropped great dollops of black pudding, turnip and string beef onto the compost. To all appearances he was industriously defecating tatie pot, great turds of blood puddings, great excremental sausages of beef…

'Hah!' I cackled. I had rarely seen Radish in thespian guise, especially in this Rabelaisian incarnation as a student of cacation. But he was very accomplished and it was very convincing. As in some freakish depiction by Hieronymus Bosch it looked exactly as if Radish was emptying his bowels onto a West Cumbrian compost heap.

After five minutes of his scatological mime, he picked up the bowl and glared at what was left with infinite disgust.

'This stuff,' he said vehemently, 'is nowt but *shite*. I've had enough of it. I've had enough of shite in my life, George! I'm having nowt more to do with this… this stew made out of bloody shit.'

With swaggering recklessness he walked across to the hedge,

and tipped the tatie pot into the Bode's garden. He was so careless where he flung it that half of it landed on Willy Bode's ugly
little pot squirrel and coated its tail with dripping liquid beef. I
ran up and peered over the privet, and said anxiously to Radish:
'You bloody idiot. It looks like someone's taken a fit and done
a shit on their garden ornament! They'll think it's me next door.
They'll think I've deliberately shit on their squirrel.'

Radish guffawed. Even if I did get a hiding, he sneered, it
would be nothing like his twenty-five lashes from Bloody. I
glared at him, but instead of continuing a fruitless argument
decided we should have some after-dinner recreation. Given
that Radish was bone idle and hated the exertions of blow football, never mind football, I suggested that we play a static but
satisfying game of my own devising. I took two of my father's
garden canes and a fistful of my mother's clothes pegs and
pushed the forks of a peg onto the end of each cane. Then
Radish and I stood by the clothes line and struck the line as
hard as we could with the canes. The clothes pegs went flying
a considerable distance and the general sensation was the same
as flinging a throwing arrow or releasing some catapult or
ballistic device. Radish enjoyed the ballistics immensely and
managed to get his pegs almost half as far as mine. He seemed
rapt and ready to play peg-flying for an eternity until suddenly
his face clouded over with obvious concern.

What, I asked him impatiently, was the problem. It was the
tatie pot, Squinty said angrily. Mina Johnston had ordered him
to run back with the porcelain bowl as soon as he'd finished its
contents, just in case it got lost or damaged. I glanced and saw
that the bowl was sitting safe on the compost heap, and urged
him to ignore it. But Radish knew his mother better than I did
and repeated he would have to take it back immediately. As a
frugal landlady she kept a rigid inventory of all her crockery, no
matter how old or stained it had become. But he would return
here at once, he promised excitedly, to carry on with the brilliant peg-flogging game, and might even beg for threepence to
buy two ice creams from my mother's kiosk.

He walked over for the tatie pot bowl and seeing it had compost on it wiped it on his shirt and shorts. Then he raced off to the back gate, his outsize feet almost kicking his skinny buttocks. Radish of course was the gowkiest, gangliest boy in Standard One and quite mystically inept at soccer, rugby, rounders, tag and even marbles. His farcically feeble aspect did not desert him today. What happened next was throughly incredible, a thousand-to-one chance, and yet it really happened before my disbelieving eyes. Squinty Bar Radish hurtled off towards the back gate, kicking his lopsided arse like a hectic circus buffoon. He fumbled the latch with his left hand whilst clutching his tatie pot bowl with his right. Without having the sense to check for traffic in either direction, he dived into the back lane and turned right for his mother's Wood Street guest-house.

Just as he was closing our gate, an overweight Ewanrigg fisherman with erysipelas, Wiff Minshaw, came cycling down the cobbled lane. Wiff was dawdling and puffing at modest speed, en route to the greyhounds and the garden allotments he kept at distant Grasslot. He was sucking his pipe full of Condor and daydreaming on this pregnant June evening as the gulls made their mournful sonata above. Possibly he was dreaming of monster catches of cod at Siddick, of plaice at Flimby, of mussels at nearby Risehow. Conceive his violent amazement as an ugly little wax-eared child careered straight into his push-bike and went sprawling right over his front wheel. The timing was extraordinary and immaculate. Radish couldn't have done it better if he'd tried. Minshaw's front wheel was at an exact right angle to our gate as Squinty sped onto the backs like an accurate prototype of the post-war Billy Whizz. Obstructed by Wiff's wheel, Radish went soaring right across it and was left there draped arse upwards, as if in preparation for a proper pasting from Miss Blood. As he tripped over Wiff's bike, his right arm came flying in a protective clockwise arc, tensely clutching at the precious bowl. The torque of centripetal propulsion inevitably took precedence, and Mrs Johnston's utensil came full circle to smash into a dozen shards on the cobbles below.

It was as if Radish had deliberately cricket-bowled the tatie pot dish straight onto the stones…

The unwarranted shock kept Wiff peddling amnesically a few more yards. I emerged from our gate to see spreadeagled Radish being borne along the backs like an instructive carnival float. Minshaw finally stopped his pushbike and whistled admiringly at his bizarrely reclining passenger. He turned to me patting his huge belly and said: 'Is this bugger wantin driven somewhere special?'

Radish moaned and slowly righted himself from his absurd posture. His picnic host was roaring in an ecstasy of killing mirth. Wiff Minshaw examined him cursorily and vaguely inquired if he was damaged at all.

'No,' snorted Radish. 'But I've bust me bloody tatie pot.'

Wiff wheezed very earnestly. 'Never run anywhere fast with a bowl of tatie pot. I always take it easy if I'm handling black pudding.'

The breathless fisherman also advised him to cheer up because he could easily have broken both arms. He fingered his erysipelas, then spat an assortment of mucus into the summer dust and resumed his journey to Grasslot. Meanwhile Radish's very best friend continued to dance and hoot at the painful comedy of it. Radish himself looked as glum as death. Witlessly he picked up all the porcelain fragments and seriously deliberated if his bowl could be mended with a tube of glue.

'Not a hope,' I told him pitilessly.

'I wish I had broke my bloody arm,' he muttered. 'Cos my Mam will break my bloody neck.'

Dismally he trudged off down the dusty lane. Remorseful for a fleeting second, I stopped my cackling and shouted a cheerful see you later. Radish returned a mirthless grunt. When he reached home to face his just deserts, it was to encounter his mother in the midst of an epic furious sorting out of the week's laundry. With the dolly tub boiling, the temperature in the eighties, her face like a sweating beef tomato, she was even less prepared to be sanguinely dispassionate when it came to the auditing of her household crockery.

'Tripped over a *pushbike*?' she roared.

'Yis.'

'Keeled over a mudguard and smashed me tatie pot?' she screamed.

'I – '

'Think I'd believe a crazy bloody fairy story like that? You wicked, wicked, wicked little *tyke*!'

She ranted for over two hours, and kept him in supperless for the rest of the night. For a whole month he was kept in every evening after school, and it stayed in the sweltering eighties throughout. And bear in mind that this mad draconian passion, this epic Shakespearean anger, was all because of an unseasonal and uneaten dish of Cumbrian tatie pot...

*

Radish and his infinitely tragic bowl of tatie pot affected me with all the brutal unhinging clarity of a delicately crafted film. Remember that, thanks to the fish, I had just been forced to recollect those mesmerising Christmas baubles and the little cardboard angel out of Woolworth's. Both of these childhood memories – the one farcical and the other touchingly profound – seemed in some way thoroughly illicit and to have been sparked off by something from outside, as if by a deliberate and invisible mechanism. For the best part of thirty years these perplexing, instructive parts of my childhood had been buried away in an amnesia induced by the turmoil of marriage and family life and middle age. I had been through a messy divorce and a custody wrangle with my wife, Sarah. I had undertaken a drastic career change at the age of thirty-three. So much of my inner life had been consumed by that, I had completely forgotten that George Alfred Singer had once had Squinty Bar Radish as his closest friend. I, the swaggering prodigy of Standard One, had been the bosom pal of the dunce of Ellenbank Junior School. My life up until 1947, when I commenced at Mawbray Grammar, had clearly been characterised by an intensity, a vivid and uneven poetry, that made my adult existence seem embarrassingly paltry and tepid. Recently at times I have seriously believed that the aquarium fish and its smile came as a catalytic warning, a minatory omen. Saying to me: Look George Singer, you in your funny little ice cream kiosk, do whatever you need to do to keep your head above water in your little provincial town in the last decade of this millennium. But whatever you do with whatever is left of your life, you must take great care of your past in so doing.

4

I was walking attentively around the shark and ray pool. It was just over a month since that levitating flatfish had first confounded me with its behaviour. Since then, using my life-membership card, I'd been popping in every day in the hope of seeing this unlikely creature offer me another of its puzzling benedictions. There I was regularly stationed by the pool, watching that turbot with inordinate intentness, waiting for it to do a repeat performance. To my chagrin, it spent most of its time lying inert on the pool bed. When it did consent to rise up and suffer a pat from a friendly child, it did so without any ceremony or superfluous flourish. Admittedly its human-looking expression was still there, an amiable enough one in anthropomorphic terms. But that vision of angelic facial inno-cence, I soon realised, was obviously only my crass psychological projection. After all, it wasn't visibly cordial towards its fellow flatfish, much less the sharks and gurnards and spotted rays. So it would be just as fanciful to imagine that my Morris Minor car had a 'friendly' little face, given the whimsical Noddy-like geometry of its headlamps, radiator and bumpers.

On close inspection the turbot also proved less handsome than I'd thought. For a start, since its evolutionarily adapted shape meant that it swam along a flat rather than a vertical plane, its mouth was well out of alignment with its eyes. Self-evidently if you are a human, unless you are an unfortunate freak, your mouth is situated symmetrically between the eyes. Likewise if you are a vertically-swimming cod or coley or snapper, the same holds true. But if you are a flat-swimming turbot, megrim or brill, you will demonstrate the Quasimodo grotesqueness of having a mouth well to the left of your left eye. And talking of cartoon monsters, if you are a turbot, you will have two little beady black ones that look exactly like raised-up warts or blackcurrants. These eyes are capable of 360 degree independent rotation. Stare long enough at those autonomously revolving orbs from above and you start to feel a little peculiar. Or, in my case, you suffer a touch of incredulity. Could this in close up rather gargoylish beast be the same one that a month ago emitted the radiance one normally only sees in paintings of haloed Florentine saints?

I looked at the illuminated captions opposite the pool, and read that a turbot could be up to thirty-nine inches in length and weigh up to thirty-four pounds. In passing I ended up reading about the pool's other inhabitants, and imbibed a great deal about the tope, the tub gurnard, the brill, the spotted ray, the thornback ray and the greater spotted dogfish. The last two, I was informed, are also known as the smooth hound and the rough hound. The rough hound is so inordinately rough that its skin was once used by Victorian craftsmen for polishing wood and alabaster.

I was just swallowing that nugget with admiring fascination for the tenacious industry of the unsung heroes who research and then write these educative tit-bits, when I was struck by something infinitely paradoxical. For the benefit of those pioneering foreign tourists serendipitous enough to make it as far as Maryport, the captions were all given French and German translations. On one of these I read in some confusion that the greater spotted dogfish is called in German *der gross-fleckiger Katzenhai*. Meaning of course that those zealous but myopic foreigners had got it completely the wrong way about. Because that shark species known as the *dog*fish, also known by the alternative common name of rough hound, is described by those obsessively scrupulous Teutons as a *cat*shark…

Dogfish? Catshark? Who was right and who was wrong? To

58

put it in the terms of the 1945 Ellenbank playground, was it the Brits or the Jerries, the Limeys or the Huns? I turned back to the pool and stared at the species in question. I looked at its rather saturnine face from all angles and to me it looked like neither dog nor cat. It looked rather more like a stoat or a weasel with those narrow predatorial eyes. The truth was, it looked only like itself. I sighed as I listened to the racket of the rain on the aquarium roof, and I realised that it was raining cats and dogs here in Maryport today. And as I thought of those riotous playground games of Japs and Jerries, I could not help but think of the unique physiognomy of Squinty Bar Radish. His eyes had the faintest upward slant, which perhaps explains why he was always forced to be a merciless Jap every time we played at war games. The listless turbot seemed to throw me a rather baleful, condescending glance as I suddenly found myself helplessly travelling back through a half a century.

*

It was 1945, only weeks before VE Day, and I was still being taught by Bloody. For three whole years, a third of my life, the length of my Durham University degree, Miss Blood was our sole representative conduit of the fountain of human knowledge. Hence the fact that I have turned out anything better than an illiterate pauper is little short of miraculous. As for Squinty Bar Radish, he married and emigrated to South Africa in 1964, and I've since learnt that he has prospered out there as a major dealer in secondhand cars. By 1964, of course, slide rules and rudimentary calculators had become universally available, and Squinty Bar's tables were no longer his Nemesis.

Miss Blood was inevitably a fervent patriot and she kept a bulging scrapbook of everything to do with the monarchy. When she was in a generous mood, which was surprisingly frequent for someone pathologically neurotic, she would bring in her scrapbook and allow Standard Three to peruse it. She had snipped out dozens of ancient pictures, not only of various

Georges and Edwards and Marys but of distant cousins, forgotten half-cousins, moth-eaten royal animals, majestic country houses and even of one or two foreign sovereigns. There was a striking picture of sleek and brilliantined King Zog of Albania in her scrapbook, and Bloody told us that that funny Albanian name meant 'bird'. King Bird of Albania, we all murmured wonderingly to ourselves. Some bird he was, Bloody muttered with a sneer. He had called himself a king, she told us indignantly, but he wasn't a proper monarch like ours, the issue of countless generations of blue blood. Zog had just decided to give himself that title and had also betrayed his country to the puny little Italians, something no British monarch would ever have done in parallel circumstances.

In line with this awesome devotional attitude to kings and queens, Miss Blood insisted that we learn every last detail of the hierarchies of royal titles and the ceremonious forms of address appropriate to each. As with troy weight and apothecary's weight, all mistakes were punished on the spot with her ruler. In addition, because the established Anglican Church and the British Monarchy were mystically indivisible in the eyes of Bloody and of Bloody's God, we nine-year-olds had to learn how to write a hypothetical letter to a thousand varieties of clergyman. This included not only the obvious archbishop, archdeacon, dean, rural dean, ordinary clergyman and his curate... but also such one-off obscurities as Her Majesty's Lord High Commissioner to the General Assembly of the Church of Scotland...

'Suppose you are obliged to write a letter,' announced Bloody on a breezy April morning in 1945, 'to an ordinary village clergyman, one who has no titled relations or family connections with county. Suppose also that this humble village parson is called Tom Cribbins. You write his title on the envelope simply as "The Rev. Tom Cribbins". The letter itself you begin with "Dear Sir".'

Thirty lugubrious Maryport children, most of them drably dressed, listened studiously to this helpful exhortation on epistolary etiquette. Bloody droned on indefatigably, moving slyly in my direction: 'But supposing that your Reverend Tom Cribbins is a titled clergyman, and is the son of a duke or a marquess. How would you address him, George Singer?'

I had met no aristocratic parsons outside of those satirised inside *Just William* books. Yet I answered her smartly: 'As "The Rev. Lord Tom Cribbins", Miss.'

'Uh,' she said disgusted. 'But what if he was the son of either an earl or a viscount or a baron?'

'"The Rev. the Hon. Tom Cribbins".'

Squinting with immense effort, she ransacked her dusty old brains for the furthest reaches of heraldic propriety.

'What if the Rev. Tom Cribbins happens to be a baronet himself?'

'He would be addressed as "The Rev. Sir Tom Cribbins Bart".'

Without fair warning she jumped from the titled clergy to the titled nobility, and went on catechising this arrogant little brainbox.

'Singer, imagine the unlikely situation where you become something of a success in adult life. You get away to Oxford University, say, make a name for yourself there, and eventually become familiar with several people of high social standing. Let's suppose by the time you are twenty-five or thirty you have become intimate friends with an earl's eldest son and an earl's eldest son's wife.'

'Miss?'

'One day you find yourself writing a letter to these two to thank them for a most enjoyable weekend of shooting grouse or snipe at their commodious Highland mansion. How d'you suppose you would address them on the envelope?'

'Miss,' I replied, with a demure, passably aristocratic smile, 'I would address them as if the courtesy title were an actual peerage. I would address my titled friends as if they were *actual* peers.'

Unable to restrain herself, she croaked resentfully, 'Would

you now? You shouldn't have been called George Singer. You should have been called George Burke of Burke's Peerage fame. Very well. Answer me this. How would you begin the same letter if you were writing to say thank you to a marchioness?'

I opened my mouth and looked very vacant. Just as Bloody's own mouth was dropping open and her ruler hopefully flexing itself, I shot back: 'I would address the lady as "Madam", Miss.'

'Ah?' she whispered in a distant voice. 'And you'd refer to her, the marchioness, in the letter itself as...?'

'"Your Ladyship", Miss.'

Bloody stumped her heavy carcass to the far end of the class-room. She had adopted this bizarre strategic tactic previously, assuming that by having to shout my answers some distance I would falter and thus lose my nerve.

'What about,' she boomed the length of the room, 'if you were writing to the eldest son of a distinguished English baron? How would you address this person on the envelope?'

'As "The Hon.",' I bawled back politely.

'Supposing he was the eldest son of a *Scottish* baron, residing in his ancestral home of Glenziel Castle?'

'"The Hon., the Master of Glenziel Castle", Miss,' I cried. And I sounded as if I were a nine-year-old butler in a Will Hay film.

On the same patriotic lines Bloody insisted that as part of our war effort we should memorise the exact hierarchy of officers in the three services. Here, for the first and last time, my best friend Thomas Ernest Johnston was to rise to a miraculous super-eminence. Because to everyone's astonishment, Squinty Bar Radish, who was RAF-daft and fancied himself as a future air pilot, demonstrated an anomalous brilliance at remembering every last detail. Even before Bloody could pose the precise question and select someone who was bound to get it all wrong, Squinty Bar had shot up his hand, and in one fell swoop blurted out: 'The army ranks starting from the top, Miss, are Field-

Marshal, General, Lieutenant-General, Major-General…'

'Eh…' began Bloody.

The whole of the class held its breath as Squinty rattled on regardless like a Bren gun. It was as if he was being prompted by an invisible voice, the passive conduit of a magical feat of memory.

'… Brigadier, Colonel, Lieutenant-Colonel, Major, Captain, Lieutenant, Second-Lieutenant.'

Miss Blood was so amazed that she failed to clatter him for speaking out of turn.

'RAF is Marshal of the RAF, Air Chief Marshal, Air Marshal, Air Vice-Marshal, Air Commodore, Group Captain, Wing…'

'Shut…' remonstrated Bloody, in a very worried voice.

'… Commander, Squadron Leader, Flight-Lieutenant, Flying Officer, Pilot Officer.'

'*up…*'

'Navy has Admiral of the Fleet, Admiral, Vice-Admiral, Rear-Admiral…'

'That'll do!' Bloody cried. 'Imagine a fool like you knowing all of that. If you can remember all of those, Johnston, why can't you remember what three blasted sevens is?'

Bar Radish hesitated and almost ventured a hypothesis. The words were quite beyond him, but he explained to me later what had been going through his mind. What he couldn't articulate to old Bloody was that officer titles and the whole paraphernalia of ranking signified glamorous, valorous people who stirred his thwarted imagination. Arithmetical tables, on the other hand, were neither human nor brave nor hierarchical, they were just insipid and unreal abstractions.

'Johnston, you've spoken out of turn, and you know what that means…'

Radish and I both stiffened and threw her looks of sullen reproach. We scowled resentfully at this sheer demented tyranny which even by 1945 had had its day. That glacial contempt of ours stopped even Bloody in her brazen tracks. She drummed her ruler, squinted at us uneasily, and said: 'For once, here's a chance to redeem yourself. And to learn something important at the same time. Square measure is what you need most practice in, isn't it? Along with everything else, that is. Here's a tester for you.'

'Miss?'

'Given that there are four roods in an acre…'

'Miss?'

'… and forty square poles in a rood…'

'Miss?'

'… and thirty and a quarter square yards in a square pole…'

'Miss?'

'… how many square yards are there in a farmer's acre?'

Radish lifted the end of his tie and flapped it wanly in the sunlight streaming through the window. He had given up listening halfway through the question and instead of answering in square measure he hazarded: 'Havvadooper, Miss?'

Bloody brought back her wrist before swinging it forward, drum-rolling his left ear, and shouting that the correct answer was 4840! In the same breath, she offered him further redemption, meaning inevitable further punishment, as she squawked: 'What is an *ell*?'

Squinty Bar, who always dropped his own aitches, thought she had taken leave of her senses. Scripture with Bloody was always on Monday afternoons, never midweek. His mother who was no churchgoer herself made him go every week to Evangelical Sunday School on Wood Street. The teachers there of course didn't bother to spare the children the most fiery passages of the Old Testament or even the incomprehensible apocalyptic splendour of Revelations. Radish answered obligingly: 'Where whoremongers, adulterers and idolaters go, please Miss.'

Crack! Crack! Crack!

'*What* did you say!'

'Mrs Bimson at Eyevan Jellycal School said that's who goes to hell.'

'*Ell*, not hell, you imbecile! E-l-l.' She turned to me in her quivering fury. 'Singer…'

'Yes Miss.'

'Tell him what an ell is.'

'Miss Blood,' I said politely, 'do you mean the Scottish ell or the English ell?'

'Eh?' she blinked, still flushing at Squinty's Evangelism. 'I mean both ells, you awful little wiseacre! Decimal points included.'

'37.2 inches in a Scottish ell and 45 inches in an English ell.'

'Gah!'

*

That afternoon I conveyed to Squinty Bar Radish the opinion of my socialist father, who thought all these forms of address to deacons and duchesses were a waste of bloody time. As pointless, he insisted, as all the retrogressive drivel we had to learn about pecks, bushels, roods and chains. To my surprise, Radish, who'd been caned that day for confusing linear and area measure (and for blithely telling Bloody there were twelve fathoms in a perch), suddenly played the devil's advocate and said he, or at any rate his Dad, wasn't at all sure it was a bad thing.

'You're bloody barmy,' I said. 'When will you ever need to thank an earl's eldest son for a successful weekend of quail shooting?'

Squinty sniffed and pointed out that his Dad measured his allotment in chains and that he had a Great-Uncle Willy, a farmer at Goody Hills near Mawbray, who still measured his oats and wheat in bushels.

'How old's your Great-Uncle Willy?' I said sceptically.

'Ninety-five,' declared Radish matter of fact.

I snorted derisively. 'And it's 1945 which means your Great-Uncle Willy was born in 1850, Radish! I'll bet he thinks the sun revolves round the bloody earth.'

'No he doesn't! He's great, Great-Uncle Willy. He's my favourite relation. I've stayed on my own at Goody Hills for a holiday, and you should see the things he showed me. He can fart at will for one thing, and for another he has loads of adders, poisonous snakes in his fields.'

I swallowed those two congruous facts impressed. I suggested he farted at will because he was living in permanent fear of the snakes in his fields. Radish said any time he holidayed there his great-uncle let him smoke Woodbines and had once given him a small glass of whisky. It had made him puke and Great-Uncle Willy had laughed his head off to see his great-nephew so out of control, but it had been an unparalleled experience nonetheless.

Meanwhile Radish and I had made our way up to my house. We wandered into our back yard and dallied there fooling by the outside privy. Mina Johnston was attending a funeral that afternoon so Squinty Bar had been grudgingly permitted to stay and play with me for an hour. Aunty Elsie soon heard us whooping and shouting at Red Indians and came out to tell us to pipe down as she was trying to listen to her wireless. To *Forces Requests* she added with the weary, regretful expression of an eternal widow. I looked at her morose yet complacent expression and wondered why it was I didn't feel enormous sympathy. It seemed like deliberate self-torture, now that it was four years since her fiancé had died. Four years was nearly half of my life and of Squinty's life for that matter. I said as much to Radish once Elsie had gone in, and he quoted his own mother to the effect that Elsie should give herself a kick up the behind and get herself another chap before she got any uglier and found the task impossible.

'Why does she need a man?' I asked him wonderingly. 'Why is it grown-ups always need someone else?'

'Because they need plenty of leg-over tooty-fruity,' said Radish lewdly, 'and because they're all daft, bloody desperate buggers. And I'll tell you something else, George, should I?'

'What?' I said, quietly impressed by his mature vocabulary.

He assumed a momentous confiding expression as he whispered into my ear. 'I'm busting for a shite. If I don't hurry up I'll end up skittering all over your yard.'

I smirked at him innocently as my brain made sly and rapid calculations. Radish intended going indoors to use our upstairs toilet but I hurriedly advised him against it. I told him there was Elsie's room on one side of the lav and our lodger Miss Briar's on the other, and their proximity would be bound to cramp his style. Both women were as nosy as sin and would poke their snouts out of their rooms as soon as they heard his footsteps on the stairs. Miss Briar was a junior-school headmistress of about forty-five who taught at Dearham and possessed her own car. She had a temperament sometimes bluff and cheerful, sometimes peevish and self-righteous. She also had a violent purple complexion and a scrimping Methodist piety. To my parents' amazement, she was a vegetarian, the only one they had ever met. She would regularly drive through to posh Keswick to the exclusive delicatessen where they sold under-the-counter yoghurt, something absolutely unprocurable in Maryport in 1945. Later she mixed up grated carrots, turnips, swedes etc all raw in her bowls of yoghurt and dined on these epicurean feasts alone in her room. Bar Radish had gleaned from his Dearham cousin the ironic fact that she gave sponge cake to pupils who got their tables right. Squinty remarked bitterly on Bloody's default in that particular and said if he'd been given sponge cake by Bloody he would have learnt not just his three-times table but his seventy-three-times table.

I pointed at the outside lav and said, 'Go in there, Squinty.'

He looked at me with suspicion, not to say hauteur. His own house had three inside toilets for all his mother's lodgers, and he was obviously contemptuous of all outside bogs. 'Are there rats in there?'

'Rats yourself. Not on your bloody life.'

Still eyeing me warily, he said, 'Why the hell has it got a heart carved inside the door?'

There was a ventilation hole cut into the door at adult height, to allow in extra daylight. My father had carved the hole in a heart shape in line with his generally innocent lavatorial humour.

'That's to let fresh air into the shithouse,' I explained. 'Or you'd soon stink yourself out.'

He grunted and took himself off to defecate. I took a quick look round to make sure there were no spectators. Noiselessly I crept over to the toilet door. My innocent voice belied the fact I intended to perpetrate a throughly obnoxious practical joke. Entirely justly in Squinty Bar Radish's case, as I had yet to get even with him over something which had happened last autumn.

Six months ago, while we had been baiting set lines in this same yard, Bar Radish had performed a spectacularly lethal little stunt. It happened that I was having intermittent cramp attacks from an upset belly, and was having to make frequent lightning runs to our outside lav. On the tenth such attack, I rushed for the privy, hauled down my shorts, and was instantly catapulted three feet into the air.

'Bloody hell!' I screamed in agony. 'What the hell!'

Howling pitifully, I gaped between my legs and saw how my scrawny little arse was squatting on a posy of four knotted fish-hooks...

'Radish!' I shouted in a rage. 'Bar bloody Radish!'

With brutal haste I unhooked the four barbs from my tender buttocks. There wasn't a second to spare as I was also trying to restrain what was desperate to burst from my belly. At last I let fly noisily into the pot. Gingerly cleansing my perforated back-side, I pulled up my pants and shot out of the toilet. But of course the bird had flown. Squinty Bar Radish had taken to his heels and was just a few yards from the garden gate (the same through which he'd executed a parabola across a pushbike with a tatie pot dish).

Furious at his escape I was suddenly miraculously inspired. It can scarcely be less than significant in my overall story that this magical inspiration involved... a fish. I looked at the rolled-up set lines and confirmed that there was a single cod in the bucket adjacent. It had been our only catch on the five a.m. tide, and Radish had put it aside as a peace offering for irascible Mina. With no hesitation I raced across and grabbed it. The mouldy little cod was very slimy, extremely slippery, and it danced and leapt in my fevered hands.

But no matter... I whispered to myself victoriously.

I grasped the fish by the tail and swung it far behind my head. Squinty Bar Radish had barely two yards to go to the gate as I took aim. My bum was burning excruciatingly from the diarrhoea and from Radish's garland of hooks. I flung that slimy little cod with every atom of strength I possessed.

The fish described a very beautiful arc as it winged its way with a perfect homing instinct towards cod-faced Squinty Bar Radish...

I was treasured by all at Ellenbank Junior School as an ace cricket bowler. I was also a canny virtuoso at stoning rusty oil tins as they floated miles off in the Solway Firth. Yet it smacked of the strange occult what happened next...

The fish assumed a downward trajectory just as Bar Radish had his fumbling finger on the latch. As he dithered hamfistedly with its clumsy mechanism, the codfish achieved a profound percussive impact with Squinty Bar's left ear...

Crack!

It was the whiplash thwack of Bloody's punishment ruler. Thomas Ernest Johnston had been assailed by a flying fish. Squinty Bar Radish had been concussed by a projectile cod.

'Fuck me stiff!' he groaned amazed.

All that had happened six months ago. Yet a fish in the earhole had been a very meagre retaliation, it had been nothing compared to the castration and perforated anus he'd almost inflicted on me. My punctured arse still burned for justice. Six months later, kneeling by this toilet door, I wondered how else I could avenge myself. Why not drench him through the keyhole with a water pistol as he strained and grunted on the pot? Why not fill it up with something dangerously abrasive, with undiluted Dettol say? A few drops of that fizzling on his wizened dick end and he'd watch what he did to George Singer.

Before I tried any Dettol on the dick, I needed to gauge some distances and make some important calculations. I stooped to peer through the keyhole and saw Bar Radish perched on the throne in all his glory. He was staring wonderingly into space, squinting in the afternoon sunlight that streamed through the heart-shaped ventilation hole. My shoulders shook convulsively at the sight of this sunlit angel with the army-shaved haircut, those stuck-out ears and that mordant yet vacant expression.

Bar Radish's penis was dangling absurdly, a piglet's tail of a thing, curlicued and ludicrous. His army khaki shorts were around his knees and his cracked leather braces trailed on the stone floor. There were frequent melodious plops as he did his business. As he strained and grunted, he siffled a senseless tune. His sleepy eyes were blinking aimlessly in the direction of the toilet door. Amazed by the loose-lipped siffling and that piglet's penis, I exploded into noisy laughter.

Radish noted my eye at the keyhole and squawked, 'Oy!'

I guffawed derisively and poked out my tongue.

'I can see thy beady eyebol,' he snorted in broad dialect. 'Gowpin at us as I's hevvin a shite.'

My eye stayed glued to this entrancing floor show as I informed him he'd pissed all over his braces. Radish looked down very worried and I snorted at such idiot credulity. I also cackled insanely as I imagined my hawkish gaze seen from Squinty's singular perspective.

Radish said amiably, 'Why are you starin at me having a shite, George?'

'Because you look so bloody ridiculous.'

'You think so, do you?' he said, standing up and wiping his behind. He bowed and invited me to inspect the visual effect of his labours and emitted a raucous whinny. It was a very cursory cleansing, but he advised me that I had seen absolutely nothing yet. As if to say, this is what I think of you, he turned round to

70

expose the dazzling radiance of his bare buttocks. With both index fingers he began to manipulate the two cheeks and ventriloquise a decorous if preposterous voice. Instantly, as if by magical legerdemain, his ugly scrawny little posterior became an imaginary Miss Blood interrogating the pupils of Standard Three...

'Singer!' the twin cheeks demanded in a winsome falsetto. 'Tell me how you would address a duke's *arse*? A duke's son's arse? A duke's daughter's arse? How would you address a clergyman's daughter's arse assuming she was a peer of the realm?'

'Please Miss,' I snickered, 'that's a most imaginative play on words. I believe the proper form when you address a clergyman's daughter's arse is "Miss Right Reverend Dirty Back Passage".'

'Mmm,' Radish's buttocks minced. 'And how would you address her if she was titled?'

'That's easy, Miss. "Milady Right Reverend Bare Arse the Bandit Bart".'

'Excellent, boy,' enthused Squinty's cheeks in a rapture. 'But if you'll excuse me, I have to clear my throat.'

Radish farted loudly, and Miss Blood instantly exclaimed that that was better.

'Now children,' the buttocks imperiously continued, 'it is time you all learnt some valuable dance steps for when you enter polite society. Just in case some of you rise up into high society, you will need to know how to do the Lambeth Walk with a duke's son's wife. Or with a marchioness's sister. For my demonstration I shall need to get a bit higher so that you can all get a better view...'

Radish carefully lowered the toilet seat. With trousers and galluses dangling about his bony ankles, he clambered up on top. Next he bent and touched his toes as if anticipating a bout of naturist leapfrog. With two fingers by the side of each buttock, he continued his exposition of terpsichorean etiquette.

'First you lift your left leg,' his beaming haunches continued

71

in a pedantic soprano. 'That is how you do the Lambeth Walk! Can you see children, how I've lifted my left leg? Next you cough politely.' He farted reverberantly. 'After which you lift your right leg and cough again.' And with that second spontaneous fart, I realised he must have had some lessons from his Great-Uncle Willy of Goody Hills. 'You now –'

But the pedagogic backside was striving far too hard to impress its pupils. The bent double position was so awkward that Squinty Bar's foot went skittering over the edge of the seat. In one convulsive movement he skited off the toilet, rolled across the floor, and clattered arse upwards on top of a carbolic-reeking lavatory brush.

I roared in a dangerous ecstasy, 'Squinty!'

After a long and eerie delay a hoarse statement issued from underneath his upraised arse: 'Fuck me senseless.'

'Oh, Radish!...' I sighed in unfeigned admiration.

Then something dreadful happened. A large and powerful hand suddenly seized my shoulder. Rigid with horror, I turned into a stone. Into a nine-year-old stone that found itself being dragged roughly from the keyhole and Bar Radish's matchless Satyricon choreography. Blithely oblivious, that bare-arse dunce with the outsize galluses was still drivelling on with his farts and coughs and scatological lexicon.

A familiar voice erupted behind me. 'You dirty little *beasts*! You appalling little, dirty little, abysmal little, unspeakably filthy little *beasts*.'

It was not Aunty Elsie, who apart from everything else had never heard the word 'abysmal'. Neither was it Miss Blood, who might have been justified in regaling her smutty little detractors thus. It was worse than both. It was Miss Briar. It was the prim spinster Methodist teacher, the yoghurt and raw vegetable guzzler who ate alone in her room but possessed her very own motor-car.

Crazed with shock, I shouted through the keyhole, 'Radish, it's Miss Briar. Miss Briar's stood out here with me!'

The class idiot boomed back cheerfully: 'Is it fuck, man! But it's a good imitation of her stupid old voice. That bloody old squint-eyed, wall-eyed, mangy-old, dried-up cunt! I'll bet a five-pound note she's never had a good stiff shit in her life. My Dearham cousin Willy Joe says he knows for a fact she's never had a feller anywhere up her knick–'

'JOHNSTON!' Miss Briar had turned a brilliant damson purple. 'JOHNSTON, YOU MONSTER! You incredibly perverted and filthy little *beast*...'

As we waited for the monster to emerge, I turned whiter than the clouds above. I thought of our lodger telling my parents about the perverted derangement of their demonic offspring. I imagined the scene that followed and wanted to die on the spot. I assumed that Mina Johnston would have Squinty put in penal custody after his exposure in the obscenity trial. A good hiding wouldn't be enough, he would probably be given over to a reformatory as being beyond all parental control. My fervid imaginings were obviously nothing compared to Squinty's as he emerged from the lav. Neither white nor grey, he was a brackish green colour, the same I imagined as a terrified criminal submitting to a birching inside His Majesty's Prison.

'Miss,' he whimpered in a voice that came from the depths of his handmade Whitehaven clogs. 'I didn't mean it, Miss...'

'No?' she snarled, her eyes and mouth moving all ways at once. 'Didn't mean what? *Which* disgusting bit precisely didn't you mean? Which part of the obscene playlet that this one here was peeping at and snickering at? Which bit of that farrago of disgusting insinuations...?'

'Miss, I didn't mean that you were a cun–'

'*Silence*, you reptile!'

Squinty studied his battered clogs and stiffened his trembling shoulders.

I struggled with complete facial paralysis but eventually got out, 'I promise you we won't do anything like this again.'

Miss Briar puckered her bright purple lips in a sardonic mimicry of self-interrogation. She looked at me witheringly.

'How do I know? Why should I believe you? You vicious

little pair must be very far gone to manage this level of... of... wickedness?'

I noticed there was a wateriness in her eyes. There wasn't a breath of wind on this sunny spring afternoon and I swallowed awkwardly as I realised our corrupt one-act farce was not the only thing to offend. Radish had impugned her celibate spinsterhood as well as the robustness of her bowel movements. Miss Briar, being human, was ruffled, deeply disturbed, possibly deeply wounded. For all we knew she might have had a handsome sweetheart died in the Twenties and she might be an accomplished expeller of turds as big as a navvy's. After an eternity she scowled and said that as much as she'd have liked to have told on our misdeeds, she was incapable of repeating what she'd heard. It would have soiled her to her depths, a painful process unfortunately denied to two children who had sunk so low they were beyond remedial self-disgust. I quivered with incredulous relief and asked her humbly if she would like us to clean her car. Miss Briar gaped at me almost frightened and stalked off without another word.

Once she was safely inside the house, Squinty tittered.

'Bloody hell,' I whispered. 'That was some close bloody shave.'

Radish adjusted his galluses and leered at me diagnostically. He tutted wisely: 'The truth always hurts. Anyone can see what the trouble is. Her and your Aunty Elsie both need a pair of bloody boyfriends and some regular tooty-fruity. Then they wouldn't be nosing around while ordinary folks are having themselves a harmless little shite.'

*

Once again the chimera of the fish, the ghost of its smile, soundlessly flickered. Within an instant, a glimmering Christmas bauble followed. A second later, another kind of fish was sprily dancing before my memory. I saw myself looking at the slimy codfish in the bucket in our back yard in 1945 and I blinked as I stooped to pick it up and fling it in the direction of the fleeing Radish.

Pondering that Rabelaisian toilet episode and the precise mauve hue of Miss Briar's facial veins, I was seized by an access of something very hard to describe. It was a kind of abstracted but very meaningful sense of pity. Suddenly I felt a remarkable and unheralded affection for the memory of Miss Briar. For I also found myself slowly and uncertainly recalling a hallowed and out-of-the-blue day with that same lonely vegetarian teacher. Like a dim forgotten dream, I remembered that she had once asked my parents for permission to take me off for a drive in her motor-car. She must have used half of her week's ration of petrol as she drove the thirty miles to distant Carlisle. A kindly, unexpectedly gentle Miss Briar who led me round the depleted wartime market and afterwards round the Castle and the Tullie House Museum. In that massive red fortress, which struck me with its grim unpitying air, I saw the miserable dungeons where Scottish reivers and Jacobites had been incarcerated before being executed. In Tullie House I looked in the glass cases and studied the stuffed bitterns and whinchats. As we ascended the broad staircase I examined some mesmerising pre-Raphelite paintings, Burne-Jones and Rossetti and other friends of the Howards of Naworth. The birds, I said to Miss Briar wonderingly, had such gentle friendly eyes in their frozen state. I stood there open-mouthed aged nine and was deeply stirred. Miss Briar seemed stirred that I was stirred, especially now that I was beyond the confines of Maryport and my regular small-town routine. There and then in the museum beside the inhibited middle-aged schoolteacher, and today half a century later in my kiosk, I felt my insides slowly melting. And it was so imperative to wonder where it all was leading.

5

It was the fish that led me on to meet with Wright, who in turn was responsible for leading me back, with a great deal of guilt, to myself. However the route was not a direct one, and at two stages along the way I made false if reasonable deductions. It wasn't the first fish but the second that set me along that all important road to the North Quay. Likewise I believed at one point that I was following a trail back to those highly embarrassing wilderness years that my mother knew in the Twenties. To that piquant but painful period when she had fled her hopeless home and was living as a reluctant lodger with her peculiar aunt. To help clarify this riddle and draw all the threads of my story together, I need to explain three essential things. These are: the nature of my town, the nature of my mother's upbringing, and the nature of my father's death.

*

This town...

This town was settled by the Romans in 83 AD and they christened it with the beautiful name Alauna. Here imperial ships would dock bearing supplies for strategic Hadrian's Wall, then thievishly cart off the products of West Cumbrian forests, quarries and farms. The Romans finally took themselves away at the start of the fifth century, and things only began to come to life again when someone called Humphrey came on the scene. Anyone called Humphrey usually tries to keep a quiet profile, but this one was sufficiently sure of himself to obtain an Act of Parliament for the creation of a new town and port near the straggling hamlet of Alnefoot. It was 1749 and Humphrey Senhouse II, the owner of Netherhall mansion, rechristened Alnefoot 'Maryport' after his wife Mary, formerly of the illustrious Fleming family.

By 1765 it had a population of 1170. Fifty years later Maryport was still without a magistrate. People complained about 'ruffianish youths making plunder', just as they still do in the local papers every week in 1992. Back then it had no sewage system, few handy water supplies, and a great deal of wretched housing. In 1833 a grand public meeting was held in the Golden Lion inn, calling for the improvement of the town and harbour. Everything blossomed after that. First, massive Campbell Dock was opened in 1836. They added the magnificent Elizabeth in 1857, and ten years later three thousand vessels a year were using the port. In 1884 came the just as gargantuan Senhouse. Maryport was now a thriving, teeming coal port and, with its belching ironworks and Workington's Bessemer steelworks, a principal exporter of rails around the world.

However our docks, though vast, were too narrow, and by the start of the century were unable to accommodate the latest ships made from steel. In twenty years we went from boom to bust, which perhaps explains why the town even now has such a remarkable quantity of chapels, churches and public houses. At the beginning of the Depression in the Twenties, unemployment soared to a record 85%. Things continued stagnant and depressing until a few years ago, when the development brought a marina, a new bridge over the harbour, and some dockland housing development to rival London's East End. It also focused envious attention on me and my conveniently sited kiosk, for it sat there right at the heart of the proposed new expansion.

With regard to following in the family footsteps, my mother's kiosk was not really a kiosk, but a tin mission hut built into the side of an old chimney wall. It was knocked down as late as 1989 and with it went seventy years of trade and the cumulative memory of about a million tiny transactions. Those cramped, uncomfortable dimensions of Ma Singer's little gold-mine of a hut vividly emphasised the punishing constraints she'd always put upon herself. It was obvious that my mother would always remain resentful and uncomfortable after that mad decision of hers to make herself financially and emotion-ally independent from an early age. You could say that her tin mission hut was one of her defining geometries. Everyone has their defining geometry, needless to add. Humphrey Senhouse II had his defining geometry, a beautiful mansion called Netherhall, and the special slates he wanted for his roof had to be carted up by ship from Seascale harbour. Anyone who goes in for special ship-born slates naturally develops a feeling of being someone special, and this can lead them to the breath-taking audacity of building a town and naming it after their wife. Likewise the grey mullet and tompot blennies in their tanks in the town aquarium are very much subject to a defining geometry. Even the finest literary imagination might vainly struggle to imagine what it feels like for one of God's creatures to be swimming around the same glass rectangle day after day after day. My belief is that they transcend the limitations of their defining geometry by means of certain hidden and extraordinary faculties. But more of that later, and in its proper place...

When I had this kiosk constructed I insisted that it be designed so as to give maximum shelf display combined with optimum space within. Hence it is the size of a small marquee, and Karen and I, if we so wish, can pace around the largely empty floor. In the centre is the ice cream display with three yards of legroom either side. The rest of the stock is shelved beside or on the front counter. My mother would have taken one look at all that unused space and urged me to fill it with either a fruit and veg department or a footwear sideline or even a highly select maritime café seating a maximum of four. But I realise that while money matters, peace of mind is a more priceless asset. If I kept more stock and made more money and stayed open longer, I would need to drink at least twice as much and take twice as many foreign holidays just to cope with the worry and the exhaustion.

My mother would have had all sorts of shrewd suggestions as to how I might have made more of this place. Of course everyone is sensible and reasonable until they start making plans for others and give themselves full rein to vicarious fantasies. It is a golden art to look after oneself successfully in this life, and it's a long time since I have presumed to give anyone any unsolicited advice. In that respect I take after my father, who must have been one of the gentlest, least interfering men in the world. My mother, on the other hand, poked her nose in everywhere and advised everyone on everything, irrespective of professional specialism or simple considerations of tact. I once saw her give advice to a distinguished nuclear physicist, Professor James Berrie (the father of my college friend William who was holidaying with his parents in the nearby Lake District), on the best way to store Cumbrian reactor plutonium, even though she had never heard of either fission or fusion. As for human psychology, if you had explained to her the theories of Freud and Jung she would have effortlessly booted those revered savants out of the window as a pair of bungling, overwrought amateurs.

*

My mother's drive…

My mother's drive and willpower were boundless and incredible. Presumably heredity must have played a part in such a vehement temperament, but if it did it reached back to ancestors of whom I have no memory nor anecdotal reference. She was raised in extraordinarily topsy-turvy circumstances. Her mother Mary was widowed by the age of thirty-four when my grandfather Jack was killed by a bread van hurtling down Shipping Brow. He was on his way by foot to Ewanrigg Pit, and was lifted up and wheeled in a lopsided squeaking wheelbarrow to Maryport Hospital where he lived another hour. Mary Cannon, who was left with four young children, was guileless and credulous to the point of nil return. Legendarily eccentric in outlook before she was a widow, she was a fervent Primitive Methodist with a strong belief in practical charity. For example she would give away her last bit of ham for Jack's pit bait to any tramp who came begging at her well-known door. She would substitute tasteless haw and hip jam in Jack's sandwiches, something which ruffled my grandfather considerably, once even making him take his hand to his too Christian wife. After he was killed and Mary was living from hand to mouth with her family, instead of changing her mad habits, she increased giving and lending to the extent of full, comprehensive support for the hopeless and indigent.

My grandmother had a tiny terraced cottage along the harbour for which she was paying a rent of 6/6d in 1920, the year of her bereavement. This was also the year that my mother left Ellenbank School and rented the hole-in-the-wall for use as a shop at two shillings a week. If Mary Cannon had had any gumption she would have run the business alongside her enterprising fourteen-year-old. Instead of that, the new income allowed her to spend more time tending to the unpalatable oddities who were gradually filling up her house. There was Uncle Jimmie, for example, who was no uncle of anybody's as far as anyone knew, a seventy-five-year-old tramp with an impenetrable Glaswegian accent whose arthritis had apparently reached the crippling stage just as he was passing by 18 Harbour Villas. He was invited inside by my clucking grandmother who permitted, indeed encouraged, him to spend the last five years of his life as gratis lodger on a bed-settee in the sitting-room.

'Thass as nae bad,' Uncle Jimmie remarked expansively, though with a wary glance at scowling Mildred. 'Hame frae hame warr a sad wee man micht end his wanderin yeers.'

Uncle Jimmie, who was wall-eyed, goitrous, and had symmetrical pink moles on each cheek, rarely left his bed-settee and sometimes mournfully, sometimes brutally, battered his stick for cups of tea or sandwiches. His saintly landlady was a strict teetotaller, but Uncle Jimmie one day began pressing a tanner and a penny into the hands of the youngest of her four kids, Jim, and urged him to go and fetch him a nip of rum from either the Lifeboat or the Hope and Anchor. Jim and later Dave and Minnie did as they were bid and took the penny bribe, but when he approached the eldest, Mildred, she went straight to my grandmother and told her about the old man wasting the hard-earned pocket money she gave him on rum.

'No,' exclaimed Mary incredulous.

From behind her back Mildred brought out a dirty old medicine bottle that reeked of Lamb's. My grandmother turned grave and sorrowful. She walked through and gently reproved Uncle Jimmie, but when he went into loud tears and a self-flagellating, wholly unintelligible monologue, she forgave him instantly and quietly explained that, though she did not strictly forbid his vice, she'd welcome it if he abstained. Uncle Jimmie immediately broke into incredulous smiles and shouts of joy, and bumptiously commanded Dave, aged eight, to go and get him the Lamb's which was a far from adequate analgesic for the hell of a lifelong mendicant's rheumatism.

'Hell!' said Mildred disgustedly.

The young breadwinner was justifiably frightened by her mother's dangerous gullibility. It doubtless explained the ferocity of the adult Mildred Singer's legendary shrewdness with regard to the hidden motives of others. It probably determined my mother's unique blend of massive generosity and unnerving vigilance when it came to treating with new acquaintances. Besides, as a very young shopkeeper open day and night, she was learning a great deal of life's worrying secrets. The coarse and immoral ways of certain colliers and sailors, both married and unmarried, who tried to make sordid propositions and lewd grabs at her inside her cubby-hole. The desperation with which both the poor and the feckless would try to seek credit. Mildred allowed credit to the reliable, the virtuous poor and the absolutely destitute. To all the rest and especially the feckless, she allowed nothing but her adamantine advice, which was to do what she had done aged fourteen.

'What I did,' she informed them slowly and threateningly, 'was to pull myself up by my bootstraps.'

Mary Cannon continued her spendthrift benevolence towards waifs and strays, and in 1922 introduced Sam Hewitt and his middle-aged daughter Tillie. Uncle Sam was eighty-eight yet he had a full head of silver hair and a phenomenal appetite for both neck of lamb and pipe tobacco. He was also dumb from birth and his daughter Tillie, who kept her hair in long braids and still had the ghost of her youthful looks, was about forty-five and stone deaf. At first they were lodged in the parlour with Uncle Jimmie, but he took angry exception to their eerie silence-cum-gabble chunter as he called it. As he paradoxically stated it, it was making him drink more rum than he could afford on Mary's handouts. Undaunted and bearing in mind the Sermon on the Mount, where Christ said you must give your cloak as well as your coat to him who asks, Mary Cannon moved Uncle Sam and Cousin Tillie into her eldest child's bedroom. Of course my mother was safely out at the hole-in-the-wall when she committed that appalling treachery. Adolescent Mildred was so enraged at having to jump into the double bed with her mother and the little ones that she threatened to go and live with her unsavoury Aunty Agnes who lived in a hovel on North Quay.

'You wouldn't dare to go and live with my sister. Think of the shame for me. Think of what people would think.'

'What do you think they're thinking already? About these smelly old freaks you're polluting our house with?'

Safely ensconced in Mildred's bedroom with its bracing harbour view, father and daughter rapidly communicated something on a bit of paper and through Tillie's consonantless speech. They intended sharing the double bed rather than troubling Mrs Cannon for two shake-me-downs. Mary was deeply touched but Mildred was deeply suspicious. That night there came the unmistakable sounds of creaking bedsprings and repetitive female groans.

'Ha!' gasped Mildred triumphantly.

She realised at once the grotesque truth of it, but her mother persisted in her angelic view that they were both tragic cripples in an innocent family relationship. The moans, she whispered to her daughter over the heads of the sleeping children, were just the innocent groans that deaf women make in their sleep. The creaking springs were troubled dreams, nothing more. If you had had a hard pauperish travelling existence all your life like Sam and Tillie, it was natural that you moaned and shuffled in your sleep. Mildred gave a hysterical guffaw and offered to burst in on them to prove the obvious hypothesis, but her mother became very angry and said that just because Sam and Tillie were poor and handicapped did not mean they were forbidden simple Christian civility and kindness.

'They are fooling you,' my mother hissed appalled. 'Just like Uncle Jimmie, the old sot who's got segs on his fat behind from lying all day on our settee. Do you really believe it's the Seaman's Bethel he crawls his way to every Wednesday night for Bible Study?'

'Of course I do,' said my grandmother staunchly. 'Why on earth would he lie to me?'

'He goes to the taproom of the Sailor's Return, not the prayer room of the Seaman's Bethel. He spends his collection on rummy and rum, not on studying Ecclesiastes and Ecclesiasticus!'

Mary Cannon replied patiently, 'We have to think the best of them. They are all God's creatures after all. He loves them all the more because all three of them are halt and lame. Uncle Jimmie has obviously read his Bible carefully. He says that weakening complaint of his is what the scripture calls dropsy.'

'If he means those bloated and burst veins in his dirty face, it's because of a lifetime of swilling.'

'Mildred, God is the only judge of mankind, not me and certainly not a child like you! Just supposing they were trying to deceive me, even if they succeeded they couldn't deceive Him. We mustn't judge the mote in our neighbour's eye. We have to remove the beam in our own eyes first.'

My mother looked for a beam in her own eye and couldn't find it. She closed her tearful eyes and fell asleep exhausted. But as the sense of maternal betrayal became increasingly unbearable, Mildred punished her mother's credulity by playing spiteful tricks on her repulsive lodgers. She put a tablespoon of salt in the milk that Uncle Sam tipped over his morning porridge, and listened delighted as a man avowedly dumb from birth swore a mile-long oath that had the c-word twice and the f-word four times.

'I'd like to break whose flicking neck did that, Tillie!' came through the door. 'Snap it like a bloody little twig.'

His accent was Mancunian even though he had written on a bit of paper that he was from Antrim in Ireland. A week later she carefully filled his baccy tin with cayenne pepper and heard him spluttering and roaring as he took a post-coital smoke in her bedroom at midnight. Mary and the little ones slept on undisturbed and my mother flexed her restless toes delighted. Mildred also invested good money on giving his middle-aged daughter-concubine a heart attack. Tillie very occasionally helped my grandmother with the cooking, and one day when Mary was out at a chapel meeting, Mildred bribed a boy of ten to approach the sluttish deafwoman with a note saying Mrs Cannon had stopped at the butchers and ordered a pound of lard to be sent to 18 Harbour Villas. She needed a great deal of shortcut pastry made up for next week's Primitive Bring and Buy and wanted Tillie to get started on it now. The boy dawdled at the step two minutes until he heard the expected scream, then shot off to report complete success to Mildred.

Mildred had instructed the boy to search for something highly specific in one of the rotting hulks lying along South Quay. After that, to wrap it up very tightly in this sheet of lardy newspaper she'd handed him…

Tillie Hewitt had unrolled Mary's pound of lard with the

84

intention of cutting it on the pastryboard. Her blood froze, the kitchen clock stopped ticking, time petrified as the hideous apparition manifested itself between the sheets of the *Maryport News*. The deafwoman had found herself unrolling the whiskers and putrid head of a dead adolescent rat.

'Agh!' she screamed, so deafeningly that it could be heard across on the Scots side.

That evening as Mary was busy getting the young ones to bed and Mildred was eating bacon and potatoes on her own in the kitchen, Tillie came in with a handwritten message which she displayed to the vindictive child. What it said was STOP PERCYCUTTINN ME AND SAM. OR ELS. YOO GON FAR ENOF WIT RATTS AND SOLT AND PEPR. YOR ONLEE A KID. YOOL ONLEE GET INTER SEERYESS DANSHA.

Mildred assumed a polite incomprehension but was very frightened by the expression on the tramp woman's face. She kept on chewing her bacon and pretended the message had nothing to do with her. She strove to look as if butter, or for that matter lard, wouldn't melt in her teenage mouth. Tillie approached her and pinched her knee painfully and shoved her face terrifyingly close. She bared her few teeth and dilated her bloodshot grey eyes, and Mildred noted the incredible density of frown lines and the sourness of her breath and the queerness of her body odour which was both saline and equine. She pushed away her plate, leant backwards in her chair, and spat out as bravely as she could: 'You're a wicked damn fake! You're not deaf and your Dad isn't dumb. And he isn't Irish. And he isn't your Dad! You and he do things together and make disgusting noises in my bed every night like a pair of filthy dogs...'

Tillie grinned menacingly in the child's face. She had kept hold of the pinch of flesh and was turning it agonisingly. The tears were welling in my mother's eyes. In desperation her mind filled with artful slanders and lies that might startle this bloody old witch.

'Uncle Sam has tried courting with me as well...'

'Uh?'

'He grabbed me on the stairs last week when you were in the kitchen making teacakes with Mam. He talked to me like a manfriend even though he's supposed to be a poor dumb chap. He said he's from Manchester and he has a rich nephew called Adam. And that he loves me just from looking at me making tea in the kitchen. And that he'll take me with him to Manchester.'

Tillie growled from the depths of her throat. She dug her other hand into my mother's knee as she continued to exercise strappado on the nip of flesh. My mother picked up her fork and carefully eased her arm around the back of Tillie's skirt. What she invented next took her breath away, never mind Tillie's.

'I saw Uncle Sam *kissing* Uncle Jimmie on the stairs last week!'

'Uh!'

'When you and Mam were buying fish on the quay!'

Tillie's huge eyes dilated and she let out a strangled grunt.

'He told him that he loved him and that it had to be kept a secret and that it might be easier to lovebird him in a big city than in Maryport. He told Uncle Jimmie that he would take him away on the train down to Manch–'

'What!' shouted the deafwoman in fully palatalised Mancunian. 'You miserable little bitch!'

All five nails went deep into Mildred's leg. My mother screamed and stabbed her fork as hard as she could into Tillie's skirt. The fork was Sheffield steel and it penetrated Tillie's sinewy backside to a quarter of an inch. Sam's daughter shrieked and my mother stamped on Tillie's foot. My grandmother came racing down the stairs and saw her eldest child trembling by the front door as she struggled to put on her coat. She watched amazed as Tillie carefully prised a fork out of her skirts. The deafwoman was also waving a scrawled message, and demanding justice in her pitiful, mumbled way.

'Where are you going?' Mary gasped at Mildred. 'What on

earth's been happening between you and Tillie?'

'She called me a b-i-t-c-h,' Mildred shouted back furiously. For without any doubt, her mother's guileless piety was a species of unwitting perfidy. It was no less insidious because it was innocent. 'I'm moving out. I'm going to live with Aunty Agnes! Look at the nail marks she did on my knee. I had to stab her fat old bum with a fork to stop her from giving me lockjaw.'

Tillie handed Mary her message. Mary read it slowly then watched Tillie's laborious mime show which confirmed the bizarre assault.

'That's disgraceful! A girl of mine stabbing one of my lodgers…'

'But she has a ton of dirt under her fingernails, and it's full of her old vagrant's germs!'

Tillie began to moan and whimper at the brutal insult. Like a helpless, dependent infant she snatched at my grandmother's protective skirt.

'How can you possibly hurt the poor creature's feelings like that? How can you?'

'Because I know exactly what she is and what she's up to. And I'm telling you something else. You can get her out of my bedroom as soon as you like! I refuse to sleep five in a bed any more while she enjoys herself and does you-know-what every night with Uncle Sam.'

Mary's drooping spectacles admonished her pityingly. 'Why on earth can't you share a bed with your own brothers and sisters, Mildred? How can you be so proud and haughty with your own family?'

'Because I've got no bloody father!' my mother answered ruthlessly. She almost swallowed the brutal words but decided on balance that telling the truth was worth any sacrifice. 'That's why I've taught myself to act so proud as you call it. Because I can't rely on someone like you to look after me. Can I? Not when you turn the house into a dirty bear garden with all these scrounging potters and drunken sots. I've got nothing to fall back on if I try to depend on you. The only thing I have in the world is my own business. You can't even provide your own breadwinner with her own bed! Can't you see that sharing a bed at my age just makes me feel like a stinking trollop or a dirty little gypsy? And I'm not one of those, am I? I don't think God expects me to be one either.'

It gushed out in a bilious torrent before my mother slammed the back door and raced out into the pouring rain. She stayed out of the house all night and would never tell anyone, not even my father, where she spent those twelve atrocious hours. The next morning, stony and rigid at her mother's mournful pleading, she removed her clothes and few little trinkets and took them round to Agnes on North Quay.

*

As for my father…

As for my father…

The crucial encounter with the second fish and my subsequent entanglement with Wright are only credible if we accept one basic assumption, viz. that I am not a certifiable lunatic subject to florid hallucinations. This notional possibility is perhaps harder to brush off in my case than it might be in many others. After all, my maternal grandmother behaved like an imbecile in a Boccaccio story when she refused to believe that Tillie and Uncle Sam were having sex in my mother's bedroom. By contrast my mother, though extreme in all things, was obviously sane to the roots of her toes. Ditto my father Joe Singer, who must have been one of the gentlest as well as the stablest people ever to walk the streets of this town. But on the assumption that genetic predispositions often slip a generation, what if I have received my hereditary endowment from my father's father, Solomon Singer?

My paternal grandfather was a fourteen-stone farmhand who spent his married life in a tied cottage on the melancholy shores of Buttermere Lake. Before his marriage he was known the length of the county as an unrepentant firebrand and atavistic anarchist. He died in 1930, six years before I was born, but I see that he is impressively blunt-featured and threatening in the photograph I possess of the 1898–99 Seatoller and Buttermere Hound Trail Committee. In his teens he went along obsessively to every barn dance within a radius of twenty miles, walking there and back in all weathers, sleeping under dykes in the summer or inside breezy haylofts in the winter. Forever the ringleader when it came to playing insane and drunken tricks, it was fitting enough that his son should end up marrying a woman who sprinkled cayenne in a tramp's tobacco tin.

My father never tricked anyone in his life, not even on April Fool's Day. But Solomon Singer devoted his best energies to outrages of varying degrees of hazard. In 1899 he ruined a Methodist Supper and Recitation at Isel by shinning on top of the roof and ramming a huge sod into the smoking chimney. Within five minutes fifty men, women and children in their Sunday bests emerged coughing and choking, the tears streaming down their blackened faces. Solomon inflicted this cruelty in return for the recent prohibition of his courting with Cicely Chegwidden, forced on her by her father Robert, a well-to-do draper. The old man was so Primitive as a Rechabite Methodist he forbade her not only a madman like Singer, but to do anything but read or sew on the Lord's Day. When morose, bearded Chegwidden himself emerged from the hall, Solomon, still up on the roof, removed the sod and flung it full in the spluttering lay-reader's face. Old Chegwidden shook his fist and roared up that he should (a) get off that roof and (b) repent. Solomon squinted leerily, then to the mortified horror of the assembled Rechabites, lowered his cord trousers to display his enormous pimpled buttocks. Whimsically he informed them that the moon had decided to come out early tonight. He jumped the fifteen feet to the rock-hard ground as if it had been three, and ran off hooting as some of the younger chapelfolk began pelting him with stones.

Solomon the lawless had no trouble staying a single man until well into his forties. Besides, like many a Lakeland farmhand he lived, breathed and worshipped trail-hounds, and spent every evening walking them miles across the fells and lanes. Embroiled as he was in dogs and betting half his wages on the trails, he inevitably neglected many of the subtler refinements of courtship and almost all other baffling aspects of interpersonal communication. But in 1888 he set his greedy eyes on a very bonny young girl called Marian, the youngest of four beauties whose parents farmed by lonely Blindcrake. As well as being beautiful, Marian was aloof, well spoken and extremely choosy. And because my grandfather was nearly seven-foot tall, flat-footed, picked his nose, broke wind and hawked snot before women just as he did before his trail dogs, she laughed out loud when he gruffly asked her to spoon with him. This was his forthright demand at a charity barn dance at Bromfield, and a hundred intrigued farming folk were on hand to hear her imperious rebuttal. Undeterred, Solomon followed her hound-like with his wistful, drooping ears into the empty tea room at the back where he urged her to change her mind.

'Please,' he said, and added without a trace of irony, 'Neck with us Marian and I'll give you a hundred pounds in your hand…'

He was lying but he almost meant it. As she brushed him away snootily, he began to embrace her. He just laughed and snorted when Marian pushed him backwards through the door. But then, pathetically unable to restrain a great burning inside him, he did something completely outrageous. A naughty ten-year-old might just have got away with it, but as a grown man it was entirely unforgivable. Guffawing noisily, more like a thoughtless child than a responsible adult, my grandfather went behind Marian and pulled down her drawers.

Just to see what was there, just to make a detailed inspection of what was not on offer. The back room was completely empty, but Marian was horrified by his incredible madness. He lifted up her skirt and examined her impressive young backside as if she had been a Galloway heifer at Wigton auction. He murmured approvingly and slapped her calves resoundingly and wondered why she didn't moo. Marian turned and struck him as hard as she could across his ruddy beaming face. In doing so she revealed down below her trembling, bristling maidenhair. Incensed at the force of the blow, shouting that she'd nearly put his eye out, my grandfather grabbed a pen he kept for trail slips in his pocket. Pinning her immobile with his great fist, he proceeded to draw a comical face with ready-made beard and moustache around the area of her private parts. Then, minus drawers and skirt, with her arms pinioned behind her, he pushed her back into the throng of the dance hall and began to parade her as if she was a dancing bear.

Four days later her two brothers fell on my grandfather and beat him senseless, almost killed him with two kebbie sticks as he walked the hounds on the deserted fellside near Rogerscale. It took over a year for his injuries to heal and for him to resume his lunatic tricks with only marginally less vigour. That penchant for insensitive recklessness continued unabated until arthritis lost Sol the use of his legs and a fit of apoplexy finally finished him off in Keswick Infirmary. The arthritis was caused by all the soakings he'd got as he walked his precious hounds, and fittingly enough it monsooned remorselessly the day that he was buried.

It amounts to this, then. I am the grandson of a bucolic madman, who was almost killed for his outrageous, outlandish behaviour. It was a well-kept family secret of course, and it was only at the eleventh hour that I was finally informed. Joe Singer had managed to swear my mother to secrecy, and I only learnt about my grandfather's disgrace when his only son was on his early deathbed…

*

Towards the end…
I have described how, by her unwitting artistic power, my mother was responsible for that Christmas epiphany of the

angel and the turning baubles. She ended her days demented of course, and was no longer capable of anything. It is now just as essential to describe my father's final days, and the symmetrical epiphany that he created on that nighttime walk by Flimby pit. That haunting symmetry, I believe, is explicable only in terms of what Kenneth Wright had to say in that incredible speech he made down on North Quay. The lesson, if that was what it was, is a tough one and cannot be explained in simple terms of temporal cause and temporal effect. Which perhaps explains why I have told so few about these matters up to now...

Towards the end my father's decline was very rapid. For over a year he'd complained of moderately unpleasant gastric sensations and a strange uncategorisable indigestion that invariably put him off his food. Never a guzzler like Solomon, he picked indifferently at his dinners and even gave them to his dog Sid when my mother turned her back. Joe Singer was a thin, fragile wisp of a man and, suffering no visible weight loss, chose not to trouble dozy eighty-five-year-old Doctor Lytollis. Joe and Mildred Singer had struggled and battled all their lives and, like all their generation, dosed the resultant headaches and dyspepsia with paracetamol and antacids. If ever she heard smooth-voiced experts on TV prating about reified abstractions like 'stress' and 'tension', Mildred Singer would laugh out loud and slap her thigh contemptuously. She had a far simpler name for these painful figments of the imagination, she boasted. She preferred to call them 'life'.

One sunny day in June her too gentle husband suddenly collapsed in the upstairs bathroom. My mother rang me at my shop sounding absolutely terrified. For the first time in my life I heard her speaking with a pleading, frightened voice. I shuddered premonitorily, telephoned 999 for an ambulance and drove round there straight away. Joe Singer was still lying on the bathroom floor looking unbelievably pale, uncannily tiny, and murmuring something about his allotments and his poultry. My unhinged mother was babbling away very rapidly with an incongruous glaze in her eyes, like an uninhibited television compère.

'We'll get you into the ambulance, Joe, and we'll make you comfortable, and we'll get you to Hensingham, and then they'll get you into bed, and then they'll get the specialist, and then you'll soon be as right as...'

It was the hopeless hysteria of the seasoned coper. As I went downstairs to meet the ambulance men I could hear her upstairs crying by his side. Predictably enough I felt more upset and confused by her sobs than I did by my father's mortal collapse. By the time they had got him onto a stretcher, the tears had been wiped away and she was seriously asking the two men if they would like to hang on a quarter of an hour for a cup of tea.

'No lass,' said the fatter one with the bloodshot eyes. He patted her arm very tenderly and comprehendingly. 'We'd have to stop off and irrigate a dyke if we did.'

My mother blinked and laughed heartily and greatly appreciated that he'd said nothing whatever about life and death. Swiftly she packed a holdall with his pyjamas, his pipe and a change of clothes. I drove her to the hospital while the two of us effortfully struggled to fend off the unthinkable.

By the time we got there, Joe Singer had regained his colour and had come round to a reasonable lucidity. Mildred Singer was mildly snappy at this welcome turnabout and chided him for giving her an unwarranted heart attack.

'You've got a dirty tie on,' she reproved him.

I pursed my lips and tutted them both. 'He should have flaked out on the floor with a clean one.'

'I feel quite alright,' he said, fingering the grubby tie. But he seemed to be losing his colour again, and the frown lines on his brow stood out in harsh relief. 'And I think I'd prefer to go home.'

He was lucid and capable of speech for another two days. As well as running my mother through to see him every evening, I closed up the shop and made my own afternoon visits. The nurses had him strapped up with plastic tubes running in and out of his nostrils, but he was permitted to leave his bed and visit the noisy hospital café with me. We sat there slowly chewing two-finger KitKats and made the halting conversation of two elderly sleepwalkers.

'This place,' he said to me wonderingly, 'I don't think much of these billets.'

'Billets?' I echoed, looking in the direction of the wards where he was pointing. It was an unusual, disquieting and anachronistic word. Besides, working as a wages clerk for the coal board, Joe Singer had been exempted from any active war service.

'Yes. Why the hell are we billeted here, George?'

This story began with Alzheimer-stricken Mildred Singer thinking she was staying in a hotel rather than a psychogeriatric ward. Through her choleric confusion she kept asking me when her husband Joe would come and pick her up. I thought to myself, twenty years from now, when I'm sitting old and dopy on a hospital bed like my Dad, will I ask someone, my daughter Anne, perhaps, where it is we are flying from this bloody airport lounge?

On the third day, as he began to decline, he was moved into a private room. With that, he retreated into an uncomprehending fog, like a wounded and ailing little bird. He looked the perfect image of a sparrow that a cat has mauled: frozen, traumatised and beyond any kind of help.

'Where have you sprung from?' he asked me in a distant puzzled whisper. The glaze across his mild blue eyes was total, as if a cruel cataract or optical parasite had decided to lodge itself there.

There was an odd levity in his voice and I thought for a second he was still the same natural joker. I gazed embarrassed at this little lost man who had once fathered me. I wondered if by some sort of magic I could summon him out of this completely diabolic fog. I did not believe in God but I wanted to believe in Him and I also wanted Him to save my father. I joked and chatted about Mildred and his grand-daughter Anne, while he squinted away uncomprehending and speechless. Halfway through my visit I decided to remain quiet myself and just be there in his presence. Perhaps my silence would elicit something that my hopeless cheery gossip would not.

Instead it just allowed him to moult away eerily, like the dying little bird he was.

'What's wrong with him?' I asked the ward matron shakily. Appalled by the speed of his decline, I had slipped out of the room for a few minutes, promising I'd be back right away. He had made no sound or movement and I realised I could have told him the world had ended for anything it mattered.

The matron was about sixty and simultaneously placid and stiff. She deliberated like a pedantic teacher or a mournful politician, as if my father's symptoms were best confronted by doleful, melodramatic headshaking.

'Well he's not getting any better,' she said with exaggeratedly pursed lips.

'No,' I said, as I imitated her stiffness. 'And I wonder what the bloody hell you're going to do about it?'

She said brusquely, 'We're going to do tests.'

'What tests?'

She stiffened her jaw and obviously had no intention of telling me. I was both amazed and incensed. Looking as frightening as I could, I thumped my fist hard on her ugly melamine desk. I demanded precise clinical information on his condition, or else.

'If you won't enlighten me, I want an immediate interview with his specialist.'

'That's quite impossible, Mr Singer.'

'Immediately! Or else I'll start throwing things around this bloody office.'

She gulped and sat down quickly and wiped her sweating brow. Then like a shaky wooden marionette she attempted a tremulous kindness and old-fashioned courtesy. 'We're going to give him an endoscopy, Mr Singer. You remember you've said he's had this long-term stomach trouble...'

I started, as if from a guilty amnesia. 'You mean that you're testing him for stomach cancer?'

'If that's what it is,' she answered, looking anxiously at a chart on the far wall.

'But he's had nothing worse than indigestion symptoms.'

She looked at me faintly accusingly, as if I and my mother should have exercised more commonsense vigilance. And it struck me just as forcefully that, yes, we should have shown more care and more sense when it came to protecting that vulnerable little man who was now a wasted sparrow.

I said, 'If he's had stomach cancer for over a year, he'd have shown much more severe symptoms? Cancer can't be confused with indigestion? Can it?'

She sighed too theatrically and fidgeted with her ballpoint pen.

'Can it?'

An endoscopy, an optical exploration into the stomach, was done on the little man who had turned into a bird. Like a bird he had no idea what was happening to him. The cancer was in a very advanced condition and had spread to his brain, as even my desolate mother was finally obliged to acknowledge. Cancer in the brain cells turns a healthy man into a broken little fledgling. The specialist predicted he would live for two more days, three days at most. He survived for just two and was buried a week later on a windy July day.

*

That first day in the hospital I reminded him of the pit buckets we'd seen in 1942. My father chewed his two-finger KitKat and nodded with a serenity which might have been interpreted as intelligent attention. I spoke at length and very carefully, very precisely, as if each word about those buckets and the father and son of twenty-six years ago might have been a helpful life-line. I felt as if an anecdote about something deeply felt might promote a miracle and restore a sick man to health. I would heal him with a true story.

The story was very simple. Joe Singer worked in the offices at Risehow pit and one fine spring evening decided to take his young son for a walk in that direction. It was only a couple of miles, but for a six-year-old it meant a marathon hike and a miraculously extended bedtime. My mother was in the shop, feverishly busy because it was Easter, and I was on holiday from Bloody and her restless ruler. Joe Singer had decided to give his only son a quixotic treat and a magical nocturnal adventure. To cap all, we would have chips from Flimby chip shop where they had free fish scrapings and cooked a wartime staple of dried and leathery salt cod.

As we walked the two miles I felt my father's gentleness, his silent tranquillity, drifting up and floating through the evening air. On our right there was the vast frieze of the dark blue Solway Firth. The delicate hills of a foreign land, of Wigtown and Kircudbright, were ruminating opposite. There was a brilliant bright orange sunset though the warm Friday evening was turning to chill. My Dad had been carrying my coat and now he bundled me up and took my hand which was cold yet tingling.

The lights of the pit offices were visible as the dusk and the icy air gathered around us. The little lights were mercury blue and they seemed as tiny and intense as in a fairy story. I looked at them gladdened. As I held my father's hand I felt that he and I were both as small and concentrated as that mercury blue. He led us past the offices and down beyond a rubbish-filled forest beck that leaked into the Solway Firth. We looked across to some of the biggest garden allotments for miles around. Some of his Flimby collier friends kept greyhounds, pigeons, hens and turkeys over there. We continued walking up the dirt path that went parallel with the pit. As dusk became dark we stared at the great spiders of pit wheels that seemed to be humming and turning in the dark. It was a trick of the light for they were stationary and the illusion of motion came from the pit-yard lamps. They shone that mild yet vivid orange because, my father said, they were filled with a thing called sodium. I looked with longing at their warm and comforting reflection, which was the nearest thing in these sombre parts to the transfixing light of the Mediterranean.

We halted as if by agreement. We lingered, the tiny one and his father, and stared at the deserted pit and that soothing orange radiance. In front of the sodium lamps were other mercury lamps that illumined the wall of the yard. The sodium was radiant but the mercury was sharp and focused. They were like us two, like father and son, both diffuse and focused, both warm and cool.

Then I saw the miracle. My Dad touched my shoulder and pointed up at the floating buckets. They were shaped like bread baskets and were the size of large coal scuttles. They were floating along pulleys and wires, self-propelled in the dark, inanimate sleepwalkers making their nighttime procession. Way above in the sky they made their small solemn way like objects in a supernatural fairground. Like a glimpse of things that go on independent of men and of time they wove their vulnerable way through the dark. I thought of them as toys come to life in the middle of the night when time and the laws of adults do not exist.

'What are they doing?'

'They're carrying coal,' he whispered.

'But where are they going?' I interrogated. 'Where are they coming from?'

'What?'

'Who's moving them? Who looks after them?'

'To the pit yard,' he said patiently. 'From the forest. A machine. They don't need looking after. They're not alive.'

'Yes they are! They've come to life, they've woken up, because it's the night.'

*

98

My father smiled ever so gently and tolerantly at my illusions. Fifty years on in the noisy hospital café I reminded him that he had allowed me to believe my childish little fairy tale. I looked aghast at his nodding incomprehension and my eyes began to prick. I was thirty-two, which seemed a disastrously young age to be losing your Dad. I felt as if I was only six instead of thirty-two and I held his hand in the same way I had held it on the allotment road in 1942. Somewhere outside in the hospital car park 'Revolution' by the Beatles was being played on a car radio. It was 1968, there was a real revolution going on in France, every night on the news we saw the vicious gendarmes busting peoples' heads in gay Paree. My father was busy commenting witlessly on the quality of the billets here in this army camp. He had nodded carefully at my long story about the pit, the Flimby chip shop, the leathery salt cod, the blue and orange lamps, but he was not there beside me, and I was quite incapable of performing the impossible.

I wanted to tell him that I loved him, as I had never been able to before now. If I did I knew I would end up sobbing and squawking all over his ill-fitting dressing gown. I also knew that if he'd been in his proper mind, he would have been deeply embarrassed by such an unnecessary and unfathomable display of womanish hysterics...

So, even though he was away with the fairies, I was quite incapable of making my confession of filial love.

'Do you want another KitKat?' I asked him miserably. 'Do you?'

He gave me a hint of a smile. 'They're not bad billets,' he said. 'But I don't know how long I'll be staying here.'

6

Now we get to the heart of the matter, meaning the validity or otherwise of a spoken as opposed to wordless message. What we had in its simplest terms was the urgent communication of a verbal imperative, a highly specific instruction, from one party to another. The dynamics of the model might have been simplicity itself but the content was explosive to the last degree. The fact that the imperative led me on to a man like Wright, wearing the thing that he wore as conspicuously as he did, can hardly be a specious coincidence. But enough of prevarication. Instead of continuing to couch my questionable story with cowardly hesitations and elaborately teasing provisos, it is best that I simply tell it as it happened.

I was back in the aquarium and lingering by the ray pool. No one seemed to mind that I was an obsessive visitor and was becoming something of a lunchtime fixture. Indeed everyone who came, whether boisterous Italian tourist or octogenarian local, seemed unselfconsciously entranced by the place. Ironically the elusive turbot had a baleful, melancholy look about it today, and was lying low on the pool bed. Watching it carefully, I decided I no longer believed it had anything truly miraculous in its make-up. Even the fact that it and the rays and sharks liked to rise out of the water and be patted on the back was no longer a touching mystery. I had read a bit more of that old library book on ethology, and discovered that rays and flat-fish are densely studded with sensory skin receptors. Banal as it seems, like any other species with a sensitive skin, these sociable flatfish are partial to a friendly massage.

There was yet another irony. My ethology book said that the turbot, like the brill, has no fixed morphology, no stable identity in the visual sense. It changes its spots to suit its background, to confuse ocean predators as well as oddballs like me stood watching it with an ulterior motive. It is camouflaged by its chromatophore colour cells, which can either contract into a central blob or diffuse throughout its body. Thus it can mimic the pattern of the sea bed and lie low until the scavenger has passed.

If it can do all that, I thought, it must be no effort whatever to dupe the likes of me with a radiant hallucination of a smile. Feeling comprehensively let down, not to say deeply ridiculous, I wandered off to look at some of the wrasse. Before coming in here, I had never even heard of this species, but several compelling reasons drew me to their tanks these days. Most vividly because, of the six-hundred recognised varieties of wrasse, a great majority of them change their sex (from male to female) in middle age. It was not so much the fact that they were capable of changing sex that made me marvel, as the fact they chose to do so at a critical halfway point during their lives. After all, I remembered enough of school biology to recall the bizarreness of parthenogenesis, and the gothic symbolism of parasitism and symbiosis. All that extrapolated easily enough into analogous human parallels, but it was the mid-life crisis of the male wrasse that really set me thinking. I was tempted to turn to the fifty-year-old German in the windcheater standing next to me and say, 'I don't suppose it'd be a bad idea to change sex at this stage in our lives. *Was meinen Sie, mein Herr?* I've had enough of being a dissatisfied man and I wouldn't mind a crack at being a dissatisfied woman from now on.'

I didn't, of course. Instead I turned my attention to the cuckoo wrasse, one of the most beautiful fish of our native waters. The male of the species is a vivid orange with blue stripes, so lustrous and intense that if you were a little boy you would wish to scoop it up and hug it lovingly to your breast. Orange and blue, the combination instantly reminded me of something from the past. Of the piercing fairytale lamps around Risehow pit during the War? A sodium in chromatic combination with a mercury? I looked at the male cuckoo wrasse and thought of my Dad, Joe Singer, and my eyes began to itch with sadness. I turned sharply to the corkwing wrasse (*Goldmaid* in German), a species which definitely does not switch genders. Then I shifted to the goldsinny wrasse, which might or might not have a sex change, marine biologists being unable to prove the case either way.

Naturally I read all that the caption had to say about this sexual indeterminacy. There was no explanation of why they couldn't be certain of a gender reversal. Feeling irritated by their lack of omniscience, I moved into the converted hulk dragged out of the dock, which houses the brook charr, the sand goby, the pouting, the snake pipefish and butterfish and the common sea squirt. However, I had studied them numerous times before, and having glanced at the lesser weever and the bullroot adjacent, I turned on my heel. With a vague sense of purpose I strode back to that highly enigmatic specimen that lives on its own at the far end of the hulk. There, in all his sullen gloriousness, reposes the magnificently ugly, indescribably inscrutable and charismatic species known as John Dory...

*

There was just the one John Dory swimming about in his capacious tank. Looking back this was an additional strangeness, for apart from the obvious antisocial loners like the conger and the octopus, all the other species were represented in the plural. I stood and stared at one of the queerest albeit exotic fish in existence. His grotesque little body was absurdly tall and compressed, circled by fierce barbed fins and quills and trailing filaments. Suddenly he flashed his silver-grey back at me, then isomerised into a yellowy brown, a yellow grey, a grey brown, a grey and silver yellow. His striping was tantalisingly indistinct, altogether elusive, but he had a lustrous beaten gold sheen and the most beautiful mottlings of blue and gold.

He opened his sage mouth and looked at me glumly. I thought of Miss Blood circa 1943 and I wilted and acknowledged a superior being. Like her he was capable of creeping up unobserved and devouring his prey with impressively hinged jaws. He was uniquely designed to slink around invisible to his prey, being very strongly laterally compressed. Like Miss Blood his greatest beauty lay in his nomenclature. He was also known as Zeus Faber and St Pierre. In various folklores, the trilingual caption explained, he had important religious associations. In pursuit of prey his mobile lips shot out like a telescope, but when he wasn't hunting for food he appeared very pensive and lugubrious. This John Dory had a huge head, a protruding jaw, and he looked both phantasmagoric and fantastic. He was Miss Imogen Blood to a tee.

Apropos mythology, he was deemed sacred to Zeus because of his legendarily divine flavour. Likewise in France, Spain, Italy, Iceland, Norway and Sweden he was also called St Peter's Fish on account of the sizeable dark spot on his flank. That mesmerising little spot was clearly ringed by a pale halo, by the signature of a saint...

Digesting that last sentence, I felt a cool shiver going up my back. I read on slowly, afraid of missing anything important. Back in the old days, certain credulous, primitive fishermen believed the following story. After Peter complained to Jesus that he couldn't pay his taxes, Christ told him to pick out the first fish from the sea nearby and inside its mouth he would find a coin. That fish, which miraculously contained his tax payment, was a John Dory. Other fishermen believed the opposite; that when St Peter first caught a John Dory in his net, it looked so horrible he threw it back in disgust. As evident substantiation of that unflattering anecdote, the French nickname for it is *L'Horrible*. Yet other bygone fisherfolk of Kent claimed that it was the fish with which Christ fed the five thousand. That spot plus halo, they believed, was the print of the

Son of Man himself. Because of its divine associations they piously refused to eat it, and they nailed it to their doors as a sign of good luck.

St Peter's thumbprint or Jesus' thumbprint?

'Good God,' I whispered, without a trace of irony.

Originally there was no 'John', it was known simply as 'dory' (from the French *dorée*, the adjective relating to the gold glimmer on the sides). In the seventeenth century the 'John' was added as an affectionate diminutive embellishment, doubtless because, on the analogy of Jack Sprat, its ugliness brought out the fishermen's affable compassion.

The John Dory, it concluded, tends to be a solitary fish…

I spent a good twenty minutes carefully examining this lonely fish of hermit habits. I was mesmerised by its ineffable, singular beauty or perhaps by its charismatic ugliness. I turned my back on it very reluctantly. I had to get back to work because Karen my assistant had her dinner hour soon. For various reasons I lied to her and said I always spent my lunch hour in the library. I knew that she knew that I went to the aquarium, as it was only a hundred yards from the kiosk. She knew that I knew that she knew, but she always kindly played the game and nodded poker-faced. Of course I had said nothing to her about smiling turbots and their ability to transform one's life, or she would have been away to the Job Centre as quick as her twenty-five-year-old ankles could take her. She obviously assumed I was an eccentric old bore of an employer with a puerile if harmless hobby. If it hadn't been aquarium fish it might have been lunchtime trainspotting or gathering shells down on Grasslot shore, even more glaring indices of premature senility.

Just as I was leaving the hulk that housed the John Dory, I heard a man's voice speaking behind me. As clear as a numinous bell I heard the following words: *'It's right at the end of the North Quay.'*

That was all. Nothing more and nothing less. No clearing of the throat or pause in mid-sentence or shifting upwards cadence towards the end. Nothing extraordinary about a statement like that. In fact a perfectly innocent, innocuous remark which half the town's inhabitants might reasonably have uttered without anyone being startled. So how then am I supposed to explain the following? That instantly my creeping flesh felt as if it had the infinitely tactile sensitivity of a young fish. That an enormous overwhelming coldness seemed to spread itself all over the sensory receptors of my middle-aged human skin. That as soon as I had heard that unremarkable declaration by that apparently unremarkable masculine voice, I received the most dreadful inkling.

'Eh?' I exclaimed.

The voice had been directed at *me* from an anomalous invisible source. I hadn't a shadow of doubt about that.

I shot round in a freezing slow motion and looked at the empty recess. I peered minutely and felt a renewed chill.

There was no one there. There was nothing there...

Of course I knew that for a certainty before I started my pointless investigation. I walked the length of this little hulk annexe first of all. The particular recess that housed the John Dory was principally lit by artificial light. Despite that, every corner, every crack and cranny, was amply illumined. There were no easy hiding places and no one was hiding. There was the po-faced *L'Horrible* pouting mournfully inside his tank and there was me stood two yards away from him, and that was it.

Crazily I peered up above for a hidden microphone. I looked to the sides of the hulk recess as if someone might have hidden himself there to play some stupid trick. I looked minutely along all the panels and skirtings and surfaces, just to make doubly sure.

I checked to see if this hulk wall was adjacent to another partition and I'd been eavesdropping on someone talking on the other side. But there was only the empty car park beyond this section. This wall was an outside wall and that bit of the car park I could see through the decorative porthole was deserted. There were only two empty cars and no one was getting in or out of them. There was no one lurking out there who might have shouted through the wall.

I was cold to the marrow and for a very good reason. I had heard a disembodied voice addressing me and me alone. And it was 1992, the cyber-age and the age of global communication, not the age of cryptic portents and primitive superstitions.

'OK,' I thought to myself defiantly. 'It's a simple diagnosis. I'm going bloody crackers! That's it then. George Singer the over-educated ice cream salesman is celebrating middle age by going bananas. So that's all right then.'

I clenched my fists in my pockets and paced about angrily in front of the John Dory tank. The occupant stared at me with a baleful, dismissive expression as I staggered to and fro.

'I'm hearing voices and seeing things,' I ranted quietly, 'but I don't even have the consolation that they are *human*.' Sweating and irresolute I unclenched my fists and headed back towards the ray pool. 'I'm hearing the voices of bloody *fish*. I'm seeing apparitions in the faces of bloody fish. I thought it was a trick of the light, but no, not at all. And oh my, what a joy for me in late middle age! Bugger me, I wish I'd been born a bloody cuckoo wrasse and been able to change my sex instead of *this*.'

I made my way furiously out of the hulk. Just as I turned my back on the tank an insistent voice addressed me once again.

'*Tomorrow night*. It's at the far end of the North Quay.'

I turned round warily to face my crafty informant.

'You what?' I cried aloud and then instantly swallowed my lunatic's words.

I stared at the John Dory and a vaporous vertiginous sensation began to affect the backs of my eyeballs.

'*Tomorrow night*,' the voice repeated sternly through my suddenly hazy vision. 'It's at the far end of the North Quay.'

I can see that I need to spell it out in black and white, for my benefit as much as anyone else's. Let it be underlined twice that I spit all over the notion of fairies or trans-species reincarnation. Also that I thoroughly dislike every anthropomorphic

Walt Disney cartoon that has ever been made. Notwithstanding which, I am prepared to swear on oath that that plug-ugly fish *L'Horrible* was my preposterous and poker-faced interlocutor!

Checking that there was no one in earshot, I whispered back guiltily like some skulking criminal. 'But I don't want to know. I really don't want to know.'

*

Of course I did want to know. I wanted to know and I didn't want to know. I was frightened out of my wits, it goes without saying. Like any other sceptical middle-aged kiosk proprietor I was biliously scornful of all New Age whimsies and supernatural emanations. Part of me wanted to take the afternoon off and drink myself into temporary amnesia. Another part felt helplessly impelled to follow this shambolic trail, as if I were studiously interpreting a puzzling clue in a teasing film or foreign novel. Despite the shameful absurdity of a university-educated man in the late twentieth century paying attention to an auditory hallucination, I was extremely impatient to unravel the significance of this extraordinary vatic utterance. Apparently addressed by a charismatic species of Mediterranean fish, I was beset by a living metaphor. Like all such rhetorical tropes it demanded to be clarified once it had entered real life itself. Otherwise the whole world, not just me, would be turned upside down...

As I pondered the exhortatory tone of that message, it soon struck me that my mother, ubiquitous and importunate Mildred, was involved in this puzzle somehow. That seven-word clause, T-F-E-O-T-N-Q, had stirred up immediate maternal associations, even though it was only when I stepped outside the aquarium that I realised what they were. In the five years between leaving home and getting married my mother had had her home TFEOTNQ, at *the far end of the North Quay*. She had survived there with her Aunty Agnes in a dilapidated, crumbling terrace, just five minutes' walk from Mary Cannon and her waifs-and-strays home. Which was also jocularly known as the Crazy Workhouse to all Mildred's hole-in-the-wall customers. Of course Mildred Cannon had smiled very stiffly if any reference was made to her mother's saintly barminess. Before long she would refuse usury to the garrulous customer, no matter how sound their credit and regardless of the bitterness of their protestations. The lesson soon spread and ultimately no one dared even mention the existence of the feckless mother to the ferocious daughter. The fact that Mildred was only seen to visit her very rarely and in the secrecy of darkness when her shop was shut led to all sorts of inaccurate and unsatisfactory speculation about their wholly unintelligible bond.

In some respects the runaway seemed to have leapt from the frying pan into the fire. Agnes Gill was no saint or philanthropist but she had decidedly inherited the Cannon fecklessness – or should we gloss it, rich idiosyncracy? I looked up the word 'feckless' in my dictionary today, assuming that, because it was never off my mother's tongue, it must be standard English usage. To my surprise it wasn't there, and I had to resort to the town library and the OED where I found it between 'fecifork' (the anal fork on which the larvae of certain insects carry their faeces) and 'feculent' (the quality of being foul). 'Feck', it transpires, is of Scandinavian and subsequently Northern dialect origin, and in 1470 meant 'effect' or 'tenor', and by 1535 signified 'efficacy' or 'vigour'. In Mildred's eyes, to be without feck was the greatest sin, and hence it was remarkable that she managed to stick her aunt's company for all those years. In reality, as a young working-class girl in the remote provinces in the Twenties, she had very little choice. Single accommodation for the likes of her was unobtainable, and if by a miracle she had found it, it would have led to suggestions of prostitution or quarantine against contagious illness, or both. At least her Aunty Agnes gave her her own bedroom and attended neither chapel nor church, and ruthlessly slammed the door on even the most pitiful tramp or beggar...

7

Trying to pinpoint Agnes's old house I bumped into Wright and spent the first five minutes thinking he was an ostentatious and unlikely species of fisherman. Wright did not fish for cod or bream or plaice, of course; he pursued something very different. Sedulously searching for my great aunt's old shack along the harbourside on that sunny summer evening, really I was looking for poignant souvenirs of my dead mother. In doing so I evidenced a heartfelt, sonly devotion I had never really shown when she was alive. In essence, I was retracing Mildred Singer's old path to freedom, though the freedom I eventually stumbled on was nothing at all like hers.

But back to 1920, when it all started. Agnes Gill made almost no comment and evinced almost nil surprise when tearful Mildred came begging sanctuary from her mother's house. Agnes was a surly, corpulent fifty-year-old spinster who by her victorious admission 'did not bother with men'. Instead she bothered with hens, and as well as the considerable allotment she maintained at Grasslot full of hens and bantams, she kept half-a-dozen white Wyandottes in the back garden. She sold secondhand furniture from a warehouse she rented adjacent to her terrace, as well as a miraculous assortment of household and garden paraphernalia. The furniture stock showed some system and she always had any amount of beds and chests of drawers and dressers and linen presses. The motley bric-a-brac and garden tools were acquired on a more serendipitous, impulsive basis, depending on which auction, house sale, farm sale or bankruptcy clearance Agnes had managed to drag herself to in the last month. Taciturn fifteen-stone Agnes didn't like getting off her vast backside to any extent, not unless it was in the context of tending to her poultry. For their sake she would do almost anything. She would accept lifts in motor-cars from well-to-do fur-and-feather fanciers travelling to competitive shows in Cumberland, Westmorland and Lancashire. In practice these fanciers tended to be bachelor farmers like Willy Bellarby who was seventy-eight when Mildred first knew him and had proposed to Agnes at least seventy-eight times. Bellarby, who by his open admission dosed himself with bromide to temper a superfluous libido, not only bred show poultry but also reared rabbits, guinea pigs, cavies and anything else that could be contested and judged. At least once a week he would descend from his farm in the woodland wilds between Maryport and Flimby, and sit in Agnes's shop for long atmospheric hours. His conversation would meander between scurrilous conjecture on the corrupt practices of other poultry fanciers and the unintelligible stoniness of a broad-beamed beauty like Agnes Gill towards an uxorious, still handsome catch like Willy. Being a rough old farmer his discourse was edited neither for the sensitivity of Agnes's maiden niece or for the trickle of gratified evening customers in Agnes's warehouse.

*

Five years passed this way at TFEOTNQ and Mildred was just one month short of her majority. On a highly significant Friday evening in 1926 my mother was attending nervously on her aunt and the lovelorn old farmer. Rather than drive back to a lonely widower's supper, Bellarby invariably provided his inamorata with a cold pork pie from the butcher's, whilst seated beside her at the till he consumed his favourite alternative. Bellarby's Friday night favourite was a pint of warm cow's blood fresh from the Maryport slaughterhouse, of which he was a regular supplier. Tonight as always he drank it noisily straight from a very chipped jug donated by his reluctant sweetheart. His gory elixir surprised neither Agnes nor any town citizen older than forty. After all, they ate black pudding without a second thought, so there was no logic whatsoever in doing anything but admire Willy Bellarby's back-to-the-source-of-things approach.

Mildred sat down nervously beside this preposterous old pair. She was anxious to tell Agnes something important and wished that Bellarby would either vamoose or emigrate, or, God forgive her, pass away painlessly and peacefully in his sleep tonight. Unlike these two fur-and-feather fanciers, the old cock being eighty-two and the middle-aged hen now a seventeen-stone fifty-five, the twenty-year-old shopkeeper was capable of tender embarrassment. The more poignantly now as she had recently fallen in love with a wages clerk called Singer who spent much of his free time buying cheap two-ounce twists of sweets from her hole-in-the-wall. My father did not like eating sweets, but it was the cheapest, most practical way of paying his shy attentions. He told Mildred the sweets were for the children of his favourite cousin, a Quaker from Allonby called Joel. Yet she had been thrilled to see him on numerous occasions tipping the kaleye sherbet or Uncle Joe's Mintballs down into Maryport dock.

'Can we have him round here for supper?' she rehearsed in her mind as Bellarby ordered her to make him a pot of tea to wash down the blood that was beginning to congeal in his cheeks. Before he resumed, for the third time of telling, his aggrieved dialogue with delightfully three-chinned Agnes.

'Tommy Wandless,' he snarled, and a bolus of sanguinary mucus was heard to dance around his glottis, 'took a first with a Rhode Island cock that was chowed about its bliddy feace. One eye was glimmed over. Its beak was frayed and bliddy split. This was at Egremont Show. I had my perfect little cock there, Robert, washed, combed, not a blemish and…'

'Yes?' croaked Agnes, who never wearied of his lengthy anecdotes as long as they were indignant.

'Robert just got just a Speshul bliddy Menshun.'

'Ah?' said Agnes. 'Scandalous.'

'Scandless,' agreed Willy. It was the bona fide Maryport pronunciation and pleasingly it mimicked the culprit's name and nature. 'I couldn't bliddy stop meself. I was flaming! I walked across, grabbed his neckchief, and faced him face ter bliddy face. You know what I turnt round and said to Wandless?'

'Scandless,' said Agnes.

(He's a genuine sort of man. He's not rough and he doesn't drink. He's very serious about his intentions.)

'Wandless, I said, that bliddy old cock of thine will *never* ride any hen! I tell thee, it's the knackeredest old cock I've ever seen!'

'Aha?' frowned Agnes. 'What did he say to that?'

'He got gey bliddy cottery, and said it could ride any bliddy hen in all of bliddy Cumberlan!'

(He's got saved enough to rent us a decent house up the sea brows. We'd be in among a better-off category from the start.)

'What did you say to him?'

'I said, hearken to me, Tommy Wandless! You're not even old enough to be a decent breeder. I'm eighty-two years old, but you're only a babby of sixty-seven! I been raising perfect cocks since 1852 when I was only a bairn of seven. You weren't even born then, you've only been breedin poultry for forty bliddy years. You're just a stinkin novice, Wandless, and you must have made a bribe till that judge Fidler Porteous cause he's a bliddy Mason like yerself...'

'Scandless,' said Agnes.

A fortnight later Joe Singer put on an expensive tweed jacket purchased at a Cockermouth's country outfitter's. Then with a dry mouth and a feeling of timorous wonder at the breathtaking harbour sunset, he walked to the far end of North Quay. He was about to get his feet, covered in glinting oxblood brogues, under the table of Mildred's aunt. Mildred had decided to prepare most of the celebratory food the previous evening.

After some argument she had Agnes faithfully promise to close the warehouse at seven. The evening before the betrothal supper Willy Bellarby turned up very late bearing a quart bottle of sloe gin manufactured by his 105-year-old mother, Jinnie. Remarkably, despite her great years, Jinnie did all the more complex handyman jobs on Bellarby's farm, those demanding ingenuity rather than brute strength. Throughout September she also rode the lanes towards Flimby on a spavined carthorse, gathering great quantities of sloes in a set of panniers draped across her steed. Should her baby Willy finally succeed in marrying fat Agnes, his surly young wife would have to move up to the woodland farm, Jinnie being the supererogatory blessing, the bounteous dowry for the recalcitrant bride.

While Mildred baked little steak-and-kidney and meat-and-potato pies and scones and teacakes and ginger snaps and shortbread, Agnes sat at the table with Bellarby and gradually drained the quart of gin. En route to the scullery, Mildred caught a whiff of their breaths which smelt like a vat of industrial paraffin. Had she lit a match she would have blown all three of them to Southerness or Auchencairn on the Scots side. The tighter Bellarby got, the wilder his reminiscences. These were mostly of fantastic judicial corruption at Gilsland and Falstone Agricultural Shows fifty years ago, but at one stage he told my mother he'd once possessed a Galloway bull that had *calved*…

'You mean that had a bull calf,' inquired Mildred distractedly.

'No, a bull that had a calf. It was a bliddy freak alright. I had it butchered after it had calved. I was talked into it against my will by me Mam. She thowt we'd been put under a spell by gypsies, who I told to pish off my fields the previous winter. I should have kept it and sold it to the Lancashire fair boys for two hundred guineas.'

After his twelfth glass of gin, his anecdotes became certifiably insane. Listening to his impossible drivel, Mildred had a great urge to squash a steak-and-kidney pie in his earnest but maudlin face. She looked at her heavy-eyed aunt and wanted to pelt her with a fistful of treacle scones. Tomorrow she wished to impress the young pit clerk with Agnes's relative prosperity, to point out the surplus shop antiques that adorned her seedy little house. Instead he would be met by a testy three-chinned gargoyle nursing a monumental day-long hangover. Before that, residual gin fumes would choke him as he stepped through the door. She felt a vast explosive irritation and then an equally vast relief at the thought that her marriage to Joe Singer would mean an end to all of this.

Before passing out, Bellarby haughtily beckoned for her attention. He wanted to tell her the true story of an extraordinary friend of his father's, a signalman called Thompson Gilhespy. It sounded insane this story, but it was gospel truth. Thompson Gilhespy used to keep a colony of performing fleas under his left armpit ('as true as I's sat at this oak bliddy table, Mildred!') as interesting and unique little pets. They lived there in great contentment for many years, because Gilhespy had made them a tiny but very comfortable kennel out of a little wooden box. He secured the minute box under his armpit with insulating tape and only when he was stripped to his vest on warm evenings did the fleas come out of their kennel to take the night air. Of course, Willy Bellarby conceded in a deranged and drunken whisper, everyone knew about things like flea circuses, but without benefit of little trapezes and other miniature circus contraptions, signalman Gilhespy could get his tiny pets to obey any command he wished.

One evening Thompson Gilhespy let them out for a spot of exercise inside his Marron signalbox and became so entranced and distracted by their dance routine that he accidentally let a goods train through. The train ploughed into a gang of terrified line workers and took the leg off one of them, a man near to retirement called Waberthwaite Gillerthwaite. Gilhespy was of course panic-stricken by his wicked and ridiculous negligence, and ran down to give whatever assistance he could. As it happened, a nearby bogie had already been used to ferry

Gillerthwaite towards Brigham station and only Eve, the line gang boss, was there to greet the wretched culprit with his pitiful excuse (*that he had been busy exercising his fleas*). Eve was clutching something bulky and mysterious looking inside a tarpaulin sheet and the preoccupied signalman hadn't a clue what it was.

Eve shouted, 'Oy! Cop this, Thompson.'

He pulled back the tarpaulin and flung Waberthwaite Gillerthwaite's leg in the signalman's face. It glanced the flea-lover on his teeth and Gilhespy emitted a roar of frantic horror.

'But he's still got yan left,' shouted Eve philosophically apropos Waberthwaite's leg. 'I wouldn't take it too bad.'

Eve had the wrong end of the stick. Gilhespy wasn't dismayed by the leg rattling his teeth. He was horrified because, in rushing from the signalbox, he'd left its door wide open. By the time he got back his fleas had sauntered out into the night air only to be devoured on the spot by thousands of skimming swallows. A week later, demented and inconsolable, Gilhespy hanged himself.

At the end of this harrowing and salutary anecdote ('never get too attached to anything, Mildred, just in case you gan and bliddy lose it!') and with a quarter of the quart left in the bottle, Willy Bellarby went unconscious. His sweetheart Agnes glanced at him with a heavy, wistful, witless mien. She looked to her niece for sympathetic derision, then finally fell insensate herself.

'Thank God!' cried Mildred, picking up the gin bottle. Without hesitation she opened up the kitchen window and tipped the half-pint remaining onto the compost heap outside.

*

Willy Bellarby's habit of drinking blood might have had something to do with it. What's more, in addition to her senile suitor's gory vampirism, Agnes lived in a cluttered old shack which was the peculiar epicentre of certain strange and occult episodes. For example Agnes Gill agreed to buy warts from the local children at a penny per pluke, and right enough within a few days they transferred from the childrens' hands to hers. She also claimed to have had premonitory dreams about Cumbrian pit disasters, Gretna train crashes and other local tragedies, though she never explained why she hadn't informed any civil or military authorities about these clairvoyant forebodings. Then there was the incident which involved the killing of six white poultry, and was also timed to coincide with my parents making their betrothal...

It happened in the following manner. When the nervous suitor Joe Singer arrived at the shack at eight o'clock, he carried a small box of Fry's chocolates and a large bottle of Cooperative sherry for Agnes. The stout furniture dealer took them not ungraciously but with an inarticulate comment, as if the stunned recipient of an unintelligible anthropological rite. Bellarby was also there, uninvited and with his two malodorous sheepdogs, hoping that by sympathetic magic his feet would get under the table just like Joe's. He wore an outsize ochre cardigan with pearl buttons, an outrageous garment which his sly mother assured him would act as a visual aphrodisiac. Bellarby had been much touched by Jinnie's expert assistance as she customarily spent her time slandering his beloved. Jinnie maintained that Doctor Lytollis's housekeeper, Cora Minto, had once accidentally glimpsed Agnes stripped in the surgery parlour and had been stunned to observe that the older Gill sister had not two but *three* buttocks. Hence she was not a fit wife for her Willy, but an overweight West Cumbrian witch with one and a half backsides. This had had quite the opposite effect to what Jinnie had intended, as instantly Willy experienced a fifty percent increase in thwarted concupiscence. Both fur-and-feather fanciers looked exhausted tonight and my father, who had heard about the mammoth gin session, was tactfully sympathetic.

Expecting to be interrogated about his job and his family, Joe was not asked anything. Instead Willy Bellarby commended his father Sol Singer for the sheer lunacy of his tricks. He presumed that Joe had inherited the same devilment. Joe blushed and said he did not usually bother with that sort of thing. Mildred bridled protectively and snapped that there was nothing admirable about grown men getting up to childish and often very dangerous nonsense.

'Sol always was a bliddy warlick,' said Bellarby defiantly. 'If there weren't any warlicks about, Maryport would be a sad bliddy shithoose.'

To conceal his embarrassment my father moved over to the window and looked out at the back garden. He surveyed the neat rows of cabbages, potatoes and beans and a bizarrely lopsided garden bench constructed by Willy Bellarby. He was about to venture a flattering remark to Aunty Agnes when his eyes took in something truly astonishing.

'What is it?' asked Mildred, as she noticed his bewildered expression.

'It's queer,' he said quietly, rubbing his eyes like someone in a pantomime. 'But I've never seen anything like this.'

'A back garden?' she said sharply. 'Don't you have one, Joe?'

My father stared at Bellarby's hideous cardigan as if that might be a cryptic clue. He observed the pearl buttons and noted the correspondence. The colour was different, the size a lot smaller, but the incongruity and the absurdity were the same.

Mildred walked over and followed Joe's gaze. Mildred lifted her slim fingers to her open mouth and exclaimed. At first she tittered and then turned frightened to her aunt who was tucking in athletically at the supper table.

'Why are your hens wearing *baby jackets*?' she asked.

The six white Wyandottes were all dressed in tiny white cardigans with tiny pearl buttons. They looked like immaculately uniformed infants from a pampered orphanage or workhouse. My mother and father stared at the fairground spectacle and squeezed each other's hands in wonder. Darting and clucking in among the shrubs and bushes, the birds seemed quite unselfconscious about their majestic appearance. In that respect they were rather like Willy Bellarby, who clattered his way through life regardless and assumed his diarrhoea-yellow cardigan was the height of provincial style.

'Why d'you think?' said Agnes brusquely.

'I've no idea!'

'To keep 'em warm!' snapped the antiques dealer. 'Otherwise they'd bloody freeze.'

It was the middle of summer and a very warm evening. Mildred pointed this out before Willy chipped in to save her from Agnes's indignation. The hens had been plucked, he explained matter of fact, which was why they needed cardigans.

'Plucked?' my mother gasped. 'You plucked *live* hens? But…'

Agnes furrowed her brow savagely, at even a hint of an imputation of cruelty. She doted on her Wyandottes, she roared at Mildred, and would obviously not have plucked them had she believed them to be alive…

Her niece sat flummoxed and did not touch the beautiful supper spread. Willy put two meat pies entire into his jaws as he tried to clarify matters. His speech became unintelligible so he bolted both pieces unmasticated. They stuck in his gullet and he began to turn purple and then black. Helpful Joe battered him violently on the back and after about a minute he was a healthy shade of bucolic pink. Agnes viewed the primitive woodlander scornfully, then said to Mildred: 'It was your fault! You're the one to blame for having them plucked.'

My mother flushed and she pushed away my father's protective hand. 'I've never touched your hens. I sw–'

'It's all your fault!' Agnes repeated with harshly stabbing finger. 'I know what you bloody well did.'

At nine o'clock that morning, two hours after Mildred had begun at the shop, Agnes had walked down from the warehouse to feed her Wyandottes. Each one of her darlings had a name, each one was individually recognisable. She took the scraps and mash out from the kitchen, opened the back door, and shouted for her lovely little ones. What she saw made her cry stick in her throat, her blood turn to ice. Instead of zestfully scurrying towards her, the hens lay strewn all over the garden. Heartrendingly stiff and pitiful, they were scattered in a way that suggested an attack by a fox or a stoat.

'Was there no blood?' prompted Mildred dazed. 'Wasn't there blood and feathers everywhere?'

Not a drop. Not a single feather. There was the mystery. A fox would have mauled and worried them and taken off at least one to eat. Yet all six hens were without a mark and were splatted all over the garden like swatted insects. Evidently it was a perverse kind of fox, one who liked to destroy for its own sake. Aunty Agnes knelt down on the earth in her grief and anger and began to wail a terrible jeremiad. She cursed the fox for its cruelty and swore filthy oaths of revenge. Foxes had no rightful business to stray down here to the dockside, even if they could sniff out hens in a ten-mile radius. Over the years she had lost dozens at her Ewanrigg allotments which were just down the lane from Bellarby's plantations. Bellarby just had to look out of his back window to see entire fox families running in and out of his woods.

Like a sly fox himself, having failed to sniff her out at the warehouse, Willy tracked her down to her house. She did not answer the door so he flung it open and strode inside. He discovered her in the kitchen, red-eyed and banshee wailing. As well as touching her lowest quivering chin, he ventured to brush a tender kiss across her hair. He told this boastfully to Mildred who was astonished. Aunty Agnes had struck him across the jaw for his presumption, he conceded dolefully. Bellarby then rubbed his chin and followed her penitently into the garden. He examined the inert Wyandottes, rolled them with his boot, and pronounced them dead. The most likely explanation was a fox, he said, as if he were a forensic genius. As for the lack of blood and feathers, perhaps it had been disturbed before it could get its teeth into them. Alternatively a great trauma, an enormous nervous shock of some sort, might have caused simultaneous cardiac seizure. Such things were rare but not unknown. A very loud bang, for example, from a nearby quarry. There was no nearby quarry, Mildred pointed out impatiently. No, agreed Willy, but that was the general principle. It might have been some young kid outside with a cap gun or a jumping jack.

Supposition and meta-supposition. Bellarby had turned to Agnes and pointed out that as the hens were dead they should be passed on to a butcher right away. Billy Greggains, who specialised in mutton rustled off the fells, would only take them if they were still warm. Leave them any longer, especially in this heat, and they would be no good to anybody. Fifteen bob was fifteen bob after all. Agnes pondered his calm pragmatic advice, burst out into racking sobs, and said very well but he would have to do the plucking. She could not do that mutilation to any of her little white darlings. Willy lordly ordered her back into the kitchen to make him a pot of tea for when he was finished. Meanwhile he demanded a quart of light ale to assist him with the job itself. He sat down on the ugly garden bench he had made for Agnes and without drawing breath had all six featherless within twenty minutes.

They sat sipping tea. Agnes Gill kept her swollen eyes averted from the little bald corpses and that mountain of sad white feathers. It occurred to Willy that this was a fit opportunity amidst all the grief and vulnerability to make his seventy-ninth proposal. He opened his mouth to begin, then suddenly dropped his scalding cup and leapt up from the bench in terror.

'What in hell!' he shouted at her. 'What in hell have you put in this tea?'

Agnes turned her desolate gaze and experienced the same frightening hallucination...

Winnie, the fattest of the six hens, had just begun to twitch very rapidly. A repetitive radial convulsion had begun to spread through her plump little naked body. Agnes sobbed at what she thought was rigor mortis. Then, aghast, she realised that the dead hen was actually trying to struggle to its feet. Its jerky ghostly movements were like those of a human being who has just arisen from deep hypnosis or a tragic coma.

'It's a bliddy miracle,' Aunty Agnes squawked in remarkably henlike tones. 'My laal Winnie has gone and come back to life!'

Tottering onto her feet, Winnie clucked poignantly at her extraordinary plight. She was nude, bald, ridiculous, and of course much perplexed by her incredible metamorphosis. She was also shivering.

'Oh Winnie…' said Agnes with such tenderness that Bellarby felt an enormous jealousy of the featherless hen.

Agnes's joy turned into her first ever experience of transcendent ecstasy as Winnie's sister Ginnie, who had a recognisably misaligned beak, also flapped to her feet. Willy Bellarby stared suspiciously at Agnes Gill and at those two bald hens that had died and miraculously returned to life. Suddenly he felt ill and decided he preferred hearing about impossible stories to actually witnessing them. As a token Wesleyan Methodist who worshipped twice a decade at Flimby, he really couldn't cope with the abnormal, the occult, the bizarre.

Next Minnie, whose comb was the reddest of the six, rose from the grave. Then Queenie, who had the rapidest clucks. Then Teenie, who craned her neck more emphatically than the rest. Lastly Dinah, who had nothing distinctive and was therefore most distinctive. The six naked Wyandottes stood stiffly and gravely after their brush with the infinite. They joined chorus in that complex fugal mode typical of six small hens. It was piercing and elegiac, that clucking. Willy found it terrifying and decided he wanted to go down to The Lifeboat and steady his nerves with some brandy.

Agnes, suddenly vigilant, told him to stay where he was. She had a strange inkling, monstrous as it seemed. She waddled over to the Wyandottes, squatted down on her varicose knees, and put her nose close to each. At once her skirt backside billowed up like an enormous workhouse blanket and Bellarby felt passing gigantic lust. Agnes turned her face suspiciously and spat at no one in particular: 'These hens all stink of bliddy drink!'

Bellarby glanced anxiously at the bolted back gate. He didn't argue because he was confident she was insane.

'Guess what kind of drink?' she interrogated him savagely.

'Eh?' he said, terrified by her mounting rage. 'How the buggeration would I know?'

'Who, I wonder, gave them *sloe gin* for breakfast?'

'Eh?' said Willy, and advised her to move out of the scorching sun.

'Was it you?' she roared. 'Or was it your ugly old mam thought it would be a bloody good trick to play on old Agnes?'

Bellarby trembled as she accused him of poisoning her Wyandottes with gin. He swore with shaking hands that he would never dare fool with her possessions, especially not her poultry. After all, he was a fur-and-feather fancier himself. He loved hens just as much as she did. In any case, pointing to a trail of turnip and potato skins that were strewn about the garden, she should take a sniff at those leavings before she started pinning the blame on him. Agnes frowned and reluctantly consented to pick up the bits of rotting compost which had followed the approximate progress of the drunken hens.

The rotting vegetable skins reeked of scented alcohol. She walked across to the little heap outside the kitchen window and sniffed. The stench of gin was overwhelming.

'You!' she threw at blushing Mildred. 'I didn't empty that bottle last night. Willy swears he didn't finish it! We both nodded off at this table but the bottle wasn't finished. Someone called Mildred must have gone and tipped the dregs in the compost...'

'I...' said my mother.

'The only other person here was you!'

My mother burned with shame but my father was wonder-

122

fully thrilled not to say thoroughly vindicated. For once he felt redeemed and exculpated from his hideous ancestry. It was such a relief to learn that his fiancée's family was even more embarrassing than his. Every day it seemed to Joe Singer there were fresh scandalous revelations of the hereditary Singer deviancy. Just yesterday outside the pit offices he had discovered yet another shameful family secret. An old man of ninety walking his dogs through the pit had told him the unsavoury facts next to the colliery wash-room. Joe listened in horror as he was informed why his grandfather Kelso Singer had been sacked from Risehow pit forty years ago. It was for leading two pit ponies up in the cage before selling them for five guineas to Irish gypsies. Kelso had been sentenced to three years with hard labour in Durham jail, whereas Joe's father Sol, himself no stranger to shame, coyly maintained he spent that time working as a Durham collier.

Agnes Gill nagged on unforgivingly: 'I wasted three balls of wool on them. The poor laal hens were shivering to death without their plumage. What use will them bliddy cardigans be once their feathers start to grow?'

Through a colossal mouthful of moist shortbread Bellarby advised donating them to the Cockermouth orphanage. Agnes fumed and told him to shut his trap. She said the real issue was that she had nearly died of grief, and all because of her officious niece. Not to speak of the reckless quantity of precious gin that had been wasted on her little Wyandottes. It had been Jinnie Bellarby's very last bottle and there'd be no more sloes on the hedges for another year.

My mother eventually got out, 'But it's your fault really.'

Agnes scoffed as she snapped a treacle scone in two. 'Don't talk bliddy rubbish. How can it be?'

My mother rose from the resplendent table to take this second momentous leave of this her second family.

'It's your fault for getting blind drunk in the first place! I tipped away your gin because I was bringing my... my fiancé... round, and I didn't want you getting drunk again. Joe

Singer has got himself a tidy office job. He's a proper white-collar man. He wears only handmade suits.'

'Just like mesel when I togs up,' said Bellarby coolly. 'What's more I've got over two hundred pairs of shoes in me outside shed.'

'We're going to marry in three months time! I had to stop you two frightening him away with your crazy bloody nonsense. Your insane damn stories about armpit fleas and amputated legs. And your constant swearing and your homemade booze! I had to stop you two ruining our two's chances.'

'Not at all,' said Joe Singer blushing. He turned meekly and politely to his new aunt. 'Not at all, Mrs Gill.'

'Miss,' snarled Agnes. 'Miss Gill and always will be.'

'Not at all, Mr Bellarby.'

Willy said uncritically, 'His own Dad Sol never minded what he ruined.'

My mother sat down again and assumed a quieter, more considered tone. She addressed her skinny young fiancé as much as her overweight aunt.

'Joe here's the very opposite of his Dad. Just like I'm the very opposite of my mother. I've explained that's why I'm marrying him. I've made no bones about it, I'm giving him no illusions. I decided a long time ago I was looking for the opposite in life. It's the only way to break out of the mould. It's the only way to stop things getting worse.'

8

I made my way down to TFEOTNQ as instructed. It was only a half-mile walk but I felt as if I had crossed the border into a foreign land. It sounds bizarre, given that the town is very small and my mother spent five years of her life here, but it was an area that I rarely ever visited. Indeed in the most banal and literal sense, North Quay didn't even enter my field of vision. My kiosk faced in the opposite direction towards Shipping Brow, and my house had only a limited view of the docks and the adjacent streets. Recently renovated and handsomely repaved, for decades the Quay had been one of the most forlorn and shambling parts of town. So strenuously had I avoided its embarrassing associations that now, close up, I could barely make sense of its pristine transformation. Like some long-forgotten inner landscape, that former slum aspect persisted as its enduring and uncomfortable reality. I was caught helplessly in the past and felt considerable disorientation and regretted that I'd embarked on this bizarre expedition after all.

I stood like a conspicuous private detective, for a good half hour examining the pebble-dash and double-glazed transmogri-fication of Agnes Gill's crumbling old terrace. A thin young woman with very short hair was dusting a video machine in the downstairs parlour. I wondered if I had the gall to knock and ask her if I might poke around my mother's bedroom of seventy years ago. I hadn't the nerve of course, and in any case I felt that the next stage of the family puzzle might well lie else-where. Instead I walked another twenty yards to reacquaint myself with what had been Agnes's warehouse. There was no problem entering that. The front doors had been removed at least thirty years ago and it was now just an enormous open-fronted shed which a haulage firm used for stacking all its pallets.

If I chose I could walk in and out of Agnes's premises and await some sort of atmospheric nuance, some prescient message from the past. Great-Aunt Agnes had died before I was born, a year after amazing everyone and marrying Willy Bellarby. The likeliest explanation for the melting of her stony heart was that Willy's interfering mother had died, at the mystical age of 111, after falling off her horse reaching up for sloes. Agnes the bride was then sixty and so obese that when she entered the door of Ewanrigg church she blocked all the light and the congregation was thrown into semi-darkness. My well-mannered father had taken a helpless laughing fit in the rear pew and my mother had threatened to brain him if he didn't shush. I had seen the incredible photographs of Agnes and Willy's wedding, the bride looking like a smileless thirty-stone Galloway and the groom like its very old herdsman. Closing my eyes next to the stacked pallets, I tried to picture the prenuptial couple as they sat in this place slurping warm cow's blood, guzzling sloe gin and joyously calumniating all fellow poultry fanciers...

To no avail. Trying to bring the past back to life like this was hopeless. I left the warehouse and stepped back down to Agnes's terrace. From there I looked at the acres of silt lying down in the harbour and then across to the roof of the distant aquarium. I wondered what the John Dory was doing now the place was closed, and entertained what seemed a lunatic thought. Was it somehow aware that I was down here at TFEOTNQ, early evening, just as instructed? Berating myself for such pathetic stupidity, I decided that after another five minutes I would turn on my heel and go home. If there was anything to learn and anything to encounter, it would have to find me rather than me find it.

The truth was I had been half-expecting to meet my mother's

ghost. I could picture her easily enough stepping out from one of those pallets and accosting me with a beckoning hand. Whereupon, as well as fainting with shock, I would catch the relentless strains of her virulent criticism about the unparallelled gold mine my kiosk had failed to become. To talk of feeling trepidation would be highly inaccurate. Lingering there those last five minutes, I experienced a panoramic range of guilt, discomfort, queasiness and irritation. I was having a mid-life crisis like the wrasse, but instead of changing sex and being done with it, I was left to flounder (definitely no pun intended) in a no-man's-land. Let me sum myself up in an unflattering nutshell. I had a successful, moderately profitable little business while most people round here were struggling. I made an adequate income but was bored out of my head by my daily routine. I had a couple of close women friends, both divorced like me, both of whom had a second man in their lives. One, Mary Beswick, forty-eight, volatile and thin, owned a Victorian hotel in Silloth. The two of us took regular holidays on the Hebridean island of Coll as Mary was a keen birdwatcher and would spend entire days looking for corncrakes. The other, Angela Dacre, fifty-two, tranquil and attractively hefty, ran an art-deco coffee shop in Keswick. With Angela, who had a classics degree from Cambridge, I was working my way through the least visited Greek islands and next month we were planning to explore Kimolos and Sikinos.

These relationships were intimate, physically as well as temperamentally, but by mutual consent free from most binding attachments. The three of us kept our two lovers as insurance policies against the enormous hazards of promising our all to just one. We made the best of this profligate but partial love life, and frequently and complacently assured ourselves we had it cracked, this tiresome business of algebra and eros. Deep down we didn't fool ourselves for a moment. Post-coital sadness was the least of it. Three or four times a week I visited my daughter who lived in a Victorian shipowner's mansion up on the sea brows. I observed the happiness of Anne's marriage, and delighted as I was for her and her family I was saddened. Anne Singer, given her upbringing, had confounded all the odds. The child had succeeded where the parents had failed. All through her own resources and more by good luck than good parenting.

Just as I was about to head off home, a brand-new estate car pulled up next to me. An old man in his late seventies with an alert but unassuming expression was seated at the wheel. He glanced first at Agnes's house, then at me, then back to Agnes's terrace. Apart from a full head of unusually bright silver hair, he had a surpassingly ordinary look about him. Because it was warm the window was wound down, and he raised his old hand and murmured a friendly greeting. I knew most faces in this town but had never seen this one. I assumed he must be visiting the skinny woman with the very short hair and was either her father or her favourite uncle.

'Warm enough for you?' he asked me in a musical Lancashire accent.

He could have been talking about himself as much as the evening air. Old Lancastrian males, I reflected, always seem to have the sunniest of temperaments. I nodded at him, fanned myself exaggeratedly, and returned his generous smile. I noted his shiny navy-blue blazer and light-grey, perfectly creased trousers. The tie was an ill-matched speckled tweed. His spectacles had those thick no-nonsense rims shaped like two old television screens. His hair gave out a whiff of scented gel and a couple of harbour flies were dancing around his parting. He would have impressed my mother and she would have called him a big, smart, fine, well-built, smart-looking, elderly, very smart old chap. She might well have worked another 'smart' into the panegyric, because nothing impressed her so much as seeing ordinary people decently dressed. It contrasted very pleasingly with the way many of them had been obliged to dress fifty years ago. During the Depression, from her privileged position in the shop, Ma Singer had been forced to witness some atrocious West Cumbrian poverty.

This man looked as if he might just have seen something similar in Blackburn or Bolton or Ramsbottom when he was a child. Otherwise he had an air of unrufflable serenity and his gleaming estate car suggested anything but hardship. He looked as if he might be the sprightliest volunteer in a Help the Aged shop or a leading functionary in the Oswaldtwistle Masonic Lodge. There is something about old men and blue blazers that suggests a hopeless addiction to committees, authority and institutionalised tedium. I would have bet a fiver his Christian name was either Reg or Bert.

He got out of the car, stretched himself and waggled his tie as an ineffective fan. It was only then that I made the next connection. What I'd assumed to be an unusual pattern on his tie was in fact a tiny silver badge. The badge began to glint and pulse hypnotically in the evening sun. I looked at him and then at it and could scarcely believe my eyes…

I began to quiver and ask myself indignantly what the hell was happening. Instead of saying 'Help the Aged' or 'Blackburn British Legion Saxhorn Band', his badge had the shape of – I looked at it four or five times between rapid and incredulous blinks – a beautiful little engraved *fish*…

I gulped. I sweated at the temples and felt as if I might be about to totter on my heels. The old man continued to smile, quite oblivious of my discomfort. In my experience you have to be ten shades of grey and swaying like a felled ox before anyone notices the monstrous inner tumult preceding a public faint. I wiped my brow with the back of my hand and smiled at the badge man queasily. I gave my head a slight shake.

Then a flash of commonsense returned and I realised the obvious.

'The aquarium,' I said, pointing at the ornately moulded badge.

'I'm sorry?'

'You must be a regular visitor?' I said with overdone heartiness. 'Or possibly you're a life member?'

Obviously, I thought, they must have started selling attractive promotional badges like this one in the gift shop. It was odd, admittedly, that there was no identifying motif on the fish design but it could hardly be anything else.

'Sorry?' he repeated, looking a trifle concerned.

I pointed across the harbour at the aquarium roof and the orange and turquoise lettering on the facade.

'The aquarium,' I repeated. 'I was admiring your little…'

'Is it really?' he said genuinely surprised. 'I live twenty miles off and I hardly know the town itself. To be honest I always thought it was some sort of factory or a gymnasium. It shows just how much notice I take of such things.'

I looked at him carefully to see if he was pulling my leg. Even someone wearing double bifocals and tapping a white cane would have had a job to mistake it for a factory. Concealing my growing anxiety I persisted: 'Then you must be an angler.'

He looked as baffled as if I'd accused him of being a clown or a conjuror. I pointed at his badge and I grinned a glassy grin. Feigning a ponderous struggle, the old man carefully followed my finger and then chuckled with relief.

'Oh I see. You think I must be a fisherman. No, no chance. I've never been an angler. I just haven't the necessary patience.'

I began to feel more and more uneasy as several cars drew up and parked downwind of Agnes's house. I counted four in all, all in a straight line behind the badge man's. The occupants waved at this bluff Lancastrian in a way that suggested he was a blazered official in charge of them in some important capacity. They also smiled appreciatively at me as if I were some important but mysterious friend of his. I smiled back weakly and noted that apart from a very red-faced man of about forty all of them were older than the badge man.

'A senior citizens' shindig,' I thought worriedly. 'And they are all dressed to the nines. What the hell are they doing at the far end of the Quay? If it turns out they all have fish badges I'll…'

The old folks got out of their cars noisily, awkwardly, volubly. One after another they hailed the blazered official who was not called Reg or Bert, but Ken. Two brittle, kind-faced ladies, well into their eighties and wearing old-fashioned woven hats, smiled at me and inquired if the warm weather suited. A really old woman, a fragile nonagenarian with a deaf aid, stumbled out last of all. Examining me she feigned a dry parody of the agony of old age. To my amazement she clapped me on the shoulder in mock envy of my youth and cheerfully told me she was 'really owld and breakin up'. Her male companion, a moustachioed young stick of about eighty-five, took her other arm impatiently and pulled her over towards Ken.

With the exception of the very red-faced man, I couldn't place any of them. They could only be from the surrounding villages, I decided. Obscure and unrecognisable stay-at-homes who only surface at unusual times in unusual areas, for some reason they had chosen to crawl out of the woodwork this evening. I vaguely recalled selling a quarter of barley sugars to the red-faced chap, and tonight a prepacked quarter of the same sweet was poking out of his suit jacket. They were not a brand I stocked and I felt faintly let down by the fact he had purchased them somewhere else. He nodded pleasantly but evidently didn't recognise me as the local kiosk vendor. Instead he praised the change in the weather and explained how his farm eight miles off at the far end of the hamlet of Tarns near Silloth had been waterlogged for the past week. It was a remote boggy hopeless sort of 'bit', he added disdainfully.

Then he made a most enigmatic statement. It – meaning the whole sodden hamlet of Tarns, not just his farm – should be *closed down* by the government...

'Closed down?' I repeated baffled.

'Shut down,' he said firmly. 'The whole area condemned. Then let somebody turn it into a theme park, so's I can sell up and retire. I'd give up farming tomorrow if I could find an easy way out.'

He was joking but it took some time to realise as much. While I was smiling brainlessly, the badge man seized my arm and said: 'Come on, lad. No time to waste is there? Every moment's precious on a night like this.'

I had no idea what he meant, yet I had no wish for elucidation. The old man's grip was jovial and comradely but I felt as if I'd been put under arrest. His badge was glistening fiercely in the sun and the silver fish emitted an intense pinpoint radiance. I quivered and looked from the little fish to Ken's glinting spectacles. Recollecting what had lured me here in the first place, a ventriloquial fish with a mysterious thumbprint, I instantly decided to make myself scarce.

'I'm on my way home,' I said firmly, attempting to walk in the opposite direction.

'Too right you are, my lad. We're all of us going home in this group. Best foot forward. No time to waste on an important night like tonight.'

He was obviously wishing to frogmarch me somewhere significant. Pointing irritably to the harbour bridge, I said, 'But my house is over that way.'

The old man answered with an irrelevant and hackneyed formula: 'It's always such a pleasure to see a new face.'

He sounded as if he meant every syllable of his ludicrous cliché.

'I really don't…'

'There aren't very many of us. Yet we are, remarkably, on the increase. They keep on coming every so often, and little by little.'

'I'm going home,' I said swiftly. 'I have to go right away.'

His smile was gentle but the grip on my arm remained resolute.

'What's your name?'

'What,' I said reluctantly, as if giving him something so definite could only make things worse. 'Oh it's George.'

I turned and looked at the rest of them all waiting expectantly for Ken. Immediately I experienced a self-evident revelation.

My heart sank and I began to kick myself for chatting to this bumptious old gent with the attractive smile. Seeing all those out-of-date hats, all that stiff and handicapped old age, at last it all became clear. I knew now who they were, what they were, what they could only be. I went on rapidly, almost rudely: 'You must have mistaken me for someone else. I'm not a new face, whatever that's supposed to mean. I've just been out for a walk. And now I'm setting off home.'

'My Dad's name was George,' he replied a little plaintively. 'His Dad was called George and my great-grandfather was called George, and my eldest brother continued the tradition. My Dad was a good man in many ways but he made a blatant favourite out of his first born. Every Sunday dinner he'd give him the lean bits from his ham shank and give the gristly fatty bits to me. If I broke next door's window with a football I'd get his belt and have to go round and apologise and say I'd been belted. If George broke it he'd give him the ten bob to give to the neighbour to give to the glazier. The neighbour would drink the ten bob and cover the window with cardboard and invite George to break the other one. George never got belted for anything. He once boasted to me that he could murder me any time he liked if he wanted and Dad would let him away with it. That kind of thing can leave a scar when you're a child. But later on,' he ended on a baleful but confident note, 'when you're an adult, the more scars you have the better.'

I stared at Ken and his preposterous uncalled-for logic. My expression was sceptical if not scornful. Instead of turning apologetic, he added: 'That might seem a strange attitude. But it's the only point of view that matters.'

As brusquely as I could, I extricated myself from his insinu-ating grip. But as I grunted a surly goodbye something quite extraordinary happened. Without warning the gaggle of old folk seemed as one man to bear down upon me and surround me. I blinked astounded as, murmuring sonorously like so many frail and innocent old sheep, they gently propelled me in the direction of Agnes's house.

'It's so nice,' whispered one of the brittle old ladies with the woven hats, 'to see a new face like yours. And such a young one too.'

Compared with her, I was just a child. At fifty-six I was a mere adolescent, just as the ruddy sardonic farmer from Tarns was a babe-in-arms. Nevertheless I made an indignant protest as I was helplessly borne along to the rear of Aunty Agnes's house. Beyond that there was the pallet warehouse and beyond the warehouse only an old brick building, which I vaguely recalled was something to do with marine activity long defunct. It had possibly been a one-time storehouse for the lifeboat service, a hut for keeping distress flares and rescue tackle. All of which had ceased by the Thirties, and now, as far as I knew, it was the lock-up shed of some local fishermen. Or no, perhaps I was thinking of a similar building on the far side of Senhouse Dock? The whole of this area was littered with anomalous brick edifices, some of them put to good use, many of them decrepit and abandoned. This one had fading yellow brickwork but the rear door and windows were freshly painted. The front door faced towards the North Pier and it was so long since I had walked this way I had no idea what was written above it. At a guess it might read 'Property of Local Inshore Fishermen Association. Strictly Private.'

The circle of old folks bustled me round to the front of the building. We stood there a little breathless as Ken brought up the rear. I turned to see that he was carrying an old-fashioned briefcase which he must have got out of the boot of his car. The sight of that shiny black briefcase reminded me of something. I looked at the frontage of this ancient brick barn which was approximately the size of my own kiosk. A date inscribed above the door said 1826. The two small windows revealed not stacked fishing nets, nor tins of paint and varnish for boats, but what looked like antiquated school seating. I peered more closely and saw they were the kind they had in those old dame schools described in Thomas Hardy novels. There were two parallel rows of varnished benches split by a central aisle plus a couple of odd benches going at right angles to the aisle. Long ago thirty children might have squeezed in here at a push. There was a piano where perhaps in 1826 there had been more benches. In the middle there was a raised-up lectern bearing an all too familiar and universal emblem.

'Oh my God,' I said despairingly.

A notice above the door said 'North Quay Mission Hall'.

I had last been down at TFEOTNQ over twenty years ago. I could have sworn on oath there wasn't any Mission Hall in those days. Much less was there any anachronistic relic of an infant school. Even in a town as modest and deprived as this one, no infant school had ever been as primitive. On the other hand, I reflected, little harbour towns are notorious for the variety and profusion of backstreet chapels and eccentric churches. So small and invisible are some of their congregations, so rarely is one stood there of a Sunday evening when the handful is entering or leaving, it is a matter of doubt whether they still function as chapels or are destined for slum clearance or desirable penthouse-flat conversion. I turned to the farmer who seemed closest to my own wavelength as well as age, and began to explain that I was neither a church- nor a chapel-goer and never had been.

'Ah?' he said politely, as if it made no difference one way or the other.

Disgusted by her mother's improvident Methodism, Mildred Singer had been delighted when I showed no inclination for Sunday School. Not even the charabanc trips to Annan or Kendal or Hexham, complete with strawberry teas in their respective town halls, had lured me to perfunctory attendance. However in 1950 my shameless mother had bullied me through formal Confirmation at the C of E, convinced that if I didn't have it my career prospects would be seriously blighted. But that was all fine old-fashioned hypocritical expedience, it had nothing to do with credulous faith and gullible provincial piety. To put it simply, I was not just another old lady in a woven hat. I was a middle-aged rationalist who had accommodated to his middle-aged failure. Unlike a fish I could not change sex and have another go at life. Instead of seeking solace in religion I found it in wine and women and to a lesser extent books, music and films. My difference from these folks outside the North Quay Mission stood out a mile. They all looked very simple, very unsophisticated souls, whereas I, I imagined, was a great deal more complicated. Nevertheless as Ken in his pristine blazer flapped his way towards me, there was a look in his confident eyes that seemed to say the opposite. He glanced at me and my furtive wish to rush off up Shipping Brow as fast as my legs could take me. There was nothing very complex, much less honourable, he seemed to be thinking, about *that*...

Before I knew it I was stuck there inside the chapel and wedged next to the beefy Tarns man. I had tried as hard as I could to break out of the comical circle of old folk, but Ken's heedless flock had kept on bustling me in a forward direction. To talk about being hypnotised might sound fancifully melo-dramatic but there is no other explanation for the helplessness I felt in the presence of people themselves the epitome of help-lessness. The only hale one in the place, the young farmer, shook my hand and whispered that his name was Robert Briers. Walking behind me he pushed me gently to where the bench was flush with the wall. To escape just now as Ken was opening his briefcase at the lectern meant either stepping over Briers or vaulting backwards over the pew. Feeling uncomfortable, not to say guiltily dismayed, I looked around me at the strangeness and novelty of such a humble place of worship. Of course I had been inside ordinary churches as much as anyone else. I had visited mighty and beautiful cathedrals, convents and monas-teries both here and abroad. I had been obliged to attend the local town church for my Confirmation and for my daughter's wedding thirty years later. But I had never set foot inside a tiny spartan Nonconformist barn like this.

It was of the same dimensions as one of those minuscule chapels dotted all over the Greek islands, and particularly conspicuous up on remote mountainsides. Those Greek iklesias are a touching upturned-boat shape, almost like a naive child's version of a church, and are painted dazzlingly, drunkenly white. They possess a pure and numinous Hellenic simplicity which was rather different from the relative darkness and austerity of this place. Yet oddly there was something just as affecting about the lack of ornament here. There was not a mite, not a jot of ostentation. There was virtually no ecclesiastical adornment. Apart from the bricks and the benches there was a green velvet cloth on the pulpit with a vase of carnations set on the table in front. The pulpit cloth had a simple cross woven into it and that sampler seemed as if it had been sitting there changelessly emphatic since the place was built. The bare rough plaster also seemed unaltered since 1826 and was painted a mellow autumnal brown. What struck me as imponderably significant was that this place was like a manger. It was just like the manger we all know about and have known about since we were as tiny as this chapel. As I sat there anxiously next to ruddy Robert Briers I thought of the bauble dancing on the Christmas tree, of the beautiful Woolworth's angel of 1942, and I felt I knew where I had come to. The realisation made me deeply uneasy.

The five oldest worshippers had totteringly filled up the half-dozen benches to my left. As the clock wound its way to seven o'clock a few more people arrived. Prominent was a stiff young man sporting a rough beard and wearing a dark green suit. His jerky robotic tenseness made me think he was going through a protracted crisis, perhaps a divorce or a bereavement. I had never seen him in the town and Robert Briers told me that he had driven over thirty miles from beyond Carlisle to get here. I gave a low whistle and was sincerely baffled that anyone should drive all that way to come to a tiny manger at the far end of the North Quay. Finally there was a couple about my own age with plodding countrified Derbyshire accents and short-sleeved shirts. They both had lined but friendly faces and nodded at me very warmly. The stumpy husband joked with Robert and asked him if his farm had been condemned and knocked down yet. Briers whispered that Joe was manager of a farm shop near Keswick and that his wife Edna had had a brain tumour that had been successfully operated on…

'Oh,' I said, feeling chastened.

Ken took off his blazer and stepped up to the lectern.

'Tonight,' he said, 'I want to ask you all something.'

'Here goes,' I thought to myself. 'Here goes, here goes, here goes.'

'I want to ask you, what do you think you are worth?'

9

As soon as he'd posed his question, with an imperious sense of timing Ken stopped and said we were going to sing a hymn. After we'd sung that, he promised, he would continue his provocative line of interrogation. I opened my little red book entitled *Redemption Choruses* and sheepishly inspected Number 7. Robert Briers sang along vigorously as if to prove he really was a red-faced son of the soil, despite his wish to sell up and abandon his unprofitable farm. His voice was surprisingly melodic, childlike and tender, and I listened dismayed to my own abrasive croaking. I sounded like a hundred-Woodbines-a-day man, whereas all it was was nerves and stiffness and irreligiosity. I felt a damn fool singing a redemption hymn, to put it mildly. I felt woefully embarrassed by all this naive adoration and obeisance issuing from old people in hats and open-necked shirts. I was supposedly addressing an all-powerful, infinitely loving Lord, telling him he was everything that mattered, and in all heartfelt veneration that I adored him. No wonder my voice was in my boots.

I thought of my two girlfriends chuckling uproariously when they heard of old George being corralled into a tin mish chapel in among the hats and hymn books down by Maryport docks. Skinny, sardonic Mary Beswick who had been educated by nuns and couldn't mention the Catholic Church without appending the adjective 'fucking' and foaming at the mouth. As for the breathy articulate scepticism of hefty, bosomy Angela whose father had been an Anglican vicar with a private income: her polysyllabic antagonism would be just as damning. In fact I wouldn't dare tell them I'd been in a place like this, not unless I lied and said it was for purposes of quixotic research or as an inspired joke. If they had caught sight of me entering a wretched edifice like this they would have thought I was pushing my menopause beyond all sensible bounds. If I were fool enough to tell the whole truth and mention the John Dory and its connection with Preacher Ken and his badge, I would be out on my ear with both of these guarded, intelligent and uncompromising women.

Suddenly it struck me that Ken had no dog collar, no surplice, no clerical apparel whatever. He looked just like a brilliantined golf-club steward of pensionable age who'd impulsively decided to step out of his mundane role and talk about God. Given that Ken lived twenty miles away, obviously this tiny dusty place had no stipendiary preacher. From an unsympathetic point of view it lent the place a dubious, provisional, unsanctioned aspect. So this, I reflected, was what my grandmother's embarrassing Methodism was all about. This was what Mary Cannon, my mother's loony mother, was all in favour of. It was all about cloaking yourself in an austere lack of show. It was all about taking the message to heart and acting on it. You chuck away the surplice and the incense, you roll up your sleeves, and you get stuck in…

Ken did that literally. When the hymn was finished he took off his tie, draped it carefully across an empty bench, and rolled up the sleeves of his Double Two shirt. He was about to get stuck in good and proper. Before he did, Robert Briers handed me a small printed card which gave the North Quay Preachers' Rota for the next three months. I squinted in the weak light and saw there were twelve of these laymen (there wasn't a single woman among them). The bracketed details indicated they came from various Methodist, Evangelical and Free Church of Scotland churches the county wide. Ken, I saw, was down as a Mr K. Wright, visiting speaker from Gosforth Hebron Hall.

'Oh,' I thought, as I looked at his heavy, sober glasses and that outstandingly ordinary, anonymous face of his. 'Wright by name but wrong by...'

Ken coughed and cleared his throat. He resumed his rhetorical theme. Between alternately gentle and interrogative glances at his audience, he would raise his mild eyes up to the one who gave him his inspiration. At first I thought it was a trick of the light that as he lifted his gaze upwards a kind of rarefied mistiness seemed to emanate from his face. Yet his speech also began to lose some of its clipped briskness and to take on a resonance and dustiness which seemed acoustically almost impossible. His voice then sounded as if coming up from his toes, from the very depths of the very depths.

'*What do you think you are worth*?' he repeated. 'What do *you* think *you* are worth?'

His insistence set me going on various rapid fiscal calculations. Of course I knew that wasn't at all what he meant, but it was a starting point of a kind.

'Eh?' he chivvied us. 'If I were to approach anyone strolling down Maryport main street and ask them out of the blue precisely what they were worth, I know what kind of rejoinder I'd get. A gobful of indignation and possibly a split lip and a black eye for added emphasis. After all it's a very rude and uncompromising question, isn't it? They'd wonder what on earth gave me, a very ordinary and ugly old gadger like me, the right to pose such a thing. Most of them would immediately assume I was referring to what they had to leave to their squabbling children on their deathbeds. Only a reflective minority would realise I was talking about something approximating to self-worth. Though even they would probably interpret what I was after in the wrong way. They would think that I meant it in the limited sense of secular self-regard, how they privately rank themselves in terms of their life's achievements.

'Some people think they have inordinate personal value because they are a bigshot boss with half a dozen phone lines, fax and internet and personalised stationery and a different coloured mobile phone for every day of the week. In the case of our own local success stories, they will strive to make visible their "worthiness" by purchasing the gleamingest bungalow or most imposing Edwardian villa in the finest West Cumbrian suburb. Camp Road or Fleming Square if it's Maryport, Stainburn or Portland Square if it's Workington, Lorton Road or Highfield if it's William Wordsworth town, Cockermouth. Alternatively there are those minority individuals who are highly educated, who have left this humble county and been through college or university to get themselves some qualifications. They perhaps might pride themselves simply on the power of what's inside their brains. For this last category, their sense of worth usually lies in the brilliance of their minds and the powerful and profitable things that their intelligence can do.'

I tensed as I waited for the threatened explosion. His tone was presently mild but obviously he was going to break out into a rant. This blazer man seemed to be building up to a splenetic castigation whereas conventional church preaching usually struck me as a species of take-it-or-leave-it twittering. Also, as one who demonstrates a characteristically late twentieth-century gulf between his mundane profession and his expensive education, I felt obliged to prick up my ears at all this stuff about intelligence and brains. Robert Briers, I noted, was listening with raised eyebrows and an open mouth.

'St Paul the apostle possessed one of the subtlest philosophical minds of all time. Even the university professors who are Marxists and humanists will consent to acknowledge the obviousness of that. Anyone who doubts it only needs to give a close reading to the letter to the Ephesians, especially in the Authorised Version, to see how colossal the man's brain was, irrespective of his massive spiritual gifts. Yet he, and for that matter his finest commentator, Martin Luther, also proclaimed that to rank yourself according to the size of your brain is the highest foolishness.

'*For it is written, I will destroy the wisdom of the wise and will bring to nothing the understanding of the prudent.* And right after that, *Where is the wise? Where is the scribe? Where is the disputer of this world? Hath not God made foolish the wisdom of this world?*

'In sixteenth-century Germany, when Martin Luther was still in the Catholic monastic system, the teaching of theology had adopted the philosophical method of Aristotle. Pardon me but I'm going to educate you with a few big words. As soon as you've heard it you can forget it, but you need to know it first before you can forget it. Aristotle, in case you didn't know, was a famous Greek philosopher. The system as it was taught to Luther was called Nominalism. It worked by the application of syllogism. If such and such is true, then such and such follows, and such and such and so and so ad infinitum. It was meant to support the theological truths that the monastic authorities subscribed to, but it was, after all, an intellectual method that came from a Greek pagan. Now Luther in his mighty God-inspired courage turned his back on all that. He turned his back on philosophy entirely, whether of Thomas Aquinas or William of Ockham, the university teachings current at that time. He disputed with his teacher at Erfurt University, a brilliant chap called Jodokus Trutfetter, who had taught him his Greek method of reasoning. Luther said that on the contrary the only theology worth anything was *theological* theology. God's theology, not Greek philosophical theology. Indeed Martin Luther used far stronger words than that. Just listen to how much spiritual contempt this man of genius showed when he railed against the stiffnecked intellectual method. This is what he said.'

He began to read from some handwritten notes in his halting Blackburn accent. I looked sideways at Robert Briers who was doggedly drinking in all this history of the Reformation and the battle for uncorrupted Protestant souls. At the far end of the North Quay, in a tin mish hut, a Tarns farmer was listening to what a man in a blazer had to say about Nominalism, Thomism and Ockhamism. The scenario was surreal and utterly preposterous. Surely, I thought, I must be dreaming all of this?

"'It is an error to say that without Aristotle no one becomes a theologian. On the contrary, one only becomes a theologian when one does so without Aristotle. The assertion that a theologian who is not a logician is an abominable heretic is itself abominable and heretical... in short the whole of Aristotle is related to theology as darkness is to light.'"

Ken sniffed victoriously, as if it were he instead of Luther who had formulated the trenchant manifesto. Hand in hand with the astringent reformer he went on boldly: 'Minds are ten a penny is one way of putting it. It's a blow to the brainy ones and even more so when it comes from an authority like Luther. Everyone knows that looks and beauty fade and that no one ever got to heaven through winning a beauty contest. Maybe it's because the mind and the soul seem such natural and sympathetic partners that the majority of people are deluded by the importance of the intellect. Of course the human brain is handy for solving mathematical equations or for making a well-constructed rabbit hutch. But when it comes to human conduct and human morality, it is wickedly ineffectual. That's what outstanding intellectual geniuses like Paul and Martin Luther both believed. But try getting the idolatrous world at large to acknowledge it. We live in an age of mind worship, of mania for education and qualification, in a society where the ability to reason and dispose of things is regarded as the highest achievement.'

Slowly I turned my neck to see if the fine-featured woman in her nineties was paying any attention to any of this. Expecting to see her fast asleep, I blinked at the sight of her studiously drinking in every word. So intent she was, her face had taken on the alert receptiveness of a girl of twenty.

'During my seventy-eight years,' Ken continued, 'I have met quite a few brilliant men and women. Some of them simply by the power of their tongues could have convinced me I was Alexander the Great or Nat King Cole if they'd wished. Some of them, just as in Luther's day, were capable of cooking up the subtlest argument for or against the existence of God in five minutes flat. Without recourse to notes or props or anything outside their, you might say, supernatural eloquence, they could do it just like child's play. God disposed of and swatted like a fly, if you like, or God patted on the back and allowed there as a hypothetical but meaningless presence if you prefer. Playing God to that extent, these jet-propelled intellectuals. Capable of affirming or rejecting absolutely anything even up to and including the incalculable, the inimitable and the immeasurable. Nothing daunts these types. The mightiest spiritual concept, the greatest power in creation, is not beyond the scope of their penetrating powers of analysis, synthesis, syllogism, ratiocination. All those enormous Greek and Latin words that trip off their tongues just like the hairs off a moulting dog.'

Robert Briers grinned at the disrespectful simile. By chance I noted that his own suit had a coating of what looked like dog hair. He also smelt very much of the farmyard, a highly pungent aromatic mix of mud, cows, cow dung and engine oil.

'A sure sign of their spiritual pride is that it is usually quite matterless whether it is for or against they are arguing. Whichever side of the divide their reasoning leads them, it confirms them in their sure conviction that the brain is the be-all and end-all. For them it is an even greater diversion and excitement than alcohol or drugs or sex or fame or notoriety. Using this precious possession inside their heads, they confidently believe they can conquer everything from family tension to a breaking marriage. They can use it to win themselves a serene old age, or to find the best way of structuring society, or to cure all economic ills, or to teach a dog to come to heel, or to teach themselves to see in the dark...'

Briers broke into an open guffaw and then whispered a curious anachronistic reference to the bald-headed television magician David Nixon.

'Some things they'll never be able to solve with their brains of course. The operations of time and chance, to use a good old-fashioned phrase. The intellect is not much use when it comes to coping with serious illness or an unexpected tragedy.

Let's say your only six-year-old daughter is run over by a drunken teenage joy rider, no amount of logic or cerebral reflection is going to do much to ease the pain of that. Or looking outside the confines of this Cumbrian backwater, suppose you are living somewhere like Bosnia and the government suddenly decides to boot you out of your house and incarcerate you in a concentration camp. Or alternatively they choose to exile you beyond the borders. When you are pushing all your few possessions on a handcart through a rutted minefield with your exhausted pregnant wife and four little kiddies hungry and crying behind you... time and chance, you'll rapidly discover, is a mighty thing.

'Time and chance! Time and chance! There's only one person, one almighty power, who knows how to deal with that. Forgive me for being shy about spelling things out. As you know, one irritating thing about preachers like me is that they always talk in generalities, they never talk about specifics. They rant and they admonish and they urge and they explain, but they rarely talk about precise examples of anything drawn from their own lives. If they are preaching about greed or selfishness they never get down to the embarrassing truth and talk about their own greed or their own selfishness or their own immorality, complete with vivid examples. They'll quote from parables, but they won't quote from their own sinful history. Sticky ground isn't it, dangerous ground when it comes to home territory? But we all know that one lively example, one truthful authentic personal testimony, is worth a thousand textbook illustrations...'

Puzzled and distracted halfway through his harangue, I suddenly found myself intensely alert. I couldn't wait to hear this old man's most intimate and disgraceful confessions. One look at him and I knew his sins would be no bigger than cherries and no darker than snowflakes. If Ken Wright's misdeeds were anything worse than cheating at a tense point in a beetle drive, I would eat one of those old ladies' woven hats in front of me.

'So let's change all that for once. I've been asking you what you are worth, but let's turn to me and ask me, what am I worth? What is Ken Wright worth? And to anticipate the answer in advance, let me say the proper spiritual reply for one who follows Him is... nothing. I am worth nothing. *I am worth nothing.* Nothing at all.'

I pondered that gentle insistence of his and repeated to myself mentally, *The man with the fish badge is worth nothing at all.*

Yet, as a credo, I did not comprehend its logic. No matter how vehemently I repeated it, it made no sense at all to me.

'There's an important qualification accompanies that nothingness. I shall deal with it later. For the moment let's stick to uncomfortable rather than comfortable things. *What am I worth?* is a sadistic question in some respects. It's all to do with appearances and the way they mislead and distract. A few of you know me and you know a bit about me, but to anyone else I must look like a completely uninteresting specimen. In fact if you were invited to point to a textbook case of a boring-looking individual with nothing to recommend him on the outside, you would need look no further than this dull old gadger before you. Regarding "what is *he* worth?" the first thing you might think is, "Well as far as I'm concerned, he isn't worth a second glance."'

Thwarted by the dry sincerity of his self-abasement, I tried to play the devil's advocate and see him as more interesting, more elusively original than he appeared. I tried and tried but all I could see was the incarnate epitome of elderly and irritating conformity. At that precise moment the badge man appeared to nod dolefully in my direction, as if to confirm the truthfulness of my uncharitable thoughts.

'There are thousands upon thousands of frighteningly insignificant old gadgers like me. In some respects we are so monumentally anonymous, so much of a type, that we don't have a real flesh-and-blood existence. We exist in other people's minds just as a lump category. We register with such absolute vagueness that really we are closer to walking ghosts than human beings. By the way, talking of ghosts, I was once a real ghost. I really was. You're looking surprised, you're grinning one or two of you. I'll explain more of that later on. Suffice to say that one glance at me and, as you give one big yawn, my probable CV leaps to mind without much struggle. Probably worked three shifts for the gas board for twenty-five years and maybe has a little retirement job as a supermarket car park attendant. Watches three TV soaps a week with his old wife and discusses the plots of them before, after and during each performance. Has framed pictures of his five gorgeous grandkids over the mock-coalfire gas fire and a calendar with a picture of the centre of Torremolinos by night. Has a big sweet jar full of five-pences and maybe a rhyming poem about home and hearth displayed above the mantelpiece.'

Robert Briers hawked his throat and whispered that he had once spent a stupendous fortnight in Torremolinos with the Silloth Young Farmers. 'Even though I'm not young,' he qualified pensively.

Ken heard both the throat clearing and the whisper. He lowered his glasses and surveyed us rather like a melancholy Fifties comic. He looked like a morose Ted Ray or a dour Jimmy Jewel or even an overgrown Jimmy Clitheroe.

'Much of that guesswork would be accurate. I really am as boring as I look these days in 1992. Though I don't watch three soaps, I only watch two. Unfortunately one I used to watch, *Emmerdale Farm*, has gone right down the drain in my view. It was once a wholesome, amusing sort of television version of *The Archers*, a saga of comical Yorkshire farming folk. Now it has so much immorality and lasciviousness in its plots, I find it completely unwatchable. It makes me into a sickly voyeur if I watch it. And I can't say I follow Him, can I, if I am a voyeur? As a matter of fact and to call a spade a spade, I was flicking through a French dictionary the other day for a crossword clue and I came across the French verb *emmerder*. It means, forgive my candour, performing a private and not very pretty function in the toilet. That particular soap, *Emmerdale Farm*, is now living up to its name in a perverse sort of way. Instead of soap in the sense of offering cleansing, it should signify soap in the sense of needing a profound cleansing.'

I gulped in foggy disbelief. Not only philosophic references to Thomism and Ockhamism, but intellectual puns, too, and in a foreign language at that. *Emmerder*, if you please. It was the one French verb that no one could forget. Wait, I thought to myself with delirious anticipation, till I tell Angela and Mary *this*.

Ken readjusted his glasses so that he no longer looked like Will Hay playing the admonitory headmaster. Focusing his eyes unnervingly in my direction he went on: 'That's enough of made-up television soaps. I have a more instructive and frightening soap opera for you. It's the tale of my own former life. First of all would you like to hear something incredible? Would you believe that when I was twenty years old, I was the dead spit of Beau Brummel or Rudolf Valentino? I was a real bobby dazzler. I was such an incredibly good-looking young man, with my jet-black hair and my almond eyes and my fine slim muscular body, I literally had to fight off half the females of Blackburn. Not only that; sometimes in public, certain jealous and enraged young women would fight tooth and nail over me. It all sounds like outrageous bragging but it's so long ago, fifty-five years, I think I'm entitled to talk about that callow and immoral young man as someone existing in his own right. I can appraise him objectively, with a candid and disinterested eye.'

I snorted to myself. I almost guffawed. The badge man who was once a Blackburn Lothario? I tried in vain to metamorphose Ken Wright into a haughty Adonis who prowled the pubs of downtown Ramsbottom looking for skirt. For the moment I believed he was lying and had been instructed by his Bible College correspondence course to invent these paradigm confessions. They were simply a tested means of stopping potential converts nodding off in the pews.

'I was once sat in a compromising situation in an extremely

seedy and disreputable drinking club in Bacup, when one of these jealous women, a stunning good-looker of eighteen called Miriam, such a beautiful Old Testament name, a complete misnomer in her case, came in with a full gross – you know what a gross is, don't you, especially if you read the Bible – came into the club with 144 bantam eggs! She blocked us in at our table and pelted both me and this married woman who were canoodling together shamelessly in the snug. I got at least half of them all over my lovely suit and in my eyes and hair, and Sheila, the married woman, got the other seventy-two all over her.'

With that I knew he was definitely lying. No eighteen-year-old, not even in the old days, would have had the patience and stamina to fling an entire gross of eggs. Not to mention the incensed publican standing by idle and letting all that mayhem proceed unchecked.

'When I say fought them off, what I really meant was that I played them off. I played them off against each other. I led some on and allowed others to lead me on, and God forgive me I made no distinction between married women and single women. Part of my apparent magnetism was not just my handsome looks, but my handsome money. I was a very well-off young man, considering I came from the dirt-poor working class of Blackburn. I had trained as a fitter at the pits up until I was twenty. If I'd stuck to that, I might well have stayed on the straight and narrow and escaped the terrible fall that overtook me. But a colliery fitter, though reasonably paid compared with a bus driver or factory worker, didn't have money to burn.'

Gradually his mordant self-scrutiny had softened and he was smiling at us in a way that made me feel distinctly uneasy. I was worried because I realised that he really wasn't making any of this up. It was self-evident that somehow something profoundly indescribable had freed him from the weight of a shameful, painful past. It was the naked charity in that old man's misty, gentle smile that made me feel so uncomfortable. Surveying the rapt and silent congregation I wondered how easy it would be to vault the pew and do a lightning dash through the latched doors.

'I was rolling in it for two reasons. Firstly, I had a remarkable aptitude for all things mechanical. I was a genius when it came to working on motor-cars. I could do anything that a trained mechanic could do and I also had a natural eye for design and original modification. My Dad's brother, my Uncle Jim, had a pal who owned the biggest garage in Blackburn. This wealthy proprietor was called Giddings but he was nicknamed Muttonchop because he had the old-fashioned sideburn whiskers. He also had more expensive rings on his hairy fingers than a gypsy out of a Verdi opera. Muttonchop Giddings used to let me hang about there and watch his half-dozen mechanics at work on the splendid automobiles owned by the local nobs and the richest Blackburn businessmen. Dirty great Rolls and custom-made Bentleys and plush leather-seated Rileys and beautiful MG sports cars. Those were my favourites, those lovely MGs. I owned one myself eventually, a 1938 job, until it was taken away from me in the bitterest circumstances. It was like losing a wife more than losing a car, it was such a beautiful, perfect little thing. That's jumping a bit though. Once Muttonchop's lads saw I understood what they were doing, they let me give them a hand. When I had taken to bits and put together a few of these expensive cars, I was capable of putting together my own creative modifications, of designing and building custom-built sports cars. I was offered jobs down in Surrey and Suffolk with top manufacturers, but instead of that I stayed with Muttonchop up in Blackburn and did expensive specialist jobs for him. He charged his clients an arm and a leg but he paid me a flat rate of twenty quid a week, which in 1937 was a royal fortune. On top of which I got tips and sweeteners from these delighted Rolls and Riley owners.'

He paused and winced a little. It wasn't clear whether he was wincing on his or our behalf. Possibly he was coming to the painful sting in his tale.

'As well as being an obsessive womaniser, I was an obsessive gambler. From the age of twenty I was a pitiful slave to the cruellest addiction on earth. Don't you people find it very confusing to be told that a very harmless old man was once a very harmful young man? For the first few years, up until the start of the War, I was well ahead of the game. Unfortunately for me and all I had dealings with, I was winning a good deal more than I was blowing. I was quids in, sometimes hundreds of quids in. And like Croesus and his gold I found it a most diabolically exciting kind of magic. With my well-paying job and my gambler's luck I was travelling on wings in my early twenties. My eyes were always staring out of my head, people regularly remarked on it. Literally they were glowing like a madman's or a drug addict's, with the overwhelming physical excitement. Me, this harmless old bore you see before you in the tie and the golf-club blazer, in those days I was as vain, as deludedly omnipotent as the worst megalomaniac conceivable.'

The badge man with the glib and cheerful manner who had been a boy desperado and a youthful lush. His mild blue eyes glinted mournfully at the memory of something he'd once been enslaved to and which he crudely termed as diabolic. This new glint was not vaunting or wicked but was openly contrite. Outside of certain tragic Japanese films and harrowing performances of Shakespeare I don't believe I have ever experienced such epic contrition in the raw. His penitential face had that same misted and inscrutable purity as when he raised his eyes up for his preacherly inspiration. Swelling his frail old chest with the strength of his remorse, he invited us all to share in the weight of his emotion. He went on huskily.

'Why was I so successful at the start? Because I was so ruthlessly, so diabolically methodical, so tirelessly diligent when it came to studying form. I took many an outrageous risk on a rank outsider, but always based on a meticulous and obsessive knowledge of every single stable between Newmarket and Ayr. I worked very hard at the specialist skill and the science of it. I worked extremely hard in my own degradation. I put in a lot of time studying half a dozen different racing papers and carefully mooching around in the pubs where the trainers and jockeys and hangers-on liked to drink. I learnt all the insider stuff about jockeys who took bribes and how dope could be administered to men as well as horses. On top of which, like a true gambler, a born gambler, I would bet on anything and everything. Like any punter with any sense, I bet mostly on horses, but I also bet on greyhounds when the horses weren't running. I also played all-night card games in dozens of drinking dives. I'd bet small fortunes on poker, brag, pontoon and rummy. My eyes would be red and bloody by the end of it, my throat so dry and parched with chainsmoking, I would have to drink half a gallon of tapwater before I drove off bog-eyed to Muttonchop's garage. But there weren't enough possibilities in the world to satisfy my craving entirely. If I'd had enough to drink and I felt in a crazy mood, I'd bet ten pounds, half my week's wages, on an arm wrestle in a pub. I had to bet on something virtually every minute of the day, and if I ran out of sensible things I would bet on completely idiotic ones. Which of two schoolboys dashing by the pub window would win the race to the schoolbus. Which of two flies would be the first to drown in the beersops on our table. Which of two beermats would hit the floor first if the old blind woman in the corner with the Sweetheart Stout would agree to drop them for us. Once when I'd had a terrific skinful I bet five pounds in an argument over the word 'rhythm'. Was it spelt with one 'h' or two 'h's? It was one of the rare times in the early days that I lost, and I never bet again over words as I was always a hopeless speller...

'I should have gone on winning the geegees for evermore, because my flair for picking the form never seemed in any danger. But believe you me, addictions never come singly. As the pace of my gambling increased, so did the pace of my obsessive womanising. I felt as if every cell in my body was consumed and fired with lust, and as if the carnal greed for winnings and the carnal greed for women were an interchangeable disease. As the womanising got more and more complicated, so did the strain of these myriad affairs start to derail me. It got so complicated trying to satisfy and lie to three or four women at once that I had to increase my whisky drinking to cope with the emotional strain. If I hadn't I might well have gone doolally and ended up sedated in a mental hospital. It's possible to get to the stage where darting between women and dodging between assignations you can moither yourself completely brainless with your incredible fabrications and your astonishing deceitfulness. You forget what lie you've said to which woman. The technical term for it is cognitive overload. It gets so bad you feel as if you will have to write it all down to remind yourself. Then you think if anyone gets their hands on this atrocious notebook you'll be even more in a mess, you might be blackmailed till kingdom come. If this strain on your nerves were a case of work instead of women it would be called a workaholic's overload and the prelude to a breakdown. It only needs to see one of your conquests crying her insides out for you to plummet instead of soar. Then you feel the need to anaesthetise yourself against the consequences of your deeds. That's when you start to hit the whisky in a big way and that's when your life starts to really fall apart. That's when you realise that degradation isn't just a word, it's an abyss, an endless and terrifying pit that really has no bottom to it…

'This is how bad it got. At one stage I was courting a woman called Flor Messenger who worked in a high-class confectioner's, and who quite clearly and without boasting loved me to death. Flor was a lovely little thing, only just turned seventeen. She had a tender, shy little face, and a quaint, teasing and beautiful little laugh. She looked a bit like a beautiful antique doll, and she was a Quaker lass at that. Her Mam and Dad were real old-style Quaker farmers and as simple and straightforward as anyone could be. Sometimes they theed and thoud and bowed at you over scones and teacakes in the kitchen, just like something out of an old-fashioned play. They couldn't understand complexity. Quite rightly they saw it as a consequence of sin. They only knew what was right and what was wrong and how to say yea and how to say nay. They could see what kind I was, but I think they prayed for Flor's sake that I was otherwise. I used to take her up for drives to the Lakes, Windermere and Coniston, in my bonny little bright red MG. The thrill of that and the fact I was a few years older was enough to make any naive farmer's lass fall head over heels. But at the same time I was carrying on with two married women more than twice my age. They were not only unrepentant at their adultery, they were pandering to me with little envelopes filled with money and sometimes expensive little gifts. At the age of twenty I would have hotly denied it, but I was a species of pimp. These days the name has changed to suit the fallen times and has been dignified as *toy boy*. But there must have been some spark of decency left in me. I found soon enough that I couldn't keep on stringing Flor along, not without feeling a very painful conscience. She was too gentle, too young and too vulnerable, with those big round eyes and that pink little antiquated smile. I just couldn't keep on trifling with her. Not when I knew she wanted something serious and was prepared to keep on giving me every last thing she'd got. God love her, it was because I meant everything in her life. You know what I mean by giving me absolutely everything. For her it meant a blind and doting commitment, but for me it meant instant satisfaction of my selfish fleshly lusts.

'So I took the easy road out and I chucked shopgirl Flor. I ditched her. I couldn't do it face to face, so I wrote her a half-page letter. I spent about ten drunken minutes over it and it was all full of cheap formulas about me not exploiting her youngness and about the two of us both needing more experience of life before we saddled ourselves with responsibilities. That was baloney of course. I had already helped myself to her youngness. I'd had it all, every last treasure, on a plate. I'd had everything she had to give. I'd encouraged her day after day into furtive fornication, and I'd kept on telling her that I loved her when all I meant was I loved taking everything she had to give. My letter was a coward's letter. The more so because I should have said it, not written it, and I should have taken her terrible reaction with a grown man's courage. Instead, I was hoping that she would get over it as quick as I imagined I would. I was upset but not desperately upset. In any case I had two other much older women to employ me. Yet I wasn't prepared for the remarkable thing that happened. I would never have predicted how this very ordinary girl would try to show the extraordinary strength of her feelings for me.

'What this strictly brought-up Quaker lass did was to come round and squat herself down on the front step outside our house. She did this amazing and embarrassing business every single night for the best part of a month. Instead of being angry or shouting, she just sat there very meekly and keened on our front flags. For what seemed a biblical period, for thirty summer nights, she settled herself down and cried like in one of those primitive Irish wakes. My mother soon told me she wished I'd never been born. The whole of our street was astonished, if not terrified. It was that old-style Quaker meekness of hers that puzzled them the most. If she'd done it in a vengeful way, it might have seemed like a public protest intended to shame me. But it wasn't anything like that. She grieved on our front step like a dog might sit and howl its sorrow. There was no insistence, no blaming, no shouting or swearing at anyone. Least of all at me. She was simply showing her hurt and her grief like a little girl would do. Just like a little child after she's been beaten or abused or brutally betrayed by whoever's supposed to care for her.

'When I heard her crying her guts out on our step, I would shudder and shiver in my smart, expensive shoes. I would dart out by the back door as fast as lightning. I would set off for my conquest with Mrs Myra Pomfret, fifty-year-old wife of a very harmless old gentleman who worked in the estate management line. Or to have a sneaky liaison with Sybil Bainbridge, who had the extraordinary affectation of smoking little Cuban cigars and who at fifty-nine was literally old enough to be my grandmother. She was the spoilt wife of one of the richest machine manufacturers in Bacup. I was specially modifying his Bentley, which is how I gave the wink to cigar-puffing Sybil in the first place. I was blatantly cuckolding the rich gentleman who was providing me with work, you might say. I would dart off panic-stricken to Bacup or Rawtenstall, and my Mam and Dad would have to suffer this lovelorn girl emptying her young heart out on the step. It was a complete waste of time opening the door and asking her to come in. My mother tried that every single night but it never worked. Flor would smile a bit but keep on crying and wailing. No amount of begging or threats would budge her. Once or twice my Dad lifted her up gently and set her off down the road. But two minutes later she was back at her post on the step and pouring her soul out to the heavens. She was just like an abandoned dog, like a Greyfriars Bobby. If things hadn't altered she might have gone the same way as the dog and pined to death on those stone flags. In fact, to anyone watching, Flor lamenting for me looked as if she was sat on her own tombstone...

'One night as I was coming out of a pub I was accosted by her father, the Quaker farmer. He couldn't take his only daughter's distress any longer. Do you know how one man's sinfulness and madness can bring out a different madness in others? In Flor's case, pining to death; in his case, doing something just as crazy. Of course the old Quaker man never went near a pub and he must have wondered why on earth he was trying to please someone he knew was destroying his child. But he stepped out in front of me looking very anxious and begged me for a word.

'He begged me. He beseeched a young wilful wastrel. At the time I looked rather like a well-to-do, very ostentatious bookie's runner. I had the biggest gold wristwatch in Blackburn, and I had an engraved, pure silver cigarette case. Like all the best brashest ponces I wore an elegant diamond tie pin. Mr Messenger looked at me in my sleek pinstripe suit about to get in my perfectly gleaming sports car and he was very humble. What he should have done was take off his jacket and give me a damned good lacing. Instead of that he took out his wallet and shook it in front of my nose. I was dumbstruck. What on earth was he doing? Slowly and rather stupidly, as if he was buying a new carthorse at a country market, he counted out twenty fivers into his shaking hand. In those days a five-pound note was as a big as a tea towel. In those days that stash of fivers was as much as one of his own farmhands made in a year.

'"Look," he said at the top of his voice, "this is for you. I want you to have this money."

'I was red as a cockerel because it was in full daylight and half of Blackburn was watching. I was known by everyone as the fly boy wonder who could beat all the bookies. I was a hero though there wasn't one of them wasn't anxiously looking forward to my eventual fall. I felt so shifty and seedy, because it looked for all the world like I was harassing a dopy old coun-tryman over some terrible debt he owed me.

'"I don't want your money," I said, really rude because I was so petrified. "What on earth do you think I want with your money? I've got enough money of me own."

'He blushed and sweated at my brutal, insolent tone and said, "This hundred pounds is for you. If you'll take Flor back and court her again. If you marry her I'm ready to give you an extra five hundred."

'He forced the money into my hand in a way that appalled me. You know how market salesmen press things into your arms when you don't want them. I'd made that man so unhappy I'd turned him into someone prepared to look publicly debased and pathetic, without dignity, without his good name. He was trying to force my knuckles round the hundred pounds, the blood money for his daughter's happiness. She was losing weight as the vigils on our step went by, and she'd started not turning up at work. It was getting dangerous, it wasn't anything like a game any more. It was all about love and the depths of love, and it went to prove that even though it was 1939 people could still have these enormous unbearable passions, just like they did in Shakespeare. Of course He gives us these mighty passions for a good purpose, as we are made in His mighty image. All the same it was convenient for everyone to mock and say she was only a kid of seventeen and she'd soon get over it. But for that month of squatting on our step, she showed every evidence of being more serious than the world would give her credit for. Without saying it she was proving that consummated physical love is meant to be part of an eternal commitment, a godly covenant. Those who believe in Him will know what I'm talking about and what I mean by his costly devotion. In Flor's case she was worshipping something that was not worth worshipping as it was objectively corrupt. Unfortunately in her eyes I was angelic, she was blinded by her love. She had even revealed the buried angelic side of me on those runs up to the Lakes. Once or twice I had looked at the young tenderness in her eyes and had had a severe jolt. I'd had a recognition that I too had some of those depths and some of that capacity for adoration. It was there in me but I had leached it and bled it out of existence over the years. Meanwhile today in front of The Tap and Spile old Willy Messenger was frightened his child Flor might do away with herself. She was his only daughter, she was his greatest human treasure.

'I didn't even answer him. Even in the Blackburn of fifty years ago they'd given up the practice of cash dowries. I got into my car and shot off to the poshest house in Rawtenstall to see Sybil. I was sweating and nervously licking my lips when I told her the story of the hundred pounds and she laughed her head off until she cried. Or at least she laughed about the simplicity of the father, then she looked a bit uneasy about the continuing vigil of Flor. Sybil might have been more moved if she'd thought it was true. She thought I was making it up, or possibly exaggerating the length of the vigil, just to make her anxious about her own hold on me. Sybil was young-looking for someone nearly sixty and I could have pointed that out but never did. On some level I felt I needed to punish her for the thirty-nine-year age gap. I pretended to admire her cigar habit and I even bought her Havanas occasionally. But privately I was as old-fashioned as Flor and I was repulsed by her weirdness. That night she put three notes instead of one into the envelope, as if to demonstrate her anxiety while saving her pride. Her husband was away in London and wouldn't be back for a whole week. She invited me to turn up there every day but I made an excuse about having to drive a Riley down to the Midlands for a customer.

'Later I learnt that Mr Messenger went against his Quaker principles and used force on his daughter. One night he went and locked Flor into her bedroom. She didn't turn up on the step that night but my mother, instead of being relieved, went very stiff and rigid and then burst into angry tears in front of me. She said she felt like Flor, she couldn't explain why, but she felt as if she had been going through the same vigil and the vigil hadn't stopped. She even went and dallied there herself on the step for a few minutes, looking the length of the street and scowling at any neighbour who stared, as if paying angry tribute to Flor. She came back inside looking very peculiar, really disgusted with me. I made the mistake of saying, Thank God that's over, and that did it. She turned on me and called me things I can't repeat in the house of God. The kindest things she called me were a lush and a nancy boy. There wasn't much logic to some of her terms of abuse but I didn't dare open my mouth to rebut anything. She said if I said any more she would break my back. It was hyperbole but it was a common expression among working-class mothers when they were angry with grown-up sons. In this case she looked as if she might put words into action. She was an emphatic passionate woman, my mother, but she never used obscene language until that night.

My sinfulness made more than my mother unhinged. That night when her father wouldn't let her out of her room, Flor jumped through the glass of her bedroom window. She made a horrible gory mess of herself and she broke one of her lovely little ankles. She had to be taken to hospital and doubtless it was a toss up whether to transfer her to the nerve ward once she'd recovered. But as soon as she was patched up her parents packed her off to relatives on Walney Island near Barrow-in-Furness. For the first months she sent me dozens of letters but my mother burned them all and only told me so on her deathbed. After about a year Flor seemed to have got over it and she came back to Blackburn. I bumped into her one day in the street and by that stage I was such a hopeless wreck we both ran off without a word. Two years later Flor moved back up to Barrow and she married a Furness Quaker.

'Meanwhile I proceeded to go down the hill in royal fashion. It might have helped if I'd had to fight in the War, but I'd had TB as a little kid. I still had a weak chest and the army wouldn't have me. I was put in the ARP with on-call responsibility for Home Guard vehicles. And I was kept on by Muttonchop, even bribed and pampered by him, as all his best mechanics had been conscripted. Muttonchop Giddings was a big drinker himself and he conducted his affairs like any proper alcoholic. He could empty a brandy bottle day or night and apart from the smell on his breath he seemed frighteningly sober. Real boozers can get drunk without getting drunk, if you know what I mean. It's a true addiction, it's not just a colourful bit of dissipation. If you don't have it you feel terrible, and if you do have it you feel normal, or at least you feel as if you can function. Muttonchop introduced me to brandy for breakfast, a glass or two with your toast and bacon. It would never have occurred to me to start so early, but once I'd had breakfast with the boss I took to the habit myself. I had to move out of the house, of course, because my mother would never have permitted that kind of insane license. To see a boy of twenty-three sipping a double brandy with his plate of scrambled eggs. I bought a house at the opposite end of the town and began to do just exactly what I wanted...'

10

It's just a fine sounding abstraction for most of us. Hence its precise meaning is generally studied at safe arms' length, for somewhere in there, there is the dubious image of Roman priests, censing, superstition, mariolatry. Only in that supremely categorical faith is the baffling term meticulously formalised and sanctified. Never having been anywhere near a Roman Catholic church, I cannot speak of it at authoritative first hand...

The word I'm talking about, the thing I was vainly struggling with, was 'contrition'. Being vehemently against all Roman Catholics, Ken Wright the evangelist would probably prefer to have termed it good old-fashioned remorse.

I certainly couldn't stand it here at TFEOTNQ. I really couldn't take it and I wanted out of the place. I couldn't breathe by the time the preacher had got onto his brandy for breakfast habit. I didn't want to know any more about Muttonchop Giddings or about the badge man's going downhill during the War. More to the point and improbable as it sounds, I had known Flor Messenger myself. When Ken had talked about the young Quaker girl and her pining like a faithful bitch dog, not only was his fish badge glinting brightly through the gloom, but I could picture Flor clearer than I could see my hand in front of me. It was impossible and yet it was the same woman, for Sarah Singer and Flor Messenger were in some indefinable essence the same unprotesting victim.

I was only three years old when Flor had been performing her public vigil and shaming the cold-hearted mechanic. Also I lived over a hundred miles away, and didn't leave the county of Cumberland until the 1950s. But when he talked of Flor's vulnerable bonniness, it was identical to Sarah's, and when he spoke of her heart-melting lack of guile, it was precisely the same. In my case, to compound the merciless algebra, there was a third party, and if you include my infant daughter Anne there was also a fourth.

Referring to his early car trips with Flor, Ken had used the verb 'courting'. It seemed a quaint sort of usage, even to someone of my generation. In those two innocuous syllables I understood how much words govern the senses and how senses govern the behaviour and how behaviour governs the world. By the end of this decade, of course, no one will know that word 'court', and even if they do, they won't know in what infinitely allusive sense to use it. They will not understand any more than my tiny daughter Anne was able to understand how her parents' ten-year, rock-solid marriage could be so rapidly torn apart.

I met my future wife at an evening performance of *A Midsummer Night's Dream* given by the Junior Sixth of Mawbray Grammar School. I was sixteen, almost seventeen, she was fifteen, almost sixteen, and the year was 1952. Sarah was a student of Silloth Merchants' High School for Girls, which boasted an even more hallowed academic reputation than Mawbray. As well as being obliged to attend each other's Shakespeare productions and annual speech days, senior students of the two schools met several times before Christmas to practise the genteel art of ballroom dancing. It was obviously intended to encourage a decorous social accomplishment, to facilitate the Malthusian ladder-climbing of the cream of West Cumbrian youth. If that old-fashioned dancing was not an emotive prelude to the act of proper courting I don't know what was. At the age of sixteen I was allowed to slide my arms around a young girl's slender, tender waist. I felt as if I were touching a swan or embracing the first woman born. I was allowed to place my chest opposite a young virgin's breast. I use that word deliberately because, arch as it sounds, it indicates the flowering of the soul and a rudimentary reverence that surfaces when a boy is first allowed to touch a girl. I was permitted the smell of her hair and shoulders and a sight of the tiny gentle blond hairs that adorned a finely arching neck. I was permitted to meet an extraordinary person like Sarah Bennett, and even during that first stumbling sally with the Two Step, I knew that she was going to be my wife and no one else's.

We lived a good ten miles apart but both of us were sturdy cyclists. Most frequently we met at Allonby beach or sometimes we went inland and took long walks around the flat and melancholy pastureland between Mawbray and Abbeytown. The hamlets there have the oddest Gothic names like Aldoth, Foulsyke, Lowsay and Pelutho. We were young and serious and extremely sensitive. I felt in my case as if no one had ever had such a unique, uncluttered view on life, nor had anyone ever had such an idiosyncratic sensitivity. The lush splendour of a clump of beech trees on a warm spring evening would make my inner being seemingly melt and dissolve. The way a narrow country road would undulate ever so gently and delicately into the tenderness of the horizon would make me exclaim at the perfection of the natural world. I genuinely thought I was the first sixteen-year-old to have experienced such things. I was a pantheist in the literal sense. I believed that nature was God and God was nature and that everything else was a sham or a flop. Anything about God that wasn't about nature was not of any interest. Nature included the vividness, pungency and intensity of animals, and the good things in Sarah and myself came from our animal nature, not from our minds or our muddled personal histories. I had a mother who worked in a hole-in-the-wall in a grubby part of a run-down town. The less I thought about her at this stage in my life the better.

Sarah Bennett was transfixed by the simplicity of grass meadows, by waving seas of aromatic clover, or by the sight of a lone hare nibbling in a distant wheatfield. One day we spotted a huge one, entering the woods near a farm named Weary Hall. Hares can seem as big as a dog from a distance, and its awkward overgrown lollop made Sarah sad enough for her sharp green eyes to water. She looked at me uncomfortably and said that she saw herself in the same terms. She believed that like that hare she was too unwieldy and clumsy, too vulnerable to hazards, too conspicuous for her own good.

'I don't understand,' I said, taking her hand. 'I think of you as being graceful, as the opposite of clumsy. You're not easy game like that hare, you know how to give as good as you get. Plenty of times I've seen you calmly looking down your nose at people you dislike.'

She smiled and dropped her gaze, as if taken aback. She seemed thoroughly bemused that anyone, even her doting boyfriend, had a considered view of her temperament.

'How long is it now we've been together?' I asked her, as we studied the outside of Weary Hall.

'Nearly a year,' she said with a cautious sort of pride. 'Quite a long time.'

'My parents have just had their silver wedding. They've been together twenty-five times as long as us.' I thumped our little picnic bag dismissively against my thigh. 'Though I know our one year means a whole lot more than their quarter century.'

She nodded rather doubtfully. 'I don't suppose I'll ever know how my own parents see things from the inside. You never know. Maybe their private lives feel just as intense as ours…'

'No chance,' I answered drily. 'You and I see things that they'll never see. We feel all sorts of things that they wouldn't dare to feel. I read Fyodor Dostoievsky and my father reads Hammond Innes and my mother reads Monica Dickens. That's one measuring scale. I listen to the Third Programme whenever I get a chance and they listen to the Light. You get overwhelmed looking at the movements of a hare while your father has only ever shown emotion when he watched the Coronation. He bought a twenty-one-inch television just so that he could enjoy the royal ceremony and then he wept buckets. Don't tell me that's about his depths.'

I let go of her hand abruptly and we lifted up our bikes. Across the fields was a tidy-looking dairy farm and Sarah waved at a thin young woman who was carrying a bowl of corn for the hens in the yard.

'When my folks row,' she said in a preoccupied way, 'it's always about insignificant things. But there are deep things they dislike in each other and they never mention those. For instance he really hates the way she frowns when he's trying to explain something important. She puts on a sort of knowing school-prefect face, obviously copied from someone who impressed her a long time ago. Her voice becomes an up-and-down shrill. But her brow is much too furrowed, it's like a bad actress's expression. He really loathes, really detests her for that face. But he daren't say anything and he always shows his disgust by complaining about something else. He'll snarl at her for overcooking his carrots instead of telling her to stop smirking so idiotically.'

She was bitter rather than indifferent and for some reason this irritated me.

'How do you know it's what annoys him if he doesn't say so?'

'Because he stiffens. And then I stiffen too. I really hate that fluttery shrill little squeak of hers. I want to push her face right into the watery carrots and shout: *Use your own voice, woman, you don't need anyone else's*! I'm like the family's bloody wireless antenna, I always pick up the unspoken message. He's never once openly accused her because obviously it would hurt her too much. No one wants to be told they have so little inside themselves they have to imitate others.'

Suddenly, perversely, I began to speak with expansive warmth of my parents. I told Sarah that the one thing I admired in both Mildred Singer and Joseph Singer was the fact they aped no one and always seemed to speak with sincerity. My mother admittedly was domineering and undemocratic, but it

166

was done without disguise or unction. There was no pretence of bullying, it was overt and unashamed. Likewise my father was so contented in himself, that if he could think of nothing to say in company he would stay confidently silent. Whereupon my aghast mother would openly berate him for making no effort, and the embarrassed guest would blushingly insist that they liked Joe Singer precisely because he was a shy and quiet man...

Our parents' temperaments were important issues. As two only children we shouldered a third of the emotional freight in each home. Ma Singer very much admired my considerate young girlfriend with the old-fashioned country manners and insisted on pressing her dearest sweets upon her. Sarah was presented with 2/11d boxes of Maltesers or Bassetts' Licorice All Sorts or big shilling bars of Milk Tray and Rum'n'Raisin. When Sarah came visiting she invariably brought Mildred twenty Sweet Afton cigarettes, which shows the questionable flavour of the times. If there was any lung cancer forty years ago, it was certainly kept under the table. No one was ever rumoured to die of such a fiction. My father liked Sarah because she was the perfect embodiment of a bonny, shy, respectful young thing. Her facial bones were finely etched and the sensitivity and the infinite youth in her soft, sweet smelling skin virtually leapt across the table to proclaim themselves. It was obvious that, in her, Joe saw a dozen similar demure little country girls from his past. When he observed Sarah in 1953 he saw all the perfect sixteen-year-olds from 1923. His own favourite, shy little conquest, Mildred Cannon, had duped him roundly. She had dropped the dulcet guise after just one week's marriage and without apology had transmogrified herself into a remorseless battle-axe.

*

After a year of our courting Sarah Bennett had her feet under our table whether she wanted them or not. On Mildred's rare Sunday afternoons off she insisted that I have Sarah round for tea and put her on the last bus home to Silloth. My father always chose to sit opposite the shy lass and tease her with his po-faced jokes. Alternatively he might really baffle her by seeming to be teasing when he was in fact in deadly earnest.

It was the last Sunday of the summer holidays and the next day we would be back at school. Mildred had provided us with a sumptuous consolatory spread including strawberry tarts, lemon mould and a sherry-drenched raspberry trifle. Brushing away some treacle-scone crumbs, she decided to smoke a Sweet Afton between courses. She offered one to Sarah though she knew Sarah would refuse. It was a symbol of complete acceptance and tacit declaration of readiness to have her as her daughter-in-law in five years time. Mildred wanted another female presence in the house, she wanted a womanfriend to call her own. Elsie, her sister, had amazed the whole town by marrying a skinny bus conductor called Wilfred and settling in a two-up-two-down in dirty old Siddick. At the age of forty-two she had given birth to her first child, whereupon Uncle Wilf had lost another stone and become technically emaciated. Mildred was delighted with her lovely new niece but pretended to be chastely horrified by her sister's senile motherhood.

Sarah politely declined the Sweet Afton and instead put a small piece of angel cake to her mouth. Meanwhile my father was watching her with an embarrassing degree of attentiveness. He was visibly agog at the sight of the angel and the angel cake. She stood it for so long, not knowing where to look, and then her cake dropped from her fork. She turned to me and wonderingly raised her eyebrows at his doglike scrutiny. I smirked and mouthed that he was quietly in love with her. Oblivious of my mime and grimaces, Joe Singer kept on staring at her as unselfconsciously as a five-year-old. Eventually Mildred observed his outrageous gawping and drew in her breath to admonish. But before she got it out he leant across and said with deadly earnestness to Sarah: '*Are them your own teeth?*'

She said aghast, 'You what!'

'You chew everything so easily I'm sure they must be your own. But when I was seventeen no woman I knew had all her own teeth.'

My mother hissed, 'Thank God some things damn well change. We don't need to know about the bad old days from the likes of you.'

'Some things *don't* change,' he answered cryptically. And still looking sceptical: 'Are they really your own teeth?'

'They are, I'm afraid, Mr Singer.'

'In my day...'

'Shut up, will you. She doesn't need to know about your blasted day!'

'In my day it was a handsome present for a young girl's twenty-first. The father or the fiancé would pay to have every one of the young lass's teeth yanked out.'

Sarah froze and choked on her angel cake. 'I...'

He went on with solemn relish, 'They woke up from the laughing gas all groggy and weepy and with raw, red bloody gums. They looked nightmarish of course, for a while, like the grinning Gorgon's head if they were daft enough to forget themselves and smile. A few weeks later they went back to be fitted for an expensive set of false. Then they paraded up and down the streets grinning and smirking fit to bust, just to let folk know they had forked out all that wad of money for a full extraction.' He leant across gravely to disclose his masonic confidence. 'It was an important sign of status, you see, to have your teeth ripped out all in one go...'

*

I went up to Durham University in '55 and Sarah Bennett came up a year later. I read English and she read History, but we also read every line and hair and microbe on each other's person,

169

clothed and naked, awake and sleeping. It was indicative of the dusty mores of the time that when our parents came visiting we pretended to live in separate bedsits in the same riverside house. Of course we had been living together from the start, but we took all Sarah's books and knick-knacks and lugged them downstairs to her best friend Jenny's room. Jenny Blinco went home to York every weekend, so it could always be passed off as Sarah's place. Terrified of being discovered to be lovers, we went to eccentric lengths to disguise all evidence of sex. Incredibly, whenever the Bennetts or my parents came to visit, we would hide our week's supply of foil-wrapped condoms inside separate packets of Woodbines. I smoked a great deal as a student and at any one time always had a dozen half-consumed packs of Woodies sitting inside the ugly old chest of drawers. A Johnny was pushed inside each pack like some ribald free gift, then shoved back into the drawer as if it had been an ounce of purest heroin.

Once a term Mildred and Joe took the train across to see their only son. One Sunday just before they set off back, I carelessly offered my mother a fag and she lifted out a grinning Durex in its silver coat of armour. I blushed as fiercely as if I had soiled my trousers or had spoonerised obscenely before a parson. Sarah had just dashed off for a meeting of the Choral Society and was spared the hellish mortification. Mildred looked at this silver lozenge calmly, and instead of killing me on the spot, put it back in the packet and ferreted around for a fag without a jacket. Nothing more was said. Joe Singer noticed none of this sordid melodrama. He had been ferreting through my book-shelves and was now reading, with open mouth, an unexpurgated translation of a Zola novel. From that day onwards he was seen to hover continually around the Z shelves in Maryport Library. But today I was very puzzled. Why wasn't she outraged? Why didn't she show it to Joe and command him to horsewhip his debauched Zolaesque son? It was 1956 but she smoked her Woodbine as coolly as if it had been 1996 and 'living in sin' were some risible Dark Ages' anachronism.

When I put my parents on the afternoon train for Carlisle, Mildred slyly turned to me and whispered: 'I'm pleased to see you have a bit of common sense.'

'Eh?' I said warily.

'I'm glad you're using those shiny Woodbines so Sarah doesn't get in the family way.'

'I'm really sorry…' I trailed off feebly.

'Sorry?' she scoffed. 'I'm bloody well congratulating you. Two clever young kids with the whole world in front of you. The last thing you want is a little baby on your hands. Sarah is an exceptional young woman and you make certain she comes to no grief.'

'I won't,' I said stiffly. 'Don't you worry.'

'Are you sure of that? Now that you're helping yourself to a married man's privileges, you make sure you treat her with every consideration. It's not a game, you know. You're privileged to have her. Good women don't grow on trees. They are as rare as natural gold. Do you understand?'

'Yes,' I said resentfully. It was puerile but I wanted her to reprove me for lax adolescent behaviour, not impose this dismal burden of mature responsiblility. My father sat heedless in the carriage devouring the lurid orange Bestseller Library with its garish cover of a sultry Parisian tart. While my mother trounced me with a stern homily on sex and responsibility, my father was enjoying vicarious sex courtesy of a dead Frenchman. Dimly I understood that my parents were sexual beings as well, and I recoiled at the repulsive thought. I shuddered to realise that my own existence was occasioned by their lust. Good God, what a hopeless picture. Though it would have failed to perturb M. Emile Zola, of course. It would all have been grist to his uncensored mill.

I told Sarah about the Woodbine incident and she was so guilt-stricken she immediately wrote Mildred a four-page letter of… contrition. She explained to my mother that young as we were our commitment to each other was very strong, and that sex was as natural and untainted as helping each other with essays or doing each other's shopping when one of us was ill. However if Mrs Singer was offended and upset by our conduct, then the two of us would be happy to embrace a strict chastity for the time being. I read its touching, careful sincerity with a bloated, alienated sensation in my guts. I could no more give up our sexual relations than give up smoking my Woodbines. The two appetites were congruous as well as dependent. I offered to post the letter for her, then threw it into the dustbin on the way down to see my best friend Stokes.

Cyril Stokes was an overweight Etonian who at nineteen already had a severe drink problem. He looked rather like the bibulous comedian Fred Emney though without his monocle, that trademark sign of the lounge-bar toff. Ugly by any standards though he was, his humorous disparagement and cerebral hypersensitive manner gave him an odd sort of charisma. He was in his first year of reading Russian and drank that unheard-of stuff vodka at all hours of the day. He laughed to hear of my mother's unlightable Woodbine and even more at her down-to-earth response. He certainly liked the sound of Mildred Singer and hoped to visit 'wassacallit Merryport' one of these days. Through his fog of Smirnoff he suddenly noticed I was in a disappointed mood and offered me his pack of du Maurier. With an exaggerated smirk he emphasised how he personally had no need of contraception. French letters bedamned, he sniffed fastidiously. Talking of French letters, I replied, my more-or-less uneducated father was suddenly a rabid Zola fan. I did not spell out my response to Sarah's panicky guilt but Stokes could easily enough see the cause of my sulks.

'It's more like a marriage than a *mésalliance*,' he criticised as I refused a teatime Smirnoff. 'You seem bloody young to me to be damn near married. Though as a grubby invert who has to seek his satisfaction in public lavatories, I should definitely envy you I suppose.'

I looked at him witheringly. 'You would easily find a fellow student if you could be bothered. You can't be the only homosexual in the whole of Durham University.'

'You're right, this place is crawling with bloody nancies. Overt and covert inverts, enough to sink a fleet of ships. All this moribund Anglicanism and raucous team sport. All these Oxbridge rejects, the public-school riffraff not quite bright enough to sail through the closed schols. But they seem, even the dullest of univ homos, to want someone who looks less like a bloated baboon. My father's pots of money which I squander so prodigally for all to see, it evidently ain't enough for them, George.'

'It could be the booze,' I said bluntly. 'I'm sure your looks have nothing to do with it. Not that there's anything wrong with –'

'Ballocks. I nearly pass out myself when I come upon my reflection unawares.' Then with a weirdly childlike grimace of anxiety: 'Tell me why my reckless boozing might put people off me, Singer? I'm not hurting anyone but myself, am I?'

I scratched my nascent beard pontifically. 'An outward sign of sexual guilt, perhaps. Tell-tale evidence of inner instability?'

Stokes looked at me balefully though without hostility. I blushed at my unedited candour. 'I'm sorry. I've no right to talk to you like that, Cyril.'

'*Kiril*,' he insisted. 'I keep telling you to stop calling me bloody Cyril but you keep on doing it. It's patently obvious to me why even the most spavined, halitosis-afflicted Durham queer rejects me. It's not because I'm fat and ugly and a drunkard, but because I'm called Cyril.'

'But Kiril Stokes sounds downright bizarre.'

'Kiril *Stokowski* is how I'm to be addressed from now on.' Falteringly he held his bottle of Smirnoff next to the window and examined the evening sun through it. 'What's more, from this day forward I will communicate to my intimates and would-be intimates not in English but in guttural Russian. I will studiously promote myself as a cross between an amiable Prince Myshkin, a first-class idiot, and a neo-realist Falstaff. I will thus market myself as someone who though fat and ugly has an enduring novelty value.'

173

He put down his bottle and began to declaim in booming expectorating Russian and would not stop. He was taking one of his weekly fits of histrionics and I sat there feeling disenchanted, not at all amused. For a good ten minutes I put up with his abrasive bellowing at his swaying reflection in the wardrobe mirror. I didn't understand a word of Russian and was thus unaware he was quoting an emotional scene from *A Hero of Our Time*. Then he gesticulated at his framed picture of Lermontov and pointed back at his huge belly to indicate his own heroic dimensions. I grew more and more annoyed as he paraded around his vodka-reeking study looking and sounding like a maudlin dipsomaniac nobleman out of Maxim Gorky. Finally he braked abruptly in mid-sentence and explained in English that he was going to change to Old Church Slavonic.

'In that case I'm going back to Sarah,' I said curtly. 'To see if she's got over her panic attack. To see if she'll ever let me touch her again now my mother knows our secret.'

Stokes looked at me mockingly. 'But you are her common-law husband. What else do you expect? Personally I think if you really want to reassure her, you should go and get engaged to her tomorrow. And perhaps,' he finished in a slurred and sullen voice, 'perhaps your dear mother was right after all.'

'Right about what?' I asked.

'Oh I forget,' he said with a suddenly pitiful, quite desperate look.

'No you don't,' I said harshly. 'You're maybe drunk but you are still responsible for your opinions. What the hell do you mean?'

'Nothing at all,' he mumbled back with an odd little sniff. 'Kiril Stokowski often forgets what he's talking about. The world also forgets poor Kiril. Kiril Stokowski in turn forgets the loveless world. Stokowski justly despises the nasty bloody place. Poor dear hopeless dear Kiril. Inevitably the hapless young waif is completely forgotten by almost everyone.'

'Oh bugger off,' I said as I slammed the door behind me. Apart from anything else it felt incredibly embarrassing to see such undisguised brokenness in someone my own tender age. I kicked the solid oak door for good measure. 'You need to give yourself a bloody good shake, man.'

*

He wasn't the only one. Sarah Bennett and I were married as soon as she'd got her degree and when I was halfway through a librarianship course down in London. We had found ourselves a bargain garden flat in Maida Vale and she walked into a grammar-school teaching post immediately. In those days you didn't need any teaching qualifications to teach, and a First at Durham was viewed with almost as much favour as an Oxbridge Third. After I'd finished my library training I worked in a biology institute in Frognal for a year. It was insufferably boring, I soon discovered on the first day of being there. Running an academic science library is not quite the same as idly reading foreign novels, and to make matters worse the spanking new Gutzmann Library was full of electric static. Every time I opened a door I received a sizeable electric shock up the arm that was not so much painful as seemingly punitive. Everyone in the library received the same shocks but no one else seemed to mind them. I had read enough about behaviourism and Skinner seriously to wonder whether we were being used as empirical guinea pigs by the crafty science institute. On Christmas Eve of 1958 I gave my notice and became trainee manager of a Charing Cross bookshop.

A decade later I was back in Maryport running my own bookshop and with a four-year-old daughter called Anne. Sarah Singer was Head of History at a newly built comprehensive in her home town of Silloth. Comprehensives had only just arrived in Cumberland, and as canvassers for the Labour Party we felt like visionary provincial pioneers. Sarah of course earned a large salary, while I was struggling to scrape a semblance of an income. Anyone who has tried to run a bookshop in a remote run-down harbour town has always found it so. In the end I diversified and sold records and greetings cards, but even then making my ends meet would always be problematic. In addition I had to sell records and books I personally despised, a problem that all fastidious vendors of cultural artefacts have to wrestle with from the start. When an old chap came in asking for a double album of James Last or Miki and Griff, I had to fight the urge to grab him by the coat-tails, denounce his tastes as rubbish and shove him out of the shop. Ditto for Harold Robbins, Vicki Baum, Ngaio Marsh and Nevil Shute in the book line. I bravely filled my shop with Oxford and Penguin Classics, including Lermontov, Saltykov-Shchedrin and Turgenev, in honour of Cyril Stokes who was now a gay, if not ecstatic, civil servant and who was drinking more than ever. But no one wanted Saltykov-Shchedrin in Maryport and my bold array of Ornette Coleman and Cecil Taylor LPs was also slow in shifting.

Sarah's tender loyalty was such that she subsidised my hopeless business without a murmur. As Mildred Singer had shrewdly pointed out in the Fifties, my wife was definitely one in a million. As she rose to be Deputy Head of Silloth School, she easily made enough to keep us both. If she walked late afternoon into my bookshop and saw me happily ensconced with Stendhal, my only companion in the entirely empty premises, she made not a solitary quibble. Besides, at weekends and during school holidays, I was selling reasonable numbers of singles at 6/4d by Nirvana, Cream, Spooky Tooth and Fairport Convention. 'Progressive' Sixties rock music wasn't my chosen cup of tea but it wasn't all bad. In fact the drug-induced manifestations of hour-long heavy guitar solos – in dogged imitation of black blues musicians like BB King and Muddy Waters – those were rather to my taste. I thought of trying a drug or two myself, but sensibly never succumbed. I was thirty-two and thus in Maryport terms I was an old man. In any case I had a beautiful little four-year-old daughter, and for her I wished to stay sober and sound and everything a good father should be...

Then Corrie Millon strode into my bookshop and I found there was no going back. It was the late afternoon of a very sultry August day, and she walked in wafting some cooling harbour air. I watched her bold attractive figure as she stepped straight towards the Penguin Classics and began ferreting around with apparent familiarity. After five minutes' search she began to look frustrated and irritable. I blushed with confusion as she shouted across a couple of names I had never heard of. I was the best-read person I knew in this town, but when she said Eça de Queiróz and Pérez Galdós, I heard only Sadie Cuirass and Perry Goldlass. I thought she was wanting a steamy thriller and was at the wrong shelf. At this polite suggestion she became majestically inflamed. She said: 'Do you mind! Eça de Queiróz was only the finest Portuguese writer of the last century. Pérez Galdós was only the greatest Spanish novelist ever.'

'Oh?' I said, turning puce. 'In that case I really don't know why I've never heard of them. I always thought it was Cervantes that ah… are they very good then?'

'Good?' she snorted. 'You might as well ask if Shakespeare or Charles Dickens have anything to recommend them. Eça de Queiróz makes someone like Honoré de Balzac on a par with Mrs Belloc Lowndes. He was a dramatist, not a feeble melodramatist. He has no equal for vigour, wit, psychological insight, erotic intensity. Can you believe that this dazzling genius, rake and dandy was obliged to work for a few years in the Portuguese consulate in bloody *Newcastle upon Tyne*? Can you imagine what it was like for a man of his massive talent and refinement having to hang around bloody dirty old Newcastle?'

'I don't –'

'I waded my way through *Père Goriot* last year and as far as I could see it could have been written by Patience Strong. I wanted to shoot the lachrymose old bastard by the end of it. I didn't believe a word of it, sentimental hogwash from start to finish. But my Eça was a hundred years ahead of his time at least. Likewise Pérez Galdós puts Flaubert in the same artistic category as John Creasey or Leslie Charteris. He can describe a raucous Madrid street scene so that you can see it clearer than your own backyard. He couldn't have written anything as lifeless, schematic and idiotic as Boovar and bloody Pekewshay if he'd tried. He creates characters so fertile with life they are more real than the person next door. Of course they say that about all sorts of writers, but they haven't read Galdós so they don't know what they're bloody well talking about.'

'I see,' I gulped. 'Can you spell them for me? I'll order you anything you want. Let me look in the catalogue for you.'

I scanned through four recent catalogues and there was nothing at all by the Spaniard and only *The Maias* by de Queiróz in Everyman. This strange woman got me to order the Everyman and then relented and relaxed with an open and amused expression. She smiled with easy warmth to indicate that my insult was forgiven.

What did she look like? Corrie Millon's face was not particularly impressive in terms of symmetry or bone structure. Her beauty, if that was what it was, expressed itself in a stark almost frightening way. Her hair was short, cut tightly and severely, so that the impression was of energy, freshness and combative wakefulness. She was also very bright, far too bright for a schoolteacher, and had a reputation for rudeness and arrogance. I had this direct from one of her colleagues, who unfortunately happened to be my wife, Sarah Singer. Corrie was the flamboyant new French teacher at Silloth School, the same who was ostentatiously teaching herself Linguaphone Spanish and Portuguese so that she could read neglected geniuses in the original. As the majority of her colleagues read nothing more taxing than *Readers' Digest*, Corrie felt justifiably impatient at what she regarded as an ambient philistinism. During staffroom lunches if bored by a conversation, she would simply rise and walk away from it. She made the Head of Biology, Edna Farrell – a starchy spinster who had been at Cambridge in the Twenties and who was rumoured to wear her academic gown in bed and on the lavatory – completely apoplectic when interrupted her soporific monologue about a mortgage bridging loan. She told Edna it was an inappropriate and insufferable subject to go on about at such phenomenal length. Edna blushed and advised her that she was a remarkably insolent young woman. Whereupon Corrie informed Edna she was a first-class paradigm of a solipsistic bore. Edna clearly wasn't sure what either paradigm or solipsism meant, but prophesied to Sarah as she watched Corrie skip nimbly out of the staff room that that impudent little madam would soon come to grief.

Having compared notes with one or two other philanderers, I can confirm that starting an affair with a woman usually begins with the nose. When a man and a woman embark on the first stages of adultery, it usually begins with a barely perceptible twitching of the nostrils. The man's nose bristles and seems to say this is unambiguously exciting, this is an unlooked-for treat and a liberating anticipation of something lawless and extraordinary. If we could go to the limits as soon as possible and without anyone knowing and without either of us suffering any shameful embarrassment and without any damage to any third party, especially our children, that would be just the ticket.

Corrie Millon's nostrils were subtly playful appendages too. Her lips and her nose worked in teasing artful synchrony. Half an hour of talking to me about books and music and literature and she was aware that here in the back of this incredible West Cumbrian beyond was someone who might feed her restless mind. She told me she had a three-year-old daughter called Polly who she was picking up from an Allonby childminder in thirty minutes' time. She had a partner, not a husband she stressed, called Colin, who was a lab technician also at Silloth School. Colin was not Polly's father, she added quickly, though without embarrassment, as soon as she saw what I was thinking. Polly's father happened to be an eighteen-year-old called Lex she had met at a drunken party in London three years ago.

At the time she had been thirty, and it had served her, though not of course Polly, right. She had no idea, thank God, where Polly's boy father was these days.

'Oh,' I said uncritically. I had learnt an enormous amount about her and her mercurial character in five minutes flat. 'Well I happen to be the husband of your Deputy Head.'

Her eyes widened. 'You're really Sarah Singer's husband? Are you aware she is the one reasonable individual in the whole bloody place? It has sixty-five staff and I haven't met one apart from your wife who thinks about anything beyond their provincial nose end. Most of my pea-brained colleagues assume I'm learning my Linguaphones so that I can holiday in Costa Brava or the Algarve. When I tell them I wouldn't dream of subsidising tawdry tourism in places run by filthy Fascist despots they all turn extremely pale. They think I'm just mad, it's as simple as that.'

Sometimes looking for cowardly moral mitigation I absolve myself by recalling it was Corrie did all the running. She kept coming back to the bookshop, three or four times a week, always en route to the childminder, usually complaining about Colin her partner, the technician. She claimed he was bone idle both as a lab technician and as a handy man about the house. The late Sixties saw the birth pangs of Women's Liberation but Colin was blithely oblivious to historical challenge. He never washed up nor did any housework, but because he cooked Corrie an elaborate French or Italian meal once a month assured her he was doing his bit. After relieving herself about Colin she would frequently demand recondite authors and American textbooks she must have known I didn't have. Sometimes she would ask me to order them for her, sometimes not. The bookshop was nearly always empty, and as time went by our conversation and the unspoken lexicon of mutual attraction became freer and freer. One time she laughed and said it was all just an excuse to talk to an interesting man with an intelligent mind. The intelligent Cumbrian, she laughed incredulously, displaying sharp, tiny, perfect white teeth. A walking oxymoron. I fluttered and preened myself with an uneasy self-satisfaction. I was uneasy because I have always felt quietly disdainful of all those who take a vocal pride in their brains. Even before listening to Preacher Ken on the subject I had never been all that impressed by cerebral intelligence per se. I have met too many emotionally retarded geniuses whose social skills would embarrass a gorilla. I have known too many very bright people pathologically ashamed of the fact they do not possess a degree.

In that early period I ignored any reservations I might have about Corrie's dogmatic air and her astounding moral certitudes. She was as opinionated and categorical as my mother, and they even resembled each other slightly in some elusive facial feature. For a long time I couldn't put my finger on it. Then one day from a good distance, I saw Ma Singer in her kiosk turning her chin towards a customer in a doubtful scathing question mark. It was Corrie Millon, MA Cantab, to a tee. Contra Freud, I hadn't gone and married my mother, I had philandered with her instead. No wonder that I adored and was wary of Corrie every single day we were together.

By October of that year, two months after Russia had invaded Czechoslovakia, she was coming to the bookshop every single day. Enchanted by our ever more elaborate flirting, the febrile two-edged banter, the excitement so evident in each other's dancing hungry eyes, I was doing nothing to push things in any decisive direction. I wanted it to happen but I was powerless to initiate anything. Perhaps the reckless playfulness and the red-faced infatuation were enough in themselves. Perhaps Corrie divined this petty self-protective attitude was going to keep things at the same frustrating, tantalising level of the erotic charade. One day, looking impatient not to say moderately angry, she bristled her nose to a remarkable degree of dilation. She flared her nostrils like a rampant and fearless young mare. I was almost expecting her to snort and to pad her hooves inside the shop. The expression on her face was so definite, so insistent, I had no choice but to look the other way, deeply embarrassed. Pleased to see that I was ashamed of my cowardice, Corrie faced me straight in the eye and said: 'Well? Well Mr Singer?'

'I...'

I dried up, entirely speechless. Corrie mischievously took my hand and began massaging the palm with her mid-finger. As she did I felt myself melting into a sticky inchoate medium, neither liquid nor solid nor gas. It was pleasurable, exquisite, delicate and tender. For one as pugnacious as Corrie, her touch was very, very gentle.

'That's very lovely,' I said, with a little break in my voice.

'What happens next?' she asked, massaging with greater pressure.

'You –' I whispered.

'Me?' she smiled mock-schoolmaamishly. 'Me what?'

'I don't know.'

She became very stern. 'I've been coming in here five times a week at the same time for three whole weeks. Don't you think that signifies something? What do you think my unspoken intention is? I know I like books a lot but you never have the ones I want. I'm not coming in here for your wares, George.'

I stayed silent and rigid with lust and anxiety. She was squeezing and kissing my hand, and anyone could have blundered in at any second.

'You are silent. What a speechless man you are. Your name is Singer but you don't sing. Normally you do, but not at this moment. You are suddenly as quiet as a mouse. All I want to know is this. Are we going to take it any further?'

I sweated cobs and turned a dark embarrassed red.

'We're both married,' I said hoarsely. 'No, I mean I'm married and you're not. You're married in common law. And we both have a young child.'

'I know all that. It's an accurate resumé and I know all that.'

'I love Sarah,' I said stickily. 'You... do you love Colin?'

She glared at me and didn't bother to answer. She looked down at the floor and then back up at me. Her eyes were asking me the obvious question. If I loved my wife and my young child so much, how come I had encouraged all this feverish, dangerous flirting? No one had forced me to go so far.

'Does Sarah know I come in here to see you every day? Or is it a well-kept secret?'

'Part of me wants to,' I said with a touch of resentment. 'I do want to. I'm itching like something in heat.'

'So I've noticed,' she said pressing my fingers very tightly.

'I've kept the kettle boiling obviously.'

She guffawed loudly, and then touched me in a place where it would have electrified an ascetic monk.

'You sound like a kid describing a game of tig. Or like my Colin talking about a Liebig condenser preparation. You'd better lead us into your storeroom and bolt the door. You're about to boil over if you don't, George.'

Which was precisely what happened. I scrawled a card with green felt pen saying 'Back in Thirty Minutes' and sellotaped it carelessly to the glass. Then in the storeroom for the very first time I took part in what I had only ever seen described in the novels of Henry Miller. All stops out, half-dressed, stand-up copulation accompanied by rhetorical grunts and beseechings and in Corrie's case a series of little shrieks that sounded like a small soprano saxophone. Meanwhile the volatile American was present with us in another sense. As luck would have it Corrie had to shift half a dozen copies of *Tropic of Cancer* which I had just unpacked that morning. In those days the shocking Parisian classic was only purchasable wrapped inside a polythene cover, so that no minor could ferret between its debasing pages. I had intended doing a Miller window display surrounded by appropriately psychedelic LP covers from Cream, Traffic, Chicago and others. Vaguely intending to emphasise that my provincial shopkeeper sympathies lay with youth, rebellion and revolt, I had gone a bit further and instituted some practical revolution in my own life.

I had gone one better and gone one worse. Of course guilt came upon me as soon as we were finished. I seemed to picture

Sarah and Anne watching me in mute horror from the corner of the room. I looked at Corrie patting her hair back into place and shuddered. Never one to dawdle, she swiftly retrieved her crimson knickers and used the comparative form as well.

'That's better,' she declared, still panting.

She was scarlet and sweating. As I thought guiltily of Sarah I wondered why after sex both her and Corrie's faces looked at least thirty years younger. There was the perplexing regression to the unlined beauty of infancy, and in Corrie's case the paradoxical sight of a virginal, tender innocence. I squatted there naked and baffled in my dusty storeroom as I struggled to see any conscience or remorse in her cheerful expression.

'We'll have to meet elsewhere,' she went on in a businesslike tone. 'Perhaps at my house when Colin goes home to see his Mum down in dear old Amersham. He tries to drag me along but I always refuse to go.'

'Oh,' I said, struggling to button my shirt. 'What about Polly?'

She glanced at me sharply as she ferreted with the hook of her bra. 'What about her?

'Where will she be? Will she be at the childminder's?'

'At the weekend? Do me a favour. I do like to see my own daughter now and again.'

'But we can't... with her around.'

'Don't be stupid. Of course we can. She's only three. Three-year-olds know nothing. She doesn't understand what tomorrow means. She doesn't comprehend what yesterday means. She thinks Noddy and Big Ears live somewhere between Allonby and Silloth. She'll be playing peacefully with her Play Dough and watching the Magic Roundabout while you and I are on another roundabout. I'll be busy playing with your playd–'

'I see,' I said drily. I saw the whole fantastic picture in cutaway perspective. Innocence and gullibility on the ground floor and connivance and duplicity on the first. It was as if it were Georges Feydeau or Brian Rix on the Whitehall stage. But of course there wasn't going to be much spirit of bumbling farce in this particular enterprise.

'In a year or two's time my daughter will understand the chronological significance of today, tomorrow and yesterday. She'll comprehend the difference between an ordinary friend and a special secret friend of Mum's. In the meantime, we are as safe as houses. Colin in any case will probably be looking up an old Amersham girlfriend.'

She seemed wholly unanxious and unpiqued at the picture of Colin's possible infidelity. I tried in turn to imagine Sarah being unfaithful and felt a cold bitter wind in my insides. The wind felt icier and even more pervasive as I had another evil thought. From now on, I would have to tell lies to my wife. The minute details of the marriage vows of 1957 came back to me in a mocking whispering recitative, and I all but stopped my ears. I had no experience of hiding things from her and I had no idea how I would set about doing it now. To crown all, the other woman was also her favourite professional colleague. Corrie and Sarah were confidential intimates. Sarah Singer was Corrie Millon's chosen ally, if only because she was the only one ever to read a book outside of school. Even if I were to confess immediately, even if Sarah were to forgive me at once without a fuss, she would have to stare Corrie in the face every day at work. Gentle and resilient as she was, Sarah Singer would become justly angry, deeply resentful at all that unnecessary suffering. Even assuming she tried to muffle all that painful feeling, it would convey itself wordlessly to my little daughter Anne.

I had a second, even less alluring identity. I was now Anne's faithless, adulterous father.

Corrie departed with a hasty kiss and a squeeze. She said that she would ring me at the shop in future, now that the ice was broken. After I'd unlocked the door for her, I removed the taped message and put my favourite 45 on the shop hi-fi. It was a recent number-one hit, *Whiter Shade of Pale* by Procul Harum. I glanced at myself in the lavatory mirror and saw that

I looked pale and bilious with guilt. The sound of the surreal seasick music floated out through the open door. Why did the band call themselves a Latin name that means 'Beyond These Things'? Why the hell would anyone want to be beyond anything? I felt beyond the pale already and already I wished that everything could be reversed.

11

The badge man looked speculatively at his audience. Halfway
through his ruthless exposé, it seemed to strike him that some
of us might have things worth confessing too. As his eyes
swept over me I could have sworn he sensed that I had been
another sexual adventurer. The distinguishing marks are always
there, that hungry, roving, acquisitive look, that lifting of the
ears and twitching of the snout every time a half-passable
woman is scented. He scrutinised us slowly with a genuine pity,
and as I thought of my back-room coupling with Corrie, I felt
something akin to resentment. I might have wrecked my
marriage but at least I'd never been through a pint of Bell's a
day. Nor had I ever bet a penny on a horse or a dog. I found it
quite impossible to identify with such a pointless addiction.
Just one glance through the open door of the local betting shop
was enough to reveal a tableau parody of a Dantesque inferno.
Ten years ago I had won a Christmas goose in a British Legion
raffle and that was the extent of my gambling. Not liking goose
I had given it away to an elderly customer and had never
bought a raffle ticket since.

   Confident that he must have the darkest secrets of anyone
here, Ken surveyed us with a tolerant, generous pity. He had
been talking without a pause for twenty-five minutes and we
were all in a trance. Not even the oldest ones had stirred a
muscle or cleared their congestions. Like a Dissenter or a wild
hedge preacher the badge man looked as if he had enough lung
power to go on for a month.

'So there I was. I'd flitted the nest and the restraining hands of anxious parents, and I was doing exactly what I wanted. Brandy for appetisers in the morning, then off to the garage, then whisky for lunch, then back to the garage, then whisky for supper and brandy for nightcap. I was learning my routine from Muttonchop who could soak it up but still run a successful business. It's amazing how many alcoholics can keep going, can get on famously some of them, until eventually their livers give out. Like him I developed a colossal capacity and could function after a fashion. I would get drunk all right but not in a normal way. There was a terrible lucidity about my drunkenness, a worrying sobriety. I was only a kid after all and part of me was puzzled and frightened by the way I stayed cold and alert with all that alcohol inside me. If no one was around I would do complex jobs on a rich man's Riley with a spanner in one hand and a glass in the other. I started to believe I was superhuman or, if I was in a doubting mood, that perhaps I was just an unearthly freak. Sometimes as if to prove I was only human after all, I would feign the symptoms of drunkenness and deliberately slur my voice and deliberately stagger across a room. People laughed at that, and frequently in the pub they gave a little clap so that I felt pathetically reassured I was amusing rather than tragic. Isn't it a fact that no one wants to be seen as really tragic? They don't mind seeing other folks as desperate, but somehow they like to see their own private mess as having a peculiar redemption.

'Redemption? How to describe hitting rock bottom? It seems sacrilege to relate the sordid details in this little peaceful building, but as it was the owner of this place who dug me up from rock bottom, it is the most fitting place to tell the story. You'll have to think of it in the literal sense and in terms of a literal plummet. It involves a ledge and lasciviousness and a twenty-foot fall. It would be funny if it weren't tragic and, as I say, part of the problem of tragedy is that we try to make light of it instead of looking it in the face. Instead of repenting we turn a blind eye...

'I didn't own my new house, it was only rented and in only a moderate state of repair. Don't imagine it was a seedy slum though. I started off keeping it tidy, and the area of Blackburn was respectable enough. However the avenue it was on, Brinsley Avenue, was a thoroughfare to a gigantic dance hall, one of the biggest in the whole of Lancashire. It would fill up with soldiers on leave and with all the rowdiest teenage lassies who were stuck at home and employed in war work. There were plenty of fights because of all the soldiers and because in wartime especially the fact that you were young and mortal made for an intensely rebellious outlook. Why obey all the rules when your regiment might be decimated in a fortnight or if your Blackburn factory might be bombed next week? I went along to some of these dances when I first moved into Brinsley Avenue, and I soon palled up with the soldiers as a kind of well-off mascot and hysterical entertainer. I threw my money around and gave some of them blackmarket bottles of spirits and invented a mysterious new status for myself. I hinted that my mechanic's job was to do with important warwork, that the big cars and specialist engines I built weren't just for businessmen but for people working at the communications place outside Oldham. I even said I did modification jobs for officers working at strategic sites up in the wilds of Cumberland.

'You remember how outsiders pictured Cumberland fifty years ago? During the war it was full of internment camps for Germans and Italians, and if you were trying to give a picture of something like the Sinkiang Desert, those three syllables – Cum-ber-land – never failed. I had an uncle lived in a farm round the backside of Nenthead, which is the Pennine Himalayas beyond far-flung Alston. In the Forties Uncle Ted didn't even have an outside tap, never mind mains electricity. I waxed lyrical and hinted that when I drove up to see Uncle Ted it was just a cover for work I was doing at the secret ammunition place at Barnard Castle further on. The soldiers were all paralytic on my blackmarket Scotch so no one ever accused me of being a liar. I could talk the robin off a starch box and I had a gob like a torn pocket, to use my mother's two favourite expressions.

'When I first went to the Palais I used to take along a lass called Petty. It was an unusual name, her proper name was Petunia, and her father was a retired stationmaster who'd won prizes for his legendarily beautiful station garden. He was a ferocious old man with an oily slicked-down centre parting and an expensive meerschaum pipe he used to get to draw with an ornamental metal lid. He had retired from his perfect station up at Nelson and in his old age he tried to keep a perfect household. He was what they call strict. Petty was nineteen and he insisted she came in every night at ten o'clock or else. He was over seventy and not very big so he could hardly have thrashed her. But he had a really loud voice and he could terrorise with his temper. It was immaterial to him if there was any audience when he was flaming and screeching...

'I'd been going to the Palais for about a year when I first made a terrible scandal. For six months me and Petty Allbright were going as steady as I was capable of going with anyone. She would hang around the dance until a quarter to ten, then run off home like a panic-stricken Cinderella. Petty laughed a lot, she giggled so much she often got hiccups. She had a terrible fondness for peanut brittle and monkey nuts. She had jet-black hair and big wide eyes that were beautiful but always looked stunned. It was as if spending nearly twenty years in the company of her Dad, Wilkie Allbright, had left her permanently amazed. Sometimes I walked her halfway home, sometimes I set her off with a girlfriend. Other times leaving the Palais, I told her I was going home myself but then dawdled outside and sneaked back into the dance to find a replacement for Petty.

'This night I disgraced myself she had tried to go home at the usual time. But I was in a mean argumentative mood and I grabbed hold of her arm on the dance floor and told her to blazes with her crazy old Dad. She was to stay to midnight, like a real Cinderella, and I would escort her home, and if he took his hand to her he would have me to deal with. Petty was visibly impressed as well as horrified and she struggled half-heartedly to get away. It was obviously going to be tiring for me to keep hold of her arm for the next couple of hours, so then I did a terrible thing. I got a soldier pal Frank to get her her usual lemonade but to spike it with rough gin, a double. Petunia wasn't used to spirits of any kind and by a quarter past ten, after another lemonade, she was buckling at the legs, her eyes were all over the place and she was laughing very shrilly at nothing. And of course she had her hiccups. I tested her and said you don't care about your mad old father now, do you, and she hiccupped and blasphemed and said she couldn't care a bee. She sneered that he was old enough to be her grandad since he was well over fifty when she was born. She also said that he liked to compare this war very unfavourably with the Siege of Mafeking and thought that all the young men, including me Kenny Wright, were effeminate.

'Effeminate? That was the worst possible insult fifty years ago. I laughed as hard as Petty but inside I was boiling with rage. I couldn't wait till midnight when I planned to fling that slander in his face on his doorstep. But I didn't have to wait that long. It had got to eleven when suddenly a quite incredible apparition manifested itself before us all. It was like something off a Victorian carnival float. It looked so fantastically out of place in a modern dance hall like this one. Almost all the men, soldiers included, were dressed very smartly and fashionably, carefully in tune with the times. Lots of imitation Yanks: crew cuts, neckshaves, quiffs, gallons of gel. Here strolls in someone in his seventies who last toffed up for an outing in 1888. Instead of a quiff and a fifty-bob suit he's pint-size, wizened and shrivelled to the bone. He has his coarse moleskin trousers tucked inside his knitted fisherman socks. The moleskins are furrowed and bulged up with rusty old bike clips. This grotesque midget has a flat cap rammed so tight on his skull his tiny ears poke out like flags. He's wearing an ugly old station-master's raincoat buttoned up to his quivering nose end. To complete the charming portrait he's carrying his bike-pump, with the valve and tube dangling out of it, and he's waggling this dancing little snake like he means business. He's seventy years old and a touch rheumaticky yet he strides through all these young ones like they're so much chaff he's about to stamp under foot with his boots.

'Frank the drink-spiker saw him first, guessed who he was, and stuck his foot out to trip him up. To everyone's hilarity Petty's father spotted the squaddie's great boot and stamped on it as hard as he could. Frank roared out with terrible tears in his eyes and wanted to thump this brutal dwarf, but drunk as they were the soldiers wouldn't permit it. They felt protective towards a peculiar old man who looked a bit like their Dads, even if they didn't mind jeering at his idiotic appearance. Wilkie the prizewinning stationmaster bowled straight towards me and his errant young daughter. He shoved all the slewed couples to one side with complete contempt. He dug great big men viciously in the back. He poked hefty lassies out of the way with his knee in their backsides. He butted soldiers with the crown of his head, looking just like a little pixie in a rugby scrum. He cleared himself a decent space and squared up to me with the most quivering, threatening mouth I'd ever seen. He wasn't much more than five foot but he put the fear of God up me. He might have been an angry old dwarf, but he was also an outraged father who'd gleaned something of my nasty reputation. He lifted up his bike-pump and I thought he was going to bring the little tube down upon me like a miller's flail.

'I flinched, I suppose. At that he sneered, and said I wasn't worth being brought up for. Not that they would ever have jailed a seventy-year-old for protecting his young daughter from a youthful lush. He turned round to Petunia who was still hiccupping and ordered her to get up and follow him outside. Amazingly he pulled two old bungee straps out of his gaberdine and told her he was going to use them to strap her onto the crossbar of his bike. It was as if he was a Christmas postman and she was a heavy outsize parcel. She was so tight, he said disgustedly, she would fall off if he didn't tether her on. Petunia giggled and squawked another hiccup and struggled to her feet. You could smell the gin off her as if she was a distillery.

'"Tyke! Runt! Trollop!" he bawled at her, incensed.

'Wilkie promised she'd get a first-class hiding when he got her home, and if she didn't hurry herself she would get it on the spot. Petty kept on laughing impudently, she was so marvellously drunk. True to his word the disciplinarian took a few nasty swipes at the back of her legs with his bike-pump. They must have stung like hell with the metal valve bit because Petunia began to shout and roar blue murder. All the soldiers guffawed helplessly, overpowered by hectic mirth. In between the terrible swipes he told her there'd be no more courting with derelicts and jailbirds like Mr Kenny Wright.

'His cruelty as well as those sneering insults had me demented. I grabbed hold of Wilkie Allbright by the back of his neck and roared at him: "Come here you ugly little Rumpelstiltskin. It's time you were properly taped, you disgusting little Hitler."

'I paused to assure all the soldiers that I wasn't going to hurt him. But I wasn't going to let anyone, not even her father, beat my little Petty like that. I asked them to step back a few paces and clear a path towards the door. He was wriggling like a fish on the end of my fists and for want of any weapon was flailing around with his ridiculous bike-pump. Wilkie was trying to turn it through 180 degrees to batter me with it, you see. Of course it all looked painfully farcical and the entire dance hall was in helpless stitches. Even Petunia joined in the laughter, once she'd finished rubbing the backs of her nylons. As soon as a convenient tunnel was cleared, I primed myself like an athlete, took a massive breath and set off to give the old man a bum's rush towards the exit. Frank was there at the end of the gangway, grinning hugely and holding the doors wide open. I galloped at great speed up the tunnel, with everyone cheering wildly and the old chap's legs accelerating to a terrific speed. Frank stood sentinel at the exit, pulling a hideous face like a leering elephant and pretending to block the road. Then he danced and cavorted to the side and pretended to stick his foot out again. It was all drunken horseplay, of course, and nobody under the age of sixty would have been seriously alarmed. But Wilkie was seventy-two and had weak eyesight and perhaps he thought Frank's fooling was for real. Powerless in my grasp he was worried he would end up colliding with Frank, trip over him at forty miles an hour, and break his skinny little neck.

'Suddenly the farce turned into nightmare. I froze as Frank turned horribly white and came running the length of the tunnel. He was bawling *Stop! Stop!* and frantically waving his arms. *He's deed, he's deed,* he shouted…'

The badge man paused and there at TFEOTNQ there was an awful silence. Perhaps, I shuddered, our extraordinary silver-haired preacher was just a reformed killer after all…

'I stopped in mid-rush…'

Once more he carefully contemplated his fellow transgressors and smiled on us with pity.

'I turned the old man round and saw that his face had gone blue. Where it wasn't blue it was ashen grey. Frank the soldier had sobered up as if by magic. He got down quickly and listened to Wilkie's heart through all that dirty gaberdine. Then he shouted across terrified to Petty Allbright who was also stone sober by now.

'"It's makin neah noise, Petunia. Thee father's heart's stopt goin."

'She came up to Frank whimpering and gibbering. He patted her gently and started gibbering himself. She knelt over her Dad, shaking with hysterical panic. I stood there completely stupid and completely helpless. Of course I hadn't the faintest clue about First Aid. I didn't know how to give artificial respiration. I'd never even heard of the kiss of life. I was feeling down to my depths this great chill of stupidity, of abysmal irresponsibility. I wanted Petunia Allbright to turn on me and rail at me. But instead of that she just began crying and grieving over the corpse of her Dad. It sounded all the more hellish because she also started hiccupping between the sobs. Frank took Wilkie's dirty cap off and put it under his tiny lifeless head. He loosened the old man's crumpled gaberdine and his shirt and tie. The manager, who was called Monty Pasco, came racing up terrified. Pasco looked at me as if he wanted to murder me on the spot. Then he ran back and telephoned for an ambulance. I suddenly envisaged being hanged by the neck until I was dead. I muttered as much to another soldier, Dick Savage, who'd sauntered up drunkenly behind me. He gawped at me as if I were a childish halfwit. Manslaughter, man, he grunted. Witnesses, hundreds of them, who heard you say you didn't mean to harm him. He hadn't sobered up at all and it was as if he was talking about a theoretical point of law. Savage wasn't upset one iota. Meanwhile Wilkie still wasn't breathing and the bungee straps were still clutched there in his hands like a pair of Morris dancing ribbons. Petty tried to prize them out of his fingers, the things that would have strapped her onto the crossbar. But the ridiculous things wouldn't come loose. That must be rigor mortis, I thought to myself, in a leaden sort of uncomprehending stupor.

'After about twenty minutes an ambulance and a solitary policeman arrived. The policeman was only about thirty and he even looked sorry for me as he led me off to Pasco's office. But just as his hand touched my shoulder there was a squeaky unearthly little whimper came from Wilkie's deathly corpse. The corpse had started to groan and whimper and everyone jumped out of their skins. Frank went on bravely massaging away at his chest, hell for leather. He'd been rubbing away for what seemed hours and he was panting and gasping like an athlete with the massive effort.

'"You might not have copped it after all," said the policeman. "Him down there maybe hasn't copped it either."

'Monty Pasco looked at him angrily. "He's banned from this place whatever the outcome. Whatever happens this piece of scum'll never set foot in the Palais again."

'I spent over three hours in the police station being questioned about myself and the soldiers and the exact amount of drink we'd consumed. The police were visibly impressed to hear about my good job involving motor cars. The detective who grilled me was an important local Freemason. One of his fellow Masons was a builder whose Bentley I was busy on at the time. He rang the hospital for me twice, and the second time I almost embraced him with tearful gratitude. Wilkie was barely conscious but he was managing to make intelligible replies to their questions. He was still very poorly but he didn't seem to be getting any worse. It was more or less certain that he'd had a heart attack in the Palais, but he'd already had three heart attacks in the last ten years. The detective dithered and frowned for a long time, then decided to let me go home after he'd scribbled something down. He said if Wilkie's family were to press charges, he would have to see me again. He advised me to court my women quietly inside my house, not among drink-crazed soldiers and Blackburn wideboys. I was a highly skilled young man, a mechanic in a million by the sounds of it. I shouldn't be wasting my God-given talents.

'That had an obvious biblical ring about it. The phrase stuck in my head, as biblical phrases usually do. Though I soon got rid of it with drink. Two days later I hung about Petty's insurance office, the place where she was a junior receptionist. She came out in a rush at five o'clock but refused to stop and talk. She said her Dad was still very sick but was likely to make a partial recovery. He would possibly be let out of hospital tomorrow but would have to stay in bed for at least the next six weeks. I invited her to my house that night, but she said she'd promised him she'd have nothing more to do with me. It had looked as if he was lying on his death bed, so she'd made a promise, a vow. I said it wasn't his death bed now so the vow didn't count, but she said a vow was a vow was a vow. Also Frank last night had told her about my charming habit of sneaking back to the Palais and dancing the night away with a variety of other women. Then calmly strutting off with them down Brinsley Avenue in the wicked small hours...

'So I took to staying at home every night and damning the lot of them. I was grieved with Petunia and even more enraged with Frank for informing on me. Before long I saw the pair of them arm in arm and I was told that Frank was spending his spare time weeding and raking invalid Wilkie's garden. Frank was a big colossus of a corporal so I could hardly challenge him to a duel. I thought seriously about lying in wait down some dark side-street and getting my revenge. Then I had a vivid picture of how gangs of soldiers exact their vengeance on civvies and I changed my mind. I didn't want to be a blind or broken cripple for the rest of my days. Even though I nearly succeeded.

'I should have been properly chastened, eternally grateful for the fact I hadn't killed a man. If things had gone otherwise, I could easily have been banged up for manslaughter for the next ten years. But instead of counting my blessings I decided to become a pathetic and self-pitying recluse. It was a long, very warm summer that year, and this aided the process of my incubation. It was roasting in the early evenings and especially up there on the top floor of my house. What I used to do was sit all alone sweating in my singlet vest and feel very very sorry for myself. The big double bedroom I spent my time in faced out onto Brinsley Avenue. What I liked best of all was to open both windows wide and gaze down like a disdainful, wounded monarch on the road below. With a glass in my hand, many a sweltering evening I would sit there at the window, gawking down as if I were a victorious general inspecting his serried ranks. I had a fine new Bush wireless and I liked to listen to dance-band music. Joe Loss, Cyril Stapleton, Victor Sylvester, all nice and deafening for the benefit of the whole street. Sometimes I had angry complaints from some of the more assertive neighbours but as they were all elderly couples I paid nil attention whatsoever. Quite the opposite in fact.

'Because I was an electronics whizz I eventually managed to rig up a pair of old-fashioned amplifiers. It was only 1943 but I had succeeded in having a primitive stereophonic system attached to my wireless. It was preposterous what I did, but I lugged those speakers onto the ends of my two window ledges and gave a free concert to anyone walking past. In a way I was competing with the Palais though it didn't actually occur to me then. If it was men or soldiers down below on their way to the dance I gave a respectful *how are you, how's tricks?* It was my mascot-buffoon performance again. If it was girls parading by on their own, I would whistle and shout at them and sometimes far worse. I was so sunk in the mire, I sometimes regaled them with the most revolting lewdness, ugly suggestive comments about their bodies and their underwear. Most of them blushed or scowled and hurried away, but one or two of them replied in kind. The worst ones stood there brazenly bantering with me. Me up above perched and swaying like degradation itself, and them down below cackling and hooting away. I would invite the hardest cases upstairs to my bedroom, and usually of course they came. In effect I was operating a one-man bordello...

'Incredible as it seems, this went on for about two months. It's a miracle I wasn't arrested for procurement or at the very least for being a public nuisance. You'd have thought the fathers of some of the lassies I shouted at might have come round and hauled me out of the house and given me a public hammering. But like many a flagrant and shameless crook I got away with murder. In the end the licentiousness only ceased because of my ridiculous recklessness.

'It got so intolerably hot that August I put more than my amplifiers out there. I decided to perch myself out on those ledges as well. It was so incredibly baking I finally placed a cushion and a blanket on one of the sills and sprawled myself the length of the window. I had my whisky glass to hand, of course, and the radio blaring at either end. I had a lurid Yankee detective novel on my naked hairy chest and a hungry eye cocked for the female talent below. Given the narrowness of the window ledge, I was extremely careless each time I turned over to make myself comfortable. Likewise I was ludicrously blasé every time I craned forward to shout my filthy remarks to the young women. I ought to have gone plummeting out of my eagle's nest over a dozen times at least...

'But it was the masonry that undid me. The house was over a hundred years old and all the plastering and the roof flashing were in a very sorry state. The landlord, a Mr Bone, ought to have done something about it, but of course they didn't have the housing laws then they do now. And as Mr Bone remarked to me later, those crumbly old window ledges weren't really meant to have grown men using them as aerial sunbeds.

'One night I was having a very suggestive conversation with a tartish blond lass called Flossie, all about the overwhelming abundance of her sideways silhouette. Suddenly Flossie put her hands up to her mouth and shouted out in terror: "Tha's slipping. Tha's going. Ooh my dear God!"

'She didn't mean it metaphorically. The ledge I was on had finally cracked and sheared off clean. It all happened in about half a second, just like in a waking dream. If I'd been sober I might just have had the sense to vault backwards inside and let the ledge go down without a passenger. But because I was addled I went flying with it. I plummeted about twenty feet, though ironically I was half-anaesthetised by all that alcohol inside me. Then everything went as black as hell. Only the lass's terrified scream came piercing through my darkness.'

*

'I came to in hospital feeling as if I'd been run over by a fleet of steamrollers. I was cased in plaster like an Egyptian mummy. Both my legs were broken, as was my left arm. Three of my ribs were smashed in. It was a fluke I hadn't broken my back as well. All that drink inside me had made me loose and floppy enough to land in the most auspicious, least damaging heap. The nurses looked at me very disgustedly. One of them was a cousin of Petunia's, and she not only knew about my habit of catcalling to the street, she also knew about Uncle Wilkie's heart attack. They all looked at me as if I was dirt. I couldn't wait to be out of the place because immobile in the plaster I had nowhere to hide from myself and my nature. I was desperate for a drink and I even tried bribing a nurse, but she flung the five half-crowns on the bedside table and said I needed to give myself a very hard look in the face.

'I looked in the locker mirror and all I could see was a good-looking young man with an unusual disfigurement. I had been in a serious accident but it wasn't that had disfigured me. The red blotches, the cyanosed vessels all over my face, had come about through the whisky. One day a specialist came and did some blood tests. A few days later he came back shaking his head and said if I kept on drinking the amount of Bell's I'd been putting away I would certainly kill myself within a year. Petty's cousin was there when he told me and I saw her start a little at his old-fashioned candour. I disgusted her of course, but she and I were about the same age, early twenties, and for me to have a death sentence was the same as imagining her own.

'It would be nice to say that the specialist's words shook me out of my death wish, and they did for the best part of a day. Then the next day and the day after, all I could think about was getting my hands on a drink. I tried bribing a cleaner but she ran off when I got insistent and reported me to the specialist. I couldn't understand why Muttonchop hadn't come to visit me because the first thing I'd done was get a message to him about the fall. I knew why my parents and George didn't visit, because my behaviour by now was the talk of Blackburn. Nearly killed a frail old stationmaster after spiking his daughter's drink, then nearly killed himself, drunk and falling out of a window. Shouting filth out of windows until he was a laughing stock. Taking tarts up to his room until no one knew if he was a professional pimp or not. Best to give our Kenny a wide berth. I had a note from my mother saying if I stopped drinking and mended my ways she would keep in touch, but that my dad refused to see me again under any circumstances. If I were to start singing and collecting for the Salvation Army tomorrow it would make no difference to him. As for brother George, Dad's favourite, I guessed he thought it was my just deserts. He was a pit manager and so exempt from war service like me. He was starting to move in rich men's circles and the last thing he wanted was any tarnishing association with a scandalous drunk.

'Eventually I got an illiterate, almost comic sort of note from Muttonchop saying he didn't want me back at the garage. He couldn't even spell 'garage' right and he'd been running one for thirty years. He said I might be an unreplaceable mechanic but I was a professional liability with my behaviour. 'Liability' was spelt 'l-i-a-r-b-i-l-l-y-t-e-a'. One or two of his clients had cancelled jobs when they learnt it was me was working on their Jags and Rollses. He didn't mind me liking a drink but it was obvious that at twenty-three I couldn't hold it like my boss could. That gave me pause for thought. I knew that I couldn't buy whisky if I didn't have a job. Once I was out of hospital and had got shot of the crutches, I made a considerable effort and managed to get myself a position as a humble park attendant. It involved running the ticket shed for the clock golf and the putting golf, and lending out deck chairs and sweeping the bandstand. In the winter there was cutting the grass and tidying the shrubs and borders. The money was poor, it was barely enough to let me bet on the horses. I even enjoyed the loneliness of the job and the fact you were mostly left to your own devices. I wasn't the genius I used to be as a gambler, simply because I didn't have the same amount to bet. Now that I was putting down two bob instead of two guineas, it was as if the horses didn't respect me any more. I felt feeble with the smallness of my stakes and that translated into a nervous insecurity when it came to judging the form. I lost my absolute confidence, my big-headed certainty. I saw that I was flawed and that my impregnable skill was no longer impregnable at all. Success at gambling only comes through risk-taking and high-wire walking, through bravado and Humphrey Bogart swagger. Once you're poor you might be as addicted as ever, but your risks are pitiful and your tightrope is only two feet off the ground. No one's fooled. The bookies and the other punters see you now in your shorn glory. You're no longer wearing good suits but traipsing about in scuffed shirts and raggy ties. You're not smoking black-market Players but those terrible Turkish things, Pashas, they always reckoned were made out of camel's dung. You're not buying rounds any more, and if you play the comedian and the rowdy it all looks laughably empty when you can't back it up with any money.

'The drinking got worse. I'd been told to stop or I'd be dead before I was twenty-four. I tried, believe me, I tried. But no matter how hard I tried I couldn't stop. Sometimes in fits of lucidity, sometimes in my dreams, I'd realise I was heading for an awful darkness, a perpetual night. When I realised that I couldn't break the addiction, I got really angry at everyone under the sun. I decided one night I would speed up the process. I stopped blaming myself, I blamed the heartless rotten world instead. By now I couldn't afford a bottle of Bell's. I was busy rotting my insides with the roughest gin and navy rum, the kind of poisonous muck that tastes like industrial cleaner.

'Often after work I would stagger home up the steep hill to my house not knowing who I was or what I was. I kept thinking, *I'm not going to exist this time next year.* Once or twice despite myself I started to break down and have a weep. I would go behind a tree or a postbox to hide myself from the loveless world. Even blind drunk I was ashamed of being a grown man found in tears. Once someone, an old woman, found me sniffling and tried to comfort me. She asked me gently if I needed help, but I swore at her and ran off up the hill.

'I'd reached a total degradation, there was nowhere lower to go. I still had my job and my house but the house by now was like a festering midden. I never cleaned it. I never washed my dirty dishes from one month to the next. My pitiful park job was meant for an invalid or a pensioner, not an intelligent young man. I had no friends left now that I had no money to spend on them. One Saturday morning in the middle of Blackburn I bumped into Muttonchop Giddings, and give him his due he hesitated. He didn't reject me immediately. He almost spoke, he thought about holding out his hand, as you would to a long-lost friend. Then with his expert connoisseur's nose he smelt the kind of stuff I was drinking, and he shuddered and smiled at me terrified. Before I could open my mouth he'd shoved a pound note in my hand and raced off up the street. As he ran he shouted in a worried but disgusted voice: "Get thisel summat decent down thee neck!"

'I still had the capacity to feel humiliation. I had a brief fantasy of hurrying after him and ramming the quid down his neck. But I soon shrugged my shoulders and changed my plan. I would take his connoisseur's advice and get myself a proper drink. Uplifted yet horrified, I trudged off up the hill to a late-hours off-license. I knew the road so well I closed my eyes as I staggered along. As I stumbled my way there, I seemed to slip into a walking trance. Or was it a memory or something like – what shall I say? – a prophetic daydream?

'In my waking dream I found myself wandering around a strange seaport. I was feeling anxious and lonely and in need of simple human company. I was looking here, there and every-where for a friendly stranger. Suddenly, for no clear reason, I left the top of the town and began to walk down some very steep steps. Below lay a harbour area, a bit like the place where we find ourselves now. Down by that quay I could see it was pitch dark, blacker than any normal night. It was truly appalling, that infernal harbour darkness. The steps were impossibly, frighteningly steep, and I was the only one going down them. Down and down and down I walked, propelled by an irresistible force. The horror of my situation was precisely this. I was the only person in this town who was making this terrible descent. Yet coming the other way up the steep incline I could see two striking-looking characters. Both of them were in a somnambulistic trance. There was a shy young woman and a shy old woman who were moving up towards the light above. How I envied them, the fact they were going away from the darkness! Whereas I had no option but to keep on penetrating this dreadful depth. It was like going down a pitch-black pit shaft. But without benefit of a pit cage, lamp or railing, or anything as banal and reassuring.

'Then through my trance I heard something miraculous. I heard some voices singing. Faint at first, then clearer and clearer, I heard a chorus of people singing. It wasn't just any old singing. It was a hymn. For a second or two I thought I must be dead and these ghostly folk were singing at my funeral. Then I almost wept as I realised there might well be nobody at my imminent burial. I was going to die of alcohol poisoning in the next few months, and no one would be singing for me. But the hymn singing carried on very tender, very clear, as if it were struggling up towards the daylight and away from the depths. I felt as if it was carrying me up on a clear wave of tenderness towards the comforting light. It was lifting me up like the silent young woman and the silent old woman. Up those terrible harbour steps and into the bright white light.

'I shuddered when I opened my eyes. I was still drunk but I knew that I was nowhere near any harbour. I was in the middle of dirty old Blackburn and I was passing an old redbrick church. I'd passed this same church umpteen times every day, but there had never been any people inside. Tonight for some reason there was a midweek service...

'Doubtless you think I'm going to say I ran inside and threw myself upon the startled churchgoers. It wasn't as simple as that. It came to that in the end but not on that evening. All that happened was I stood there outside that rather ugly Victorian church feeling completely alone, utterly broken, yet somehow utterly still. I felt stilled by the sound of that old-fashioned hymn. The stillness wasn't at all painless or serene. I felt there was a mysterious peace inside that holy place. I was stuck agonisingly on its outside but everyone inside it was experiencing its special holiness. Mine was hardly the peace that passes understanding. But it signified, however weakly, a feeling of connection. I felt joined to something as a baby might be joined to its mother by the navel. Though I didn't know what the something was. And I certainly didn't conceive of it in maternal terms. The music wafted through the church door. The electric lights through the stained-glass windows seemed faint but gentle and... enduring. Meek, steadfast, not assertive. Not proud, not... overbearing. I was still drunk and still tearful. I felt such pity for myself. There was the painful fact that I was on the outside and they were on the inside. I didn't just think of the invisible congregation. It applied to the whole of Blackburn, the whole of the world. I was the only one going downhill in this life. Everyone else was striding firmly uphill.

'I staggered away from that gentle singing. Religiously, you might say, I called in at the off-license for the Bell's. It was the publican's daughter served me, a polite good-looking girl of about seventeen. She smiled but she looked very uneasy. She was harrowed by the sight of my boozer's shakes and my purple face. I tried to say thanks as she gave me the change, but the words wouldn't come. Instead I just grunted, like a pig or a dog. She looked very embarrassed. I thought, if I stay here much longer she'll ask me am I feeling ill, do I need to see a doctor? I hurried out feeling the most hideous creature alive. I was the ugliest insect that had ever existed. I felt myself crawling with vermin like a beast with fleas or like a cow tormented with ticks or scabs.

'When I got home I kicked on the door as if demanding to be let in. It was madness because I lived on my own, yet there seemed to be some meaning to it. I fumbled for my key and pushed the door open. Then, great calamity! I tripped over a couple of milk bottles and flew forward onto my face. The bottle of Bell's shot out of my hand, sailed ten feet and smashed on the stone flags in the hallway. I moaned at the sight of it spilling all over the floor. I tried to raise myself to get in there among the shards of glass and lap it all up regardless. I couldn't lift myself unfortunately. I felt weak as an invalid after my dream and my limbs just refused to function.

'But as I lay there weeping an incredible thing happened.

The faintest sound of the singing returned. I don't know where it came from. Was it inside me or outside me? I was a mile from the church by now, of course. There was this torment of a connection that wasn't a connection. Instead it was a faint life-line to a source, to an imagined parent, to a font of life. I saw myself down on the dirty floor, twenty-three, completely finished. Sprawled in my own saliva, my face purple with burst vessels, my liver and stomach diseased. How could I hope to connect with anything? How could I hope to be cared for, much less loved, by anyone in the whole world?

'Until it finally happened. And then he came. In the pit of that darkness a little pinprick of light seemed to hesitate. I saw the memory of the church window. But the light there was yellow, and this light inside my head was purest white. The whiteness started to grow. Like a swelling patch of water or an ink blot, it began to grow and spread inside me.

'"Help me," I begged him. "I don't want to die like this."

'The light grew brighter until it shone inside me like a burning jewel. It spread outside my aching head and through my neck, my breast, my legs, my whole being. While it shone I had the maddest but the truest realisation. I had only received the light because I had descended into the darkness first! The precondition of this reassuring light was my initial descent into the abyss.

'I was lying there safe with him, though I didn't know it at the time. I felt miraculously safe and still for the first time in my twenty-three years. I was as still as eternity. I was full of something best described as radiance. I was full of brilliant light and I knew for a certainty that all my blackness had been purged.

'There's another way of putting it. Unfortunately for those who don't believe, it's very difficult to comprehend. A believer understands but an unbeliever can never understand. That's called a solipsistic argument, but you could call it a didgeridoo and it wouldn't help an unbeliever. An unbeliever tries to grasp it with his brain, while a believer grasps it entire with his heart.

An unbeliever doesn't even know what a heart is. A believer knows that a heart is a spiritual, not a fleshly, organ. An unbeliever scoffs. Never the two shall meet, it seems. Unless of course he intercedes and then a miracle happens. As it did with me that night.

'What had happened to me? What do you think? What do *you* think?'

Suddenly the badge man seemed to be staring me, George Singer, very hard in the face. I flushed and fidgeted and tried to hide myself behind Briers.

'I was down in the deepest blackest pit. So how did he, the owner of this special building on the North Quay, how did he manage to lift me out of it? You'll need to listen hard to the answer. I believe it's the most important thing you will ever need to know and might ever wish to communicate to the hosts of the unbelievers.

'He didn't reach out his omnipotent arm to pull me out of the pit. He could have done so if he'd wanted. But he didn't. He can do anything he likes, of course. The depth of the deepest pit cannot frighten someone like him.

'He didn't reach in with a stick or a net. He didn't urge me to grab hold or to leap inside like a goldfish. He didn't hook me out and throw me down safe on dry land. He could have done all that if he'd wanted to. But he didn't resort to any of that.

'This is what he did. He observed Kenny Wright spreadeagled at the bottom of a very dark abyss. He saw him lying helpless at the bottom of a very dark set of steps. The steps leading to a harbour that wasn't a safe haven but an inferno. He could have stood up at the top in his sovereign safety. He could have shouted down to me, "Listen to my voice and get walking! Come up this way. Come on."

'Equally he could have tossed me a lifeline, a piece of rope. With all the ease in the world he could have hauled me up into the welcoming light.

'But he didn't...

'*Instead he leapt into the pit himself.* He descended into the depths of the darkness with me. Unafraid, omnipotent, divine, he went down there beside me, drunken Kenny, who was oh so finite and fearful. Down those terrible, those oh so awful harbour steps. That had no protective railing or any other kind of safety…

'*As he did the light broke brilliantly across the harbour…*

'It was dawn by then. The light had arrived. A little white sliver split the sky. A bright white radiance was soon covering all the dockside. Now, of course, the harbour was transformed. It was full of painted ships and human bustle and the sight of people working…

12

Corrie sent me regular love letters that thrilled me to the bone. They were not posted to my house of course, but to the shop, and as infallible identification she typed in red on the envelope, G. Singer, Prop. BETTABUX. 'Bettabux', it occurred to us, had an alternative lurid translation in line with the way local youngsters talked about sex. That tickled Corrie and pricked at my guilt each time I opened them. The notepaper was scented ever so delicately. She used an elegant cursive hand without a tremor or a hesitation in any stroke. Each letter was six pages long and invariably an impassioned meditation on the addictive intensity of our affair. They were not explicitly erotic but chaste, abstracted accounts of the unique depth of her feeling. She would write, *I think about you and your hopeless shop and the way you stand puzzled sentry behind your counter, all those hours I'm not with you. Sometimes I deliberately try to picture you as ordinary and unalluring as I can, so as not to torment myself with impatience. I'm so desperate to be there beside you on weekday afternoons, listening to the new rock singles and sniffing the damp pages of those secondhand classics. Apart from working away at my language records, I'm living for nothing but those few little hours that we spend together.*

The time we had together was one weekend a month, when Colin drove down to see his mother. I spent a couple of hours with her on the Saturday evening and most of Sunday, and had to think hard each time when fabricating excuses to Sarah. As I'd started to sell a few secondhand books in Bettabux, I claimed to be attending auctions and bookfairs in conveniently distant towns: Appleby, Brampton, Haltwhistle, Hexham. Once or twice I really did go to these events as a preliminary to the real business back at Corrie's house. On the second occasion I forgot what I was doing and ended up bidding for expensive first editions for my own private reading. To my surprise I found I was not so much a consummate liar as a natural actor. I believed my own inventions to Sarah simply by flexing my imagination. My lies were so fluent and sincere that they must in some sense be an authentic form of the truth.

Perhaps, unremarkably, this was how Corrie functioned herself. Unlike me she was untouched by guilt. There was something in the business of sexual deception she found ineffably comic. She found a relishable playfulness in telling her flagrant lies to Colin. She enjoyed a mischievous liberation at hoodwinking someone she thought should put more backbone into their partnership. He was unromantic in that he showed insufficient gratitude for having an old-fashioned Romantic on his hands. Corrie burned with the Sixties spirit of promiscuous upheaval, but she was also devout, almost pious, in the confessional simplicity of her letters. She made uncompromising reference to binding love, binding passion, binding devotion. It read like a spiritual lexicon and her terms all seemed to be written in heartfelt capitals as well as in blood.

What finally undid things was the sight of a child unaware she was being observed. Sufficient trails were left by both of us for an easy detection, but for different reasons Colin and Sarah chose not to take the scent. Her partner, as Corrie liked to point out, was a willing dupe. For a lethargic man like Colin the act of being deceived, the condition of being made a fool of, suited some part of his general abasement. In the old days, she added, in Ben Jonson's day, when they were obsessed with infidelity and damaged honour, there was a special term for it. If you were a man who desired to be deceived you were called a 'wittol'. Colin then was an example of a Home Counties 1968 wittol. Sarah meanwhile knew all along there was something malign in the air. Common sense told her there was an unpleasant three-act drama unfolding somewhere close to home. I was a husband of predictable habits, after all. For a full decade without variation I had spent every Sunday morning reading the *New Statesman* and playing my Dizzy Gillespie records. Suddenly a man who hated driving further than Carlisle was on the road every Sunday to Hexham, Newcastle and further afield. Where once I was an easy and accommodating husband I now seemed brittle and irritable. I made an excessive fuss of Anne every night and went to ridiculous lengths to spoil her. At her imperious request I would get down on the mat and crayon with her, even though Sarah was exhausted and wanted her tucked up in bed. I brought her a little present home not just every day but every time I went in between house and shops. On a good day she might get as many as six little dollies or card games or pencil sets. I looked at her anxiously as we made snakes out of plasticine or when I allowed her to cheat uproariously at Animal Pairs. As I hugged Anne I felt my deceitfulness like some pernicious lethal fungus. I was her father who was doing things I should not be doing. Sarah glanced up from her marking and tried to be touched by all this adoration and intent scrutiny of my daughter. I was looking at Anne to see if she was somehow picking up the echoes of the lie, its inaudible signature tune. After all if her mother sensed something was wrong, perhaps a sensitive four-year-old had guessed it all from the start. I wondered if she really was more peevish and fretful than usual. When Sarah finally dragged her to bed Anne reached out babyishly to me and went into the sorrowing whine of a two-year-old. At once I held out my guilty arms in response.

'Oh,' I said tenderly.

'No you don't,' said Sarah sharply to both of us. 'It's half past nine, and I'm taking her upstairs.'

'Do you think she's OK?' I said in a woeful voice.

She frowned at my pitifully maudlin tone. 'Of course she is. She's a thriving little girl. Why on earth do you want to treat her as if she's so fragile?'

'I... I feel protective.'

'Really? Protective against what?'

'I don't know,' I said blushing.

'I wouldn't mind some protection,' Sarah said flatly. 'I feel vulnerable at the moment though I can't articulate the cause. Perhaps I'm just worn out of a Sunday night. I don't feel particularly happy though I don't really know why it is...'

That was a timely confession, a prod for me to do the same thing. I shook myself into vigilance and opted for a brisk evasiveness. I said I would get Anne off to sleep while she got on with her marking.

One sunny November morning I drove round to Corrie's where I was grabbed by the lapels on the doorstep. After a month's abstinence, she was impatient to get me upstairs. Polly, who normally greeted me at the door, was nowhere to be seen. She was through in the parlour, her mother explained, watching an ancient repeat of *Watch with Mother*. While the two of us made love above the three-year-old's head, not only was Corrie uninhibitedly vocal, she also insisted on moving in and out of the bed and clumping about like a clog dancer. The name of the programme blaring below, the solace for the innocent, was painfully ironical. Mother wasn't there watching and Colin was down with grandmother in Amersham.

An hour later I stood at the parlour door and watched Polly in front of the old black-and-white screen. Disdaining the facile mediocrity of television Corrie Millon reluctantly possessed the only twelve-inch Ekco left in Cumberland. Polly was drinking in the gentle adventures of Rag, Tag and Bobtail, a badger, a dormouse and a rabbit. They were cumbersome, antiquated little puppets and their amorphous woodland setting looked as if designed by a twelve-year-old. The public school narrator's voice was kind but effortful. And yet I found the clumsy little Fifties film painfully moving. Despite the thinness of the means it had a storyline that stirred the poignant depths. They seemed such feckless, delicate things, those clumping little puppets. The badger and the rabbit and the dormouse were the epitome of all vulnerable forest creatures, those without any human protector. Little Polly was thankfully unaware that in real life badgers and rabbits were often hunted and mauled by men and dogs. The child was the very spit of her mother with her wide eyes and prominent jaw. It must have been her teenage father who had given her that sleepy gentleness and calm passivity. Her fine brown hair was tied up with a butterfly slide. Her face was serene, remote, perhaps gipsyish. She seemed to bear the inheritance of an infinitely complex ancestry. Staring at her intently, I saw that at least fifty ancient forebears were hovering there in fifty separate smiles or frowns or stares.

That was all it took, those three separate elements, to bring about the inevitable first step. The three elements were *Watch with Mother,* the silent child and the guilty adult. Ken Wright called it contrition and repentance, the stirring of the soul as it acknowledges the distant source from which it has come. I saw the vulnerable small girl watching the frail tiny puppets, and I understood the appalling truth that an unprotected infant is as alone in the world as anyone else. I meanwhile had been a self-deceiver. I had been telling myself that if I didn't have Corrie as my lover there would just be someone else. Corrie did not disguise the fact she had an impulsive, remorseless appetite and really couldn't help herself. She had betrayed Colin several times already, and to no one's disadvantage. Didn't he expect to be deceived and therefore truly deserved it? I was no longer convinced by the casuistry. Assuming the lab technician really was a willing dupe, what did that say about a woman who chose to be the partner of such a compliant fool?

But why judge others at this stage? I looked at the infant watching the twelve-inch screen and felt my own hellish guilt. My deed was before me like a running sore. I was doing this beautiful little girl no good at all. I wasn't making my furtive visits to improve the quality of her life, I was simply out to look after myself. I had just slept with her mother, though I was neither her father, her stepfather nor even her imaginary uncle. I was just a roving man, a species of ghost. I presumed to fornicate crudely above her trusting head while she, the oblivious infant, watched the most innocent story in the world.

*

Ken Wright brought me back to the present and to TFEOTNQ. He had just finished his embarrassing life story and was now giving us a theoretical explanation of his shameful past. For the next half-hour he talked in terms which I barely understood, and I listened very hard, afraid to miss a single word. I fidgeted tensely, glancing now and again at Briers who seemed comfortably at home with the highly technical glossary. Briers didn't even flinch at that mystifying word 'justification', which confused me for weeks afterwards as it signified almost exactly the opposite of its ordinary use.

A simple typist would have understood it better than me. When you justify a paragraph of type you make the right hand margin smoothly aligned. The page seems neat, pleasing to look at, harmoniously finished. For the badge man, and his hero Luther, the justification of humans comes about thus. It is through a once-and-for-all atonement by the God who is incarnate as Man. He that is who sacrificed himself in place of all of us: those dead, those living, those yet to be. The same that is who took our pains upon himself, every one, every past, present and future infringement. By our own efforts, the badge man drily explained, fallen from our pristine state, we can never be perfect, we can never be justified, no matter how hard we strive. It took the Creator born as man to do the necessary job. It needed our Creator, who by his perfect nature cannot look upon sin, to offer himself as a vicarious, blameless sacrifice. He balanced the books of good and evil and thus solved the insoluble equation. To do this he had to risk himself and his purity in an absolute once-and-for-all battle against the appalling powers of darkness. Words can only go so far. He sacrificed his son, himself, Himself. Because, remarkably, he loved all that he had created, even the hopeless worst of it...

214

That in a nutshell was the theoretical basis of Ken's conversion. It made a strange sort of music to a secular ear. Oddly I found myself fantasising my irreligious mother sitting there beside me in TFEOTNQ, commenting rudely that it was all a load of poppycock. Ma Singer, who hated organised religion not because of its otherworldly doctrines but because it had spoiled her youth, her font, her very lifespring.

I was picturing her angry expression whenever she denounced her saintly mother. Simultaneously, I had a sudden flash of Corrie Millon's fury when she was in full spate. As I hinted earlier, at times the pair of them seemed to be interchangeable temperaments. I shuddered guiltily at that realisation, as it all came gushing back.

*

It was the same outraged Corrie who accosted me on that terrible Saturday morning. It was at the beginning of 1969, in the middle of Maryport Woolworth's, if such an apposite venue can be imagined. All the unsold Christmas stock was being sold off at give-away prices and I was stood there clutching a beautiful Christmas angel intended for next year's tree. As it happened there never was to be another family Christmas, and that angel had to stay in its wrapper. Meanwhile it had been over a month since I had made any contact with Corrie and I thought that I had got away with it.

I thought that without either of us having had to suffer too much, it was finished. I hadn't turned up for our last appointed weekend. I hadn't made my customary replies to her letters using the prepaid Freeman's catalogue stickers she had given me for that purpose. Neither had I made any of our prearranged calls to the telephone box a half-mile from her house. After her third anguished disbelieving letter she had rung me up at work, and I had had the gall to shout wrong number and put it down immediately. For the rest of the afternoon I had left it off the hook and paced around the bookshop like a fretful bear. A day after that, common sense urged me to be more explicit and I used one of the Freeman's labels to tell her our affair was over. Of course I hadn't gone off her, I explained with a painful clumsiness, it was simply because of the harrowing unbearable guilt I felt towards our two children. I could almost stomach deceiving Sarah with my playacting, but I couldn't bear to hurt her child or my child. I described seeing Polly open-mouthed and innocent before *Watch with Mother*, and how the guilt of observing that had felt like a knife wound. I felt dreadful, though of course I knew that she must feel even more dreadful, especially after I had ignored all her letters. It went without saying that I took all the blame for everything, but I emphatically wanted out of this mess before things got even worse.

There were no more letters and no more phone calls. Three weeks slowly passed and I became a little less vigilant and a lot less devious. Every night I mumbled a prayer of thanks and congratulated myself that I had somehow got away with it. I became relaxed again with Sarah and she became relaxed again with me. I stopped seeing my singing, shouting, robust little daughter as a fragile victim. Periodically it occurred to me that Corrie Millon could relieve her vengeful feelings at any time by telling all in the Silloth staffroom. Yet somehow it seemed unlikely. Corrie respected no social mores, but would not wish to ruin her career prospects by starting a fight with the Deputy Head. She would not accost Sarah at Silloth School simply because it would mean almost as much painful embarrassment for herself as her rival.

Instead she accosted me between the toys and the Pick'n'Mix. She tore into Woolworth's in the same way she had first torn into my bookshop. This time, instead of looking combative and defiant, she appeared pale and sullen and stupid. She looked haggard and almost pitiful. I turned bright red, and felt an awful heat spread all over my face. I had talked about guilt in my cowardly letter and now I was a walking picture of the universal condition. I was caught out in my sins and Corrie was not about to offer any remission.

'You bastard!' she announced at considerable volume so that the whole of the shop stopped to watch. 'How *dare* you?'

'Corrie –'

'How *dare* you brush me off like an ugly insect? You preposterous bastard. How dare you not get in touch, you bloody crook? Do you think I'm some bloody fourteen-year-old you can just send a pissy *Dear John* letter?'

'Please,' I whispered.

She turned and grinned at the old women in headscarves who were biting their lips at her words and her passion. With a wild rhetorical gesture she invited them to join in the chorus.

'Talk about puce. Look at him everyone. Just look at that! I for one have seen paler beetroot.'

I pointed her towards the doors. 'Let's get out of here. Please. This is no place to –'

'Yes it is,' she sneered. 'This is an ideal bloody place. Nothing shall be hidden that shall not be made public. I never told you I was brought up holy, did I? That my people were Plymouth Brethren. It makes for madness in the adults, you know. That's why I'm so irremediably extreme. You should have avoided me like the plague, Mr Singer. But no, you had to go and play with fire.'

'Please,' I urged her. 'Let's go somewhere private.'

'Don't insult me,' she spat. 'I haven't come to beg and beseech. Of course I know that it's bloody well finished. I know it because I can smell it in your whining letter and see it in your cowardly bloody face.'

'I –'

'I despise you because of the way you went about it and so it's finished for me as well. But I am suffering and I am angry and I need to have my final say.'

'I'm so sorry,' I mumbled. I shuddered as I found myself fidgeting with the plastic spade for the Pick'n'Mix.

'Shut up,' she shrieked. 'I don't want any stinking apologies. I don't want any creeping repentance. I only want a man who's not afraid.'

'But I'm sorry,' I repeated, like a wooden idiot.

'Quiet,' she groaned, and before I knew it she had punched me hard in the face. Her sharp little fist went straight at my nose. A judicial murmur arose among the spectators and it seemed to be all in favour of Corrie, not me. After that the nightmare grew in exponential not arithmetical fashion. As my eyes began to water and the blood began to spurt, I saw the last thing I wanted to see. I saw Sarah Singer passing the window holding wriggling Anne in her arms. I suddenly remembered that we had agreed to meet in a coffee bar two doors down from Woolies. Horrified I saw her eyes meet mine. She looked at the blood on my face and the shock in my stare. Then she saw that my assailant was no other than her firebrand colleague Corrie Millon. I watched her take note of the speechless crowd gathering round her ludicrous husband and Corrie. Without any struggle she drew the obvious conclusion. Like an unwilling sleepwalker she pushed open the doors. Next I heard Anne exclaiming with delight and fear at the sight of her wounded father. She announced to the silent shop that Daddy's nose was 'blooded', not 'bloodied'. People usually laugh when infants mispronounce, but no one even smiled at the little girl. Corrie turned to follow my gaze and took in her friend Sarah and her pretty little daughter. I stiffened as I waited for her to start railing at Sarah. Corrie hesitated, as if about to drown her with invective.

Instead she muttered something quite inaudible. It might just have been, *you can have him for ever for what he's worth, assuming he's worth anything at all...*

She raced off without a backward glance. She flung open the swing doors and disappeared into the weekend throng. Sarah, overcome with shame and indignation, followed behind her. She left me standing there bleeding and alone and humiliated in the public eye. Mystified Anne asked her why she wasn't waiting for her Daddy to come as well. The shop itself was as silent as the grave.

*

It oughtn't to have been the end of my marriage. It was my one and only fling and my remorse at my folly was total. But I had been fool enough to fall for my wife's closest colleague and the professional association was simply too much for her. The sight of my lover every day of her working life was just more than Sarah Singer could bear. She had to take time off work, she felt so ill with the perpetual reminder. These days they would call it stress, though in 1969 the word only applied to cables and a new type of concrete. Corrie for her part simply blanked Sarah out of her vision, as easily as she blanked out everyone else in the staffroom. And not only her rival's ubiquitous presence made my wife ill. Half the town had witnessed her public shame that Saturday, which meant that all the staff were aware of it by the Monday morning. She could not bear all their watchful sympathy. She didn't even relish the spectacle of Corrie Millon's now irremediable pariah status. In any case Corrie was as hard as granite when it came to shame. She stayed on at Silloth School for another five years, by which time Sarah had found herself a headship in Abbeytown and moved out there with Anne.

I tried all possible means to make amends for my crime. Sarah did not accuse or rant or throw things, she simply grieved and sometimes howled and occasionally whimpered. After a fortnight of trying to get her to talk, I realised I would be chasing her vainly around the house for evermore. If I approached her she stiffened, and if I touched her she fled. She said that she just couldn't endure it. By it she meant not so much the pain as the event itself, the history, the lie, the deed, the evil in our lives. It wasn't that she didn't want to forgive. It was simply that she could not. The means were quite beyond her. She felt ill every time she thought about me or thought about Corrie. She wanted to be left quite alone. She wanted me to go. I made her physically ill and that was that.

I found a decent four-room flat out on the Allonby road and

every weekend would take Anne to play on the nearby beach. Depositing her back in town I wanted to collapse on the front step, and more than once I begged and pleaded with Sarah to try and do the impossible. Sarah grabbed Anne and pushed the door in my face, and I heard her cries each time behind the door. By 1973 we were divorced and by 1980 she was married again to a biology teacher called Eady. If I ever try to say the improbable 'Sarah Eady', it comes out 'Sreedy', which is the mental picture I have of Sarah as she shrank and hid herself away from the world after the Corrie Millon affair.

But Sarah is remarkably happy these days and so indeed is Anne. They are both steaming successes. Sarah is not only head of an excellent school, she is also on national educational committees, a frequent broadcaster, a staple of *Woman's Hour,* and an expensive after-dinner speaker to boot. Anne has written authoritative textbooks about childcare and child psychology, a biography of Piaget and a critical study of Melanie Klein. They both managed exceedingly well without me, though I like to think that I started Anne off on the royal road to reading with my hopeless Bettabux. I bought myself the dockside kiosk in 1970 and could write an authoritative history of the boiled sweet if anyone would care to commission me.

I thought of my family as I sat at TFEOTNQ, and then looking at the badge man, thought, yes, he is also a steaming success. The badge man was a very old man but he looked in prime condition. He was as happy, as joyous, as gleaming-eyed as a sandboy. Fifty years ago he had been given a death sentence, but then in the depths of the dark he had found himself to be *justified*. His explanation left me speechless, but then so did everything else in life that mattered. Bach's Masses. Joe Pass's guitar. Summer sunsets over the Solway Firth. Especially those over the unspoilt wilds of Flimby shore where the plaice teem around the old shit pipe and the fishermen's dialect sounds as raw and old as the oldest haematite hills.

As I walked away from TFEOTNQ I had this sudden enormous urge to go fishing. I decided that next Saturday I would drive the two miles to Flimby and see if I could hook a plaice, a cod, a bream, a skate. The last time I had fished was with Squinty Bar Radish and in those days of course there was no aquarium here in the town.

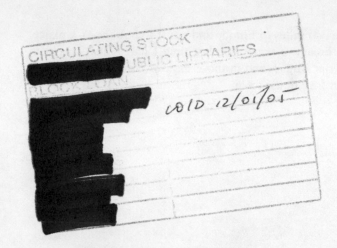